The Clifftop Murders

Rachel McLean writes thrillers that make your pulse race and your brain tick. Originally a self-publishing sensation, she has sold millions of copies digitally, with massive success in the UK, and a growing reach internationally too. She is also the author of the Detective Zoe Finch series, which precedes the Dorset Crime novels, and the spin-off McBride & Tanner series and Cumbria Crime series. In 2021 she won the Kindle Storyteller Award with *The Corfe Castle Murders* and her last five books have all hit No1 in the Bookstat ebook chart on launch.

Also by Rachel McLean

Dorset Crime series

The Corfe Castle Murders
The Clifftop Murders
The Island Murders

RACHEL McLEAN

THE CLIFFTOP MURDERS

hera

First published in Ackroyd Publishing in 2021 by the United Kingdom

This edition published in the United Kingdom in 2024 by

Hera Books
Unit 9 (Canelo), 5th Floor
Cargo Works, 1–2 Hatfields
London SE1 9PG
United Kingdom

A CIP catalogue record for this book is available from the British Library.

Print ISBN 978 1 80436 761 2

This book is a work of fiction. Names, characters, businesses, organizations, places and events are either the product of the author's imagination or are used fictitiously. Any resemblance to actual persons, living or dead, events or locales is entirely coincidental.

Look for more great books at www.herabooks.com

Printed and bound in Great Britain by Clays Ltd, Elcograf S.p.A.

CHAPTER ONE

Ameena Khan parked on a narrow lane in the quiet village of Studland and stared out into the darkness.

It wasn't quite dawn, the last of the streetlights not yet extinguished. She yawned and heaved herself out of the car, then went to the boot and took out her camera bag and a thick, waterproof jacket. She raised her fingers to feel the damp air. Last night's forecast had said it would be sunny later, perfect conditions for what she was planning. She slammed the boot shut, shrugged on her coat and pulled the camera bag over her shoulder.

Following the signs, she strode along the cliff edge towards Old Harry Rocks. Ameena stopped when she reached the headland, gazing out to sea.

The waves were loud, crashing against the rocks below, but invisible in the dark. Out to sea, she caught the occasional glimpse of white. There was a haze in the air, the damp permeating her bones, a hint of the dawn peeking over the Isle of Wight in the east. Just enough light to keep her away from the cliff edge, to show her where it was safe to tread.

She continued along the coastal path, knowing exactly where she would set up camp. She'd been here dozens of times before: it was her favourite photography spot. There was a patch of ground where the grass wasn't too long, and the views were to die for.

She reached it, stretched and yawned, and laid her jacket on the ground. The grass would be damp with dew, even without the fog in the air.

Over to the east, the cliffs of The Needles were coming into view, sunrise approaching. It was brighter over there, not blurred by fog. With luck, there would be a perfect backdrop to her photo of Old Harry Rocks. Ameena wasn't a professional photographer, but it had been a hobby for fifteen years.

She'd moved to Dorset five years earlier, and discovered she could feed her passion almost everywhere she looked. Her husband Tom was only too happy to stay in bed on Sunday mornings and keep an eye on their daughters, while she dragged herself up before dawn and trudged out into the darkness. By the time she got home, he would only just be stirring, little Brandon and Daisy still snuggled up beside him in bed. They would hardly notice she'd been gone.

But Ameena was in her happy place. Out here in the dark and the wet, staring across the sea towards a dawn that was racing her way. She took her camera out of the bag and placed it on the jacket, then folded the jacket sleeves over it. The camera was precious, she had to keep it dry. She'd screwed on the lens the night before, knowing how damaging it could be to do so in the morning mist. She hoped she'd chosen wisely.

She peered over towards Bournemouth. The sky was reddening behind the coastline, forming a thin, bright line. She felt her heart pick up pace. Time to start firing off some test shots. She removed the lens cap and brought the camera up to her eye. With the light changing so quickly, she'd have to adjust the settings every few minutes, but that was part of the fun.

Ameena had never been a point-and-click photographer; she liked fiddling too much for that. She enjoyed adjusting the settings, checking the light, consulting meters. Without that, what was the point?

She took a few shots and lowered the camera to check what she'd caught. It was OK, a bit dim. Conditions would be better in about fifteen minutes, she reckoned.

She lifted the camera to her eye again, and checked the light levels. There was a display in the viewfinder. She was using a digital camera with an inbuilt screen, so she didn't really need the viewfinder. But putting the camera to her face brought her closer to the photo. It made her feel like she was part of the landscape. It also steadied the camera and gave her a crisper shot.

She sensed movement behind her and hoped the wind wasn't picking up. It had been still when she'd left the house, driving along the country lanes in silence and darkness. It spooked her sometimes, but it also made her feel alive.

There it was again, that movement behind her. A bird, perhaps, or a small animal. Something come to watch the strange woman sitting on the cliff at dawn.

Then she felt it. A hand on her shoulder.

She tensed. Her camera was still up at her eye.

"Don't move," said a voice.

She relaxed; she recognised it.

"What are you doing here?" she asked.

"I could ask the same of you."

She smiled, still peering through the viewfinder. The light was changing, the dawn approaching. She needed to be left alone so she could get this shot.

"Give me ten minutes," she said.

A grunt came from behind her. The hand left her shoulder and she lowered her camera to check the display.

She needed to make more adjustments. She did what she had to, her mind focused on the task at hand. She would deal with her visitor after she'd got the perfect shot. With a little luck, she might get it printed in the local paper. No money, just the satisfaction. She didn't need the money.

She raised the camera, pushing it against her face to steady the shot. The hand clamped her shoulder again. She felt weight pushing onto her.

"Please." She frowned. "Just give me ten minutes."

"No," came the reply. The grip tightened on her shoulder.

She loosened her grip on the camera, desperate not to lose the moment. She'd been waiting for a day like this for weeks.

"This is important," she said, trying to hide the exasperation in her voice. She dropped the camera as the hands moved from her shoulders to her arms, pulling them into her sides. The strap tugged at her neck.

She turned, grunting. "Not now. Please."

A hand came out and slapped her across the face. She screamed and raised her fingers to her lips. Blood?

Another slap. "Don't ignore me."

"What?" she breathed. What was this about?

Stay calm. "We can talk about this on Monday. Please, not here." She cast around. The clifftop was deserted.

"No," came the reply.

She stared back into her assailant's eyes. How on earth had she been found up here? It was five in the morning, for God's sake. Who else knew that she did this? The only person she talked to about it was her husband.

Her assailant lifted her off the ground, making the camera swing out on its neck strap. She threw her hand out, trying to grab it. "Put me down!"

But her attacker wasn't listening. She kicked out with her legs as she felt herself being shifted towards the cliff edge. Her heart thumped in her ears. Her chest hollowed out and her stomach felt like butter.

She could feel the chill behind her. The emptiness, the air, the waves below crashing on the rocks. It was all there beyond the void.

"Put me down!" she cried.

A grunt. Another slap. She screamed and managed to free one arm. She flailed out, catching skin, clammy under her fingernails. She screamed again as she felt herself tipping to one side. She threw her arms out in the other direction, trying to catch her balance, aware of how little there was behind her. Just air and space and gravity and suction.

Her eyes widened as she stared back into her attacker's face.

"Wait!" she cried, the wind pulling the words out of her mouth.

"You talked," came the response, shouted into the wind. "You should have kept quiet."

A final shove, and she felt herself being hurled backwards. Gravity sucked at her as she tumbled through space.

Finally, she screamed. Loudly, properly. A full-throated scream coming right up from her lungs, but it was too late.

Ameena fell through the air beyond the clifftop. Seconds later, she thudded to the rocks below and the waves crashed over her. She stared lifelessly up at the sky, unaware of the birds that were already approaching.

CHAPTER TWO

Lesley was woken by a quiet knock on her door. Light seeped around the edges of the curtains.

What time is it? She lifted her head from the pillow, her brain muddy.

The door opened and Sharon poked her head round.

Lesley smiled. "Morning, love. You sleep OK?"

Sharon had slept on the sofa bed downstairs. This cottage had only one usable bedroom, or at least only one room with a bed in it. The other upstairs room seemed to be used as a storeroom by the landlord. It was full of junk. Old furniture, electrical items that Lesley imagined would explode as soon as they so much as sniffed a current. Blankets and pillowcases she preferred not to touch.

Sharon closed the door behind her and sat on the end of Lesley's bed. "Yeah, Mum," she said. "It was fine".

Lesley tried to remember what it had been like to be sixteen, and capable of sleeping anywhere. She could probably tell Sharon to sleep on the front path, and the girl would still get a good night's kip. She, on the other hand, at the age of forty-six, needed a comfortable bed. Preferably one with a thick duvet and a supportive pillow.

Unfortunately, this bed in her rented cottage in Wareham didn't fit that description. The mattress was lumpy, and the bed squeaked every time she moved. She dreaded to think what it would be like if she ever brought someone home. She sat up and plumped the pillows behind her.

"What d'you want to do today?" she asked Sharon.

She'd been showing her daughter the sights of Dorset, anxious to be a good mum. Since she'd caught her husband Terry with his fancywoman on a trip back to Birmingham, she'd worried about being the best mum she could. Especially with her being stuck down here in Dorset for the next five months.

"I don't fancy doing much today, Mum," Sharon said. "You've been dragging me around the county like we're on some sort of organised tour. Can't we just chill in the back garden?"

Lesley looked towards the window. "Have you seen the state of my back garden?"

The garden was tiny, about the size of a chihuahua's nose and overgrown with weeds. The landlord had made it clear that if Lesley wanted the garden improved, it was her responsibility to do it. But today, a muggy Sunday in July, she had no inclination to do anything of the sort.

"Why don't I take you down to the pub in Kingston?" she asked. "We can have lunch in their garden and look at the views."

Sharon rolled her eyes. "More views?"

Lesley laughed. "Well, they're good at that down here. Not much else to make up for it."

"It's OK, Mum. We can just stay here. Watch TV, read, stuff like that. You don't have to make such an effort."

Lesley looked into her daughter's eyes. Since when had she been so grown-up?

She stroked stray hair away from Sharon's face. "Thanks, love. But I don't really want to stay around here all day. Do you?"

Sharon nodded. "I just want to chill, Mum."

Lesley knew Sharon needed the rest. Her life was stressful right now, she'd just finished her GCSEs and her parents were splitting up. And she had the new woman at home to contend with. Julieta Villada, a visiting lecturer at Terry's university who he'd invited to move into his home – to his and Lesley's home – the moment he realised he no longer had to pretend to be happily married.

She yawned. "I'll tell you what, I'll go out to the bakery on North Street. Get us some croissants and stuff, and then we can just sit around all morning. Chat, watch some telly, read the papers."

Sharon grimaced. "Papers? Who reads papers these days?"

Lesley gave her a mock punch. "I do. So shut up."

"OK." Sharon shrugged herself off the bed and headed out of the room.

Lesley swung her feet onto the thin carpet and pulled on her dressing gown. A lazy morning would be nice. She couldn't be bothered taking a shower. She'd just throw some clothes on, go to the shop, and then come back again.

Her phone was ringing in the back pocket of her jeans. She pulled it out. *Not work, please.* Last time she'd had a weekend with Sharon, they'd been interrupted by a murder right outside Corfe Castle.

But no, it was Elsa.

Lesley put the phone to her ear, her body filling with warmth. "Hey."

"Hello, you," Elsa replied.

Lesley smiled. "What're you doing?"

"I've just woken up," Elsa replied. "Missing you."

"Sorry." Lesley pulled the bedroom door closed. "It's just with Sharon…"

"It's OK. We've only been together a month and you've got Terry to think of."

"Yeah." There was no way Lesley wanted Terry to know about her and Elsa. Their divorce was complicated enough, without bringing yet another woman into the picture.

"So are we going to see each other today?" Elsa asked. "When does Sharon go home?"

"She's on the three forty train out of Bournemouth," Lesley replied. "I can come to you after?"

"Perfect. I'll cook."

Lesley bit her bottom lip, feeling like a teenager again. "I look forward to it."

There was a knock on the door. "Mum?"

Lesley muttered into the phone. "Sixteen years old, and still asking me to go and get her food."

Elsa laughed. "You know you love it, really."

"I do," Lesley replied. There'd been a time when she'd worried that Sharon would take Terry's side, would decide she didn't want anything to do with her mum. That time had passed.

"I'll see you later, yeah?"

"You will." Elsa hung up.

Lesley plunged the phone into the back pocket of her jeans and headed downstairs.

Right, she thought to herself. *Bread, newspapers, lazy day*.

Her phone rang again. She sighed as she lifted it to her ear.

"You forgot something?"

"Err… sorry?"

"Dennis." The anticipation Lesley had been feeling left her. DS Frampton would only be phoning for one reason, on a Sunday. "What's happened?"

CHAPTER THREE

It felt like the walk to the crime scene would never end. It was late morning, the sun was high overhead, and the sky was so blue it was almost white. At least Lesley had taken the precaution of wearing sensible boots this time, not her court shoes. She'd gone into Dorchester after wrapping up the Archie Weatherton case and bought some low-heeled leather boots and was now wearing them under her jeans. No suit today: even Lesley didn't wear a suit on a Sunday.

She rounded a bend and took a shortcut through a field of long dry grass. In the distance was the Isle of Wight and The Needles. Hidden beyond the cliff edge, Old Harry Rocks. She could hear birds singing and the faint sound of cows behind her.

A cordon had already been erected, and a team of people waited for her.

Dennis turned to her. "Afternoon, boss."

She swallowed, expecting the worst. "Dennis. What have you got for me?"

"We can't see much up here," he replied. "She was found down there." He pointed towards the cliff edge, a wary look in his eyes. Sensible man, didn't want to get too close.

"So she went over from up here?" Lesley asked.

Gail Hansford, the crime scene manager, stepped forward. "Good to see you, Lesley."

"Likewise," Lesley replied. "Tell me what you've found."

Gail raised a hand to shield her eyes. "There's not much up here. A jacket, a couple of camera lenses in a bag, some snacks. No obvious sign of a struggle. I don't think she was brought up here against her will."

"What time was she found?" asked Lesley.

"About three hours ago," replied Gail.

Lesley checked her watch: it was coming up to 11am.

"Some holidaymakers out at sea spotted something on the rocks," Gail said.

Lesley grimaced. "Is she still down there?"

Gail nodded. "We've sent the Coast Guard out to pick up the body. One of my guys is going with them to preserve the evidence as best he can."

Lesley nodded. "What about the pathologist?"

Gail gave her an exasperated look. "It's Sunday, isn't it? Middle of the summer. He won't be here today."

Lesley sighed. "At some kiddies' party again?"

Last time they'd found a body, near Corfe Castle, it had been Sunday afternoon and Dr Whittaker had been at his granddaughter's birthday party. The man was reluctant to attend crime scenes, doubly so at the weekend.

"It's short notice," Dennis said. "We couldn't track him down."

"Hasn't he got a team?" Lesley asked. "Somebody who can come out in his place?"

Gail shrugged. "Not at the weekend."

"We're not leaving her to the waves while we wait for him," Lesley said.

Gail looked relieved. "We'll take her to the morgue. Brett will just have to do what he can and preserve the body as best as possible."

"You do what you need to," said Lesley. "We can't all pussyfoot around a pathologist who refuses to do his job."

Dennis frowned. Lesley ignored it.

"So." Lesley took a step towards the edge, but only one. "Has anybody had a look over?"

Gail shook her head. "I put two cordons up. One here, stopping people from going near the scene, and the other one between the jacket and the edge. I don't want anybody going over while they're trying to investigate."

Lesley peered across. The cliff edge sloped downwards, making it difficult to see where the land ended and the sky began.

"I'm not letting any of my team near that edge," said Gail. "No chance."

"Worried about rockslides?" Lesley asked.

"Not here," Gail replied. "This stretch of cliff is Triassic. Made of chalk, not the clay past Swanage."

Dennis gestured behind him. "The rockslides they get towards Lyme Regis can be dangerous. Crumbly material, volatile."

Lesley looked towards the edge where their victim had gone over. "It looks dangerous enough here to me. Do we have a hypothesis? Suicide, accidental death, worse?"

Gail's eyes were fixed on the jacket, spread out on the ground. "A woman who planned on throwing herself off the cliff would be unlikely to leave a jacket laid out neatly like that with her bag and the camera gear, but not leave the camera itself."

Lesley raised an eyebrow. "She took the camera with her?"

"It's not up here. There has to be a camera to go with all that gear. I'm assuming it's still around her neck."

Lesley shuddered. She resisted the temptation to approach the edge and peer over. If she got close enough to see the body, she would be joining it.

"OK." She pulled in a breath. "Let's have a look at this bag, then."

Gail raised the cordon and led her to a camera bag, which sat in the centre of an outstretched waterproof jacket. Lesley pulled on protective gloves and eased open the zip.

"Two lenses, a bag of crisps, a bottle of water and an apple," Gail said. "And a few bits and bobs to do with cameras. Brett would know more about it than me, but he's down in the boat with the coastguards."

"You're looking for signs someone pushed her?" Lesley asked.

"I don't think we can jump to conclusions right now. Not until the post-mortem."

"But what does it look like from what forensics we have?"

"There's a single path through the grass here, see." She pointed Lesley back in the direction from which she'd arrived. There was a line carved through the grass, where they'd walked, and possibly others before them.

"So either she was alone, or someone followed her tracks," Lesley said. "What about the outdoorsy types walking past all day?"

"Most people don't come this close to the edge," Gail replied. "But if somebody was after her, maybe they followed her path. Maybe they knew how to creep up on her."

"That's pretty precise." Lesley stood up, feeling the sun on her face. "Where will they be taking her?"

"Poole Hospital," Dennis said.

Lesley turned to him. He was peering past her, out to sea. The water was calm, The Needles clear in the distance.

"So we'll follow," Lesley said. "See what we can find out."

"No point," said Gail. "If Whittaker is doing the post-mortem, he won't let anybody near that body until afterwards."

Lesley gritted her teeth. "And just when is he likely to do the post-mortem?"

"Don't ask me. Hopefully sometime tomorrow."

"Sometime tomorrow," Lesley repeated. "So we've got a dead body, we don't know if it's suicide, murder, accidental death or what, and he's not prepared to get a shift on."

"Accidental death most likely, don't you think boss?" said Dennis. "I mean, she had her camera around her neck, she could have been walking towards the edge trying to get the perfect shot, or maybe even going backwards getting a shot back inland."

Lesley turned to look behind them. All she could see was a broad hill, peppered with daisies. "Nothing here you'd want to get a photograph of."

"If she was on the edge here," said Gail, "she was trying to get Old Harry."

"Maybe she went too close," Dennis said. "Tumbled over the edge." He was looking away from them, towards Swanage. His left eye twitched.

Lesley turned back towards the sea. Once again she felt herself drawn to the edge.

"We won't know until we've seen the results of the post-mortem." She looked at Gail. "Can you ask your colleague to take a look at her while en route to the hospital? Check for defensive wounds. Anything obvious."

"Righto," said Gail.

Lesley looked at Dennis.

"There's not much more we can do now," he said.

Lesley considered. "We can follow the body to the hospital." She checked her watch. "If we leave now, we'll get there first."

"But the pathologist—"

"The pathologist can whistle. Come on, Dennis. Let's get moving." She gave Gail a nod and the CSM went back to her work.

The two detectives hurried along the path back to Studland, Lesley grateful to be away from that cliff edge.

Just for once, could she find a body in a goddamn industrial estate or around the back of a pub? Somewhere accessible, somewhere that didn't require heavy boots? Or maybe on a weekday, so she could finish her peaceful Sunday with Sharon?

Dennis gave her something between a wave and a salute as he opened his car door. He didn't look happy not to have been sent home. Lesley nodded in return. They were both going to have to get used to some changes.

CHAPTER FOUR

Lesley watched Dennis drive away slowly. He was the kind of man who ambled through life, strolling along in his tweed jackets and his comfortable shoes, trousers cut in a way that reminded her of 1950s movies. When he was out of sight, she got into her car.

She checked Google Maps, and then headed towards the Sandbanks Ferry. Regardless of what Gail had said, she wanted to be at the hospital when the body arrived.

As she reached the back of the queue, she passed a sign warning of a forty-minute wait.

She turned off her engine and thumped the steering wheel. Her phone rang: Dennis. "Bad news, boss."

"Are you already there?" she asked.

"You've got to be joking. I'm at the front of the queue for the ferry."

"How did you get to the front?"

"We get priority. Don't tell me you're sitting at the back?"

She looked in her rear-view mirror. Already half a dozen cars had lined up behind her. "Just tell me the bad news," she told him.

"I've spoken to the morgue. They're accepting the body, but they're not doing anything more today. And they won't let us in there. There's no point going over there. We need to wait for the PM."

Wait. People were fond of waiting in Dorset.

She looked in her rear-view mirror again: over a dozen cars behind her now. At least she wouldn't have to jump the queue. "I'll see you tomorrow," she said. "Bright and early."

She turned her car in the road and drove through Studland. For a moment she considered returning to the crime scene. She itched to be busy, to make progress. But with the post-mortem not happening and no identity for the body, there was nothing more she could do. And besides, her daughter was waiting for her at home.

Sharon had been sunning herself in Lesley's minuscule back garden when she'd left. Lesley had worried about leaving Sharon alone in an unfamiliar house, but Sharon had waved her away.

"I'm sixteen Mum. For God's sake, just go." Sharon wasn't about to come to another crime scene, not like last time.

Lesley pointed the car towards Wareham, taking the B3351 via Corfe Castle. It took her forty-five minutes to do a twenty-minute drive. Traffic was heavy, holidaymakers attempting to get to their caravans and rented houses via the mainland instead of the ferry. She cursed them. Only a few weeks ago, she'd been surprised by how easy it was to get around this county. Far more straightforward than the clogged-up streets of Birmingham. But she was realising that at certain times of year, Dorset traffic could be heavier than Spaghetti Junction at five o'clock on a Friday afternoon.

She opened the door to her cottage and called out to Sharon. "I'm home, love. Sorry!"

"That's OK," came Sharon's voice from the garden. "What time is it?"

Lesley checked her watch and thought about the traffic she'd sat in on the way back from Studland. "Shit. Time we left for your train."

Sharon appeared at the back door, yawning. One side of her face was sunburnt. Lesley pointed at it. "Did you fall asleep in the garden?"

Sharon shrugged. "I guess so. Why?"

"You've caught the sun, love."

Sharon put her fingers up to her face and winced. "Oh, hell. I'm going to look like flipping Two Face."

"Who's Two Face?"

"Batman, Mum. You know."

Lesley looked at her. Of course she didn't know, but she'd humour her daughter.

"Have you packed your case?"

Sharon gave her a look of panic.

"Go," Lesley said. "Get a move on."

Sharon ran past her, thundering into the living room where she'd been sleeping. She threw clothes and toiletries into her rucksack. She hauled the rucksack over her shoulders, her breathing heavy.

"Sorted. Let's go."

"Good girl," Lesley said, hoping she hadn't left anything. "You got your phone? Your purse."

"Nobody carries a purse anymore, Mum. I've got my phone, that's the important thing."

"Is your ticket on your phone?"

"Yes." Sharon was doing that voice, the one that made Lesley feel eighty years old.

"Good. Let's get that train."

Lesley ran out of the house and jumped into her car. Sharon followed, slamming the front door behind her.

Forty minutes later, Lesley was back in the car, catching her breath. Sharon had just made her train, screaming at the guard to let her on as the whistle was blown. Sometimes there was an advantage to being sixteen years old.

Lesley pulled away from Bournemouth station. She had no plans to return to Wareham. She flicked down the sun visor and checked her face in the mirror as she waited to turn out of the station car park. She rubbed under her eyes where her mascara was blurring. Forty-six years old, and not bad for it. But Elsa was ten years younger, and Lesley could feel every day of those ten years.

She drove to Elsa's flat, which was three streets back from Boscombe seafront. It was an airy top floor flat, huge windows on both sides and modern furniture. It couldn't be any further from Lesley's pokey little house in Wareham with its heavy cupboards and narrow hallways. Elsa was cooking when Lesley arrived.

"Duck a l'Orange," Elsa announced, giving Lesley a welcome kiss.

Lesley sniffed. "Have the 1970s asked for their food back?"

Elsa gave her a light punch on the arm. "You don't have to eat any."

Lesley grinned. "Smells lovely," she said.

"Good." Elsa returned to preparing a salad. It did smell good, Lesley thought. What was wrong with retro? Dorset had plenty of it.

She sat at the kitchen table and poured a glass of white wine, relaxing into the chair.

"How was your day?" Elsa asked. "Good time with Sharon?"

"I hardly got to see her. I was called out to a crime scene."

Elsa placed the knife on the counter and turned to face Lesley. "A crime scene on a Sunday afternoon? That's not very Dorset."

"It's becoming that way," Lesley replied. "It seems people down here like to be inconvenient when they get themselves killed."

"A murder?" Elsa asked.

Lesley shrugged. "It could have been a suicide, or an accident. But something in my bones tells me it's suspicious."

Elsa took the seat opposite her and grabbed a wine glass. She filled it and took a sip. "How so?"

Lesley looked back at her. Elsa had dark hair and blue eyes, an unusual combination but a striking one. Her eyes sparkled when she looked at Lesley, something that made Lesley's skin flush.

"She was a photographer," Lesley said. "She left her gear at the top of the cliff. All neatly arranged on a jacket that she'd put on the ground, presumably to protect herself from the dirt."

"Or the wet," Elsa suggested.

Lesley shook her head. "Have you seen the weather out there today?"

Elsa laughed. "I live in a top floor flat. Haven't you noticed this place is a sauna?"

Lesley nodded. Sauna or not, it was better than her house.

"But who leaves their gear like that, then throws themself off the edge of a cliff with their camera still round their neck?"

"She took her camera with her?"

21

Lesley nodded. "Apparently. The coastguard and CSIs have taken the body to Poole Hospital. I haven't seen her yet."

Elsa's eyes crinkled. "Poor woman."

Lesley sipped at her wine. "Yeah."

Her phone rang: Gail. "News from the crime scene?"

"I've got an ID," Gail said.

Lesley whistled. "That was quick."

"Brett found it on her after they pulled her out of the water. She had her driving licence in her pocket."

Lesley frowned. Who carried their driving licence in their pocket?

"Go on then," she said.

"Her name was Ameena Khan," Gail replied. "Thirty-four years old, an address in Christchurch."

"Read it out it to me." Lesley gestured to Elsa, who passed her an envelope and a pen. Lesley turned the envelope over and scribbled the address on its back.

"Thanks," she said to Gail, surveying the address. It meant nothing to her. "Anything else?"

"Sorry," said Gail. "But at least now you know who she is."

Lesley swallowed. Somebody would need to go and tell Ameena's next of kin. She hung up and looked at Elsa. "I'm sorry, Els."

"You have to go?"

"We've got an ID and address, somebody has to tell the next of kin. It might as well be me." She pushed the envelope across the table for Elsa to see. "Do you know where that is?"

Elsa nodded. "It's about three miles from here. I'll drive you if you want."

"Best not."

22

Elsa was a criminal lawyer. She hadn't faced Lesley across an interview room table yet, but the time would come.

"I'll put it into Google Maps," Lesley said. "I'll ring Dennis first, get an FLO assigned."

Elsa nodded. "Good luck. Will you come back afterwards?"

Lesley shrugged. "Depends how long it takes." She leaned over and took Elsa's hand. "I don't want to keep you from your dinner."

Elsa twisted her hand in Lesley's so their fingers entwined. "Don't worry about that. Whatever time it is, just come back. You won't want to be on your own after this."

Lesley nodded. She wrote the name above the address on the back of the envelope.

Elsa put a finger on it. "That's the victim?"

Lesley looked up. "Ameena Khan."

Elsa looked into Lesley's eyes, her face pale. "How old was she?"

"Thirty-four," Lesley said. "We have her driving licence."

Elsa pulled her hand away. "Oh my God."

"What?" asked Lesley. "D'you know her?"

"I do." Elsa's voice was thin. "She's a colleague. She works at my law firm."

CHAPTER FIVE

Ameena Khan lived in a generous detached house in Christchurch. Lesley parked her car and walked to the front door, preparing herself mentally. She wished she had on her work uniform, a pale skirt suit and smart shoes. Here she was in jeans and a casual shirt. But this couldn't wait. She'd called Dennis on the way, but he was busy with his family.

She rang the doorbell and heard a chime deep in the house. A voice called out: "Daddy!" Lesley felt her heart dip. The victim had kids.

The door opened and a man of medium height with a round, friendly face stood in front of her.

"Mr Khan?" she asked.

He shook his head. "Tom Holroyd," he told her. "Are you looking for my wife?"

"Can I come in, please?" Lesley held up her ID.

His eyes widened. "What's happened? She hasn't been home. I've been calling and call…" His voice dropped away.

"I think it's best if I came inside."

He ushered her through, his breathing tight. Two children were in the kitchen, running around a large island. One of them, a small boy who couldn't have been more than five years old, yelled at his sister. She looked to be seven or eight. Lesley gave them the kindest smile she could muster. Both ran to their dad and huddled into his legs.

Lesley looked from Mr Holroyd to his children. "I think it would be best if we had this conversation in private," she told him.

He gave her a wide-eyed nod. "Of course." He bent to his children. "Go in the telly room kids, put *Night Garden* on."

She watched as they ran through a wide set of doors into a room with a vast television.

Their father turned back towards her. He gave her a plaintive look then looked down at the table between them. "I'm sorry. I need to tidy up." He grabbed plates and stacked them.

"Mr Holroyd," she said. She'd seen this before; anything to delay the inevitable. "That can wait."

He let the plates slide to the table. "It's not good news, is it?" His eyes were red.

She took a chair and gestured for him to do the same. He sat opposite her, his eyes searching her face.

"It's about your wife," she said. "Ameena Khan."

He nodded. "Has she been in an accident? Is it something to do with a client?"

Lesley swallowed. This never got easy. "I'm afraid we found your wife at the bottom of the cliffs at Old Harry Rocks this morning. Near Studland."

His head fell onto the table. He made a keening sound.

"I'm so sorry, Mr Holroyd. We've got a family liaison officer on the way, he'll help you. He'll answer any questions you have, and help you take care of your children if you need it."

Holroyd looked up. He gasped in a breath. "How? What? She went out for…"

"What did she go out for, Mr Holroyd?" Lesley asked.

"I didn't see her, she leaves early in the morning some-times when the weather' good."

He was stumbling over his words, barely able to get them out.

Lesley nodded. "She went to Ballard Down?"

"It's one of her spots. She likes to take photos of local landscapes. Landmarks, sites, weather, stuff like that. I don't really get it myself. That's why she does it early in the morning. She's normally back before breakfast. I just assumed she had to go into the office."

"Does she often go into the office on a Sunday?"

"She's a lawyer. You're police. You know what it's like."

"She wasn't in the office today," Lesley said.

He looked at her, blinking. He bent his head again and grabbed his hair. From the next room, Lesley heard one of the kids shouting. Mr Holroyd closed his eyes momentarily and glanced over towards the doorway. He muttered something unintelligible.

"Do you have anyone who can come and help you with the children?"

"Tell me," he replied. "Tell me what happened."

"I'm afraid we don't know much at the moment," Lesley replied. "But she was spotted by some people in a boat."

"Where?" he asked.

"At the bottom of the cliffs at Ballard Down, just south of Old Harry Rocks."

He nodded. "I know it. She took me there. All the time. Just last weekend… When?"

"This morning," she said. "We weren't able to retrieve her until this afternoon. That's why we didn't identify her or contact you earlier."

He stared back at her. "How did you identify her?"

"She had her driving licence on her," Lesley replied. "It gave us her name and address."

He nodded. His body slumped, his hands holding up his head.

"Was she…? Did she…?"

He wanted to know if she'd suffered, Lesley thought. He wanted to know how long it had taken her to die. But the truth was, until they'd done the post-mortem, Lesley couldn't answer those questions.

"I'm really sorry," she said. "But I don't know much right now. There'll be a post-mortem done in the next few days, and we may need you to identify her body."

He blinked at her, his jaw clenched. "Of course," he said.

"Have you got anybody who can come round?" she asked again. "Anybody who can help you with the children? Who you can talk to?"

He shook his head. "No."

"Where do you work?" she asked him.

"I'm a head teacher," he said. "School just around the…"

She knew what it was like to be in a position of authority and be hit by a tsunami like this. The worry about letting people down, combined with the stress of not allowing yourself the time to process it.

"Like I said," she told him, "we've assigned a family liaison officer to you, PC Hughes. He's already on his way."

"I don't need a family liaison officer," he said.

"It helps," she replied. "Somebody to open the door, to do the practical stuff. Just to help you keep going."

"Keep going," he whispered. "How am I supposed to *keep going*?"

She watched his face. His reaction was genuine. He didn't look like he'd killed his wife just hours ago. But then...

"I'm sorry, I have to ask you this," she said to him. "But where were you today?"

He shook his head. "Here, with the kids. Waiting for Ameena to come home. I called her, what, twelve times? I texted her. Check her phone, you'll find them."

Lesley had no recollection of Gail mentioning a phone. "We'll take a look," she said. "But can anybody vouch for the fact that you were here all day?"

He looked towards the living room. "The kids can."

She smiled at him. That didn't count. "Any neighbours? Anybody pop round? Any deliveries?"

He shook his head. "It's Sunday. It's not that kind of neighbourhood. People keep to themselves. I'm sorry, but I was here all day, you have to believe me."

He pushed up from his chair and turned away from her. He clutched the edge of the sink and lowered himself to the floor, his body shaking.

CHAPTER SIX

Lesley walked past her team's bank of desks and into her office. They were all here: Dennis, the two DC's, Johnny Chiles and Mike Legg, and finally, PC Tina Abbott. Lesley had brought Tina into the team after she'd helped them out on the Corfe Castle murder inquiry. Dennis hadn't been happy, influenced no doubt by an instinctive snobbery about uniformed officers. But Tina was slowly proving herself, chipping away at the DS's defences.

She beckoned for them all to join her.

The board was ready: blank, pristine, waiting for a new case. She wheeled it out from behind her desk where she kept it when not in use. She didn't like the thought of people walking past the ground floor office and seeing what was written on it. This building was modern and ugly, with vast, single glazed windows. In this heat, she was glad of the draft, but in the winter she knew she'd feel differently.

Still, she wouldn't be here in the winter. She'd be back in Birmingham, where she belonged.

Dennis took a seat and crossed his legs, waiting for her to start. Johnny and Mike stood behind him. Tina hovered by the door, looking like she didn't quite feel part of the team.

Lesley gestured towards the other chair. "Sit down, Tina."

Tina eyed the two DCs and did as she was told. Mike gave her a smile, while Johnny's eyes were on Lesley.

Lesley grabbed a marker and jabbed at the board. She wrote Ameena Khan's name at the top, in the middle. Below that, the name of the woman's husband, Tom Holroyd. To one side, she added the name of Ameena's employers: Nevin, Cross and Short. A chill ran down her back as she wrote the word *Short*.

"Right," she said, turning back to her team. "We've got a thirty-four-year-old woman, possibly suicide or accident, but I think not. She worked at a law firm in Bournemouth, no sign of any problems. Husband seemed legit as far as I'm concerned."

"How did he react?" Dennis asked.

"Shocked. Horrified. He'd have to be a bloody good actor to fake that."

Dennis cleared his throat. Lesley gave him a pointed look.

"He'd have to be a *very* good actor," she said.

Dennis nodded in acknowledgement. He didn't like her swearing. On her first day he'd threatened her with a swear box, which was now safely hidden inside his desk. But that was only because she'd said she would try to tone down her language. The two DCs spoke differently here in the office to when they were out with her. Mike in particular had developed a whole new range of vocabulary. Lesley didn't know if that was natural, or if it was his twisted way of trying to impress her. Either way, her judgement would be based on his work. If he was a good DC, she'd support him. If not, she'd give him a damn good bollocking until he became one.

"Right," she said. "Forensics, post-mortem, witnesses." She wrote these words on the board.

Tina spoke. "No sign of any witnesses, boss. As far as we can tell, it happened before anyone else was up there."

"That fits with what her husband said," Lesley replied. "She left the house before dawn."

Tina nodded. "Sunny day, it would have been busy up there later on. Plenty of grockles taking a stroll up from Swanage, or from Studland."

"Grockles?"

Tina blushed. "Tourists."

Lesley eyed the board. "But she wasn't spotted until up there."

"She couldn't be seen from the cliff," Johnny said. "Not unless you go right to the edge, and people don't do that, usually. She was only spotted from the sea."

Tina turned to him, shifting in her chair. "But there would have been boats earlier on, surely?"

"The pertinent point," said Lesley, "Is that nobody saw her up there before she was pushed. And as far as we're aware, nobody saw her assailant."

"If there was one," said Dennis.

Lesley eyed him. "Have you seen the angle on those cliffs?"

"I have." His expression was tight.

"It's harder than you think to push yourself over to where she was found. You'd have to take a flying jump. You couldn't just stroll over the edge and drop."

Mind you, Lesley thought. *It doesn't feel like that when you're up there.*

"Maybe she did take a flying jump?" Dennis said. "If she was determined enough."

"That doesn't explain the camera," Lesley replied. "It was still around her neck, while she'd left her bag neatly on her jacket. What kind of person leaves their camera kit and their jacket neatly on the grass, but keeps the camera itself around their neck when they jump to their death?"

"If she cared about her kit," Johnny said, "she'd have taken the camera off first."

Lesley pointed at him with the marker pen. "Exactly. That's why I'm sure it's suspicious. We need to know if she sustained defensive wounds. When's the PM scheduled?"

"This afternoon," said Dennis. "Whittaker's working as fast as he can."

Lesley rolled her eyes. For Dr Whittaker *as fast as he can* was glacial.

"Not until this afternoon?" she said.

Dennis shrugged. "The man's busy."

"Jesus Christ." Lesley ignored Dennis's glare. "He really doesn't know what his priorities should be, does he?"

"You could argue that he does," said Dennis. "I mean, granddaughter's birthday party, tending to his living patients before the dead. *Those* are his priorities. He knows what they are and he focuses on them."

"And you respect that?" Lesley asked.

"I'm not saying I respect it, boss. I'm just saying that's what's happening."

"It's not good enough." She wished she had the authority to find a new pathologist. She thought of Adana Adebayo, the woman she'd worked with back in the West Midlands. Adana had been efficient, intelligent, and tenacious. Nothing like Henry Whittaker, with his condescending manner and his inability to speed up for anyone.

"OK," she sighed. "So the post-mortem is this afternoon, if we're lucky. What about forensics? Has Gail gone over that camera bag for prints?"

"Not sure," said Dennis.

"She'll report back in to us as soon as she's got something," added Johnny.

Lesley nodded. Gail was good. Thorough, businesslike, professional. She knew how to run a crime scene. The contrast between her and the pathologist couldn't be more pointed. It wouldn't be long before Gail arrived in the office and gave them what she had. There was no reason to chase her. Once Gail had her information, she passed it on.

"In that case," Lesley said, "We need witness statements. Find out if anybody in Studland saw her arrive. Or her potential attacker."

"At dawn, boss?" said Johnny.

"Yes, at dawn. Somebody might have been up early: taking a stroll, walking their dog, or unable to sleep. You've never been out for an early walk and caught the eye of someone staring out from their front window? Shushing babies back to sleep, dealing with insomnia?"

Insomnia was a problem Lesley knew well, but she wasn't about to tell her team that.

She placed the marker in its holder. "Johnny and Mike, you go to Studland, knock on some doors, find out if anyone saw anything suspicious. Unfamiliar cars, people returning from the cliffs early in the morning."

"Boss," said Mike. He made for the door and Johnny followed, his gait slower. He glanced at Dennis, who nodded.

Dennis turned to Lesley. "What d'you want me on?"

"You and Tina go and see the husband."

"You've already seen him."

"He had his kids with him last night, and there's more we need to ask him. Find out what was going on in

Ameena's life. Did she have reason to kill herself? Was there somebody at work she'd pissed off?"

"Her colleagues would know that," suggested Tina.

"They would," said Lesley. "And that's why I'm going over to the law firm."

Dennis raised an eyebrow. "On your own?"

She met his gaze. "Yes, *on my own*. You got a problem with that?"

"No, boss. I'll work with Tina. Johnny and Mike can work together. You can go off on your lonesome."

She resisted the urge to bite. "That's what I'll do, Dennis," she said. "You let me know if you find out anything useful from Tom Holroyd, yes?"

"Of course. I've been doing this for a while, you know."

She stared at him until his gaze left hers. Dennis wasn't the easiest DS to work with, but he didn't normally go for open rebellion.

Now wasn't the time to address it. She knew that her predecessor, DCI Mackie, had died after going off a cliff. It would be even harder for Dennis to ignore.

"Go on then." She clapped her hands. "Chop, chop."

Dennis walked to the door then waited for Tina to pass him, ostentatiously gesturing for her to go first. Tina pursed her lips as she passed him.

Lesley watched as they grabbed their jackets and left the office. Dennis didn't even believe this was a murder case. But Lesley could feel it in her blood.

Somebody had killed Ameena, thrown her off the cliff edge. Possibly somebody who knew Lesley's girlfriend.

She needed to find out why, and whether Elsa was connected.

CHAPTER SEVEN

Tina stared out of the windscreen as DS Frampton drove round the block of houses near Ameena Khan's house.

"There's a spot there," she said.

He shook his head. "Not good enough."

She clenched her fist in her lap. They'd be here all day doing this.

"Why don't you just park up behind the squad car over there?" She pointed to a police car parked three houses along from Ameena's house.

"Single yellow lines," he replied. "We need a legal space."

Tina knew full well that as police officers working a case, they could park on single yellow lines. Any ticket they received would be cancelled. But no, the sarge wanted to do this properly.

She chewed her bottom lip, forcing herself not to speak, as he circled the block one more time. Fortunately, Ameena had lived in a neighbourhood with plenty of interconnecting roads, so the circuit didn't take long. On the second attempt, he'd done a figure of eight around two blocks, still seeking out the perfect spot.

"There!" She gestured towards to a space outside a house about ten doors down from Ameena's. No double yellows, no single yellows, no white lines, no nothing. Surely he couldn't reject this one.

He grunted and eased the car into the space.

At last, she thought.

Tina got out of the car and shook out the tension.

"Listen, Constable," the sarge said, looking at her over the top of the car. "You watch and learn. You haven't done this before, let me do the talking."

"Yes, Sarge." She *had* done this, plenty of times. She'd been assigned as family liaison officer in at least a dozen cases. Maybe she hadn't *officially* been part of CID as the FLO. But she'd had plenty of opportunities to talk to witnesses and victims. Plenty of opportunities to find out what was really going on. Tina could put an interviewee at their ease, get them to tell her things they'd withhold from CID. But DS Frampton would never give her credit for that.

She tugged down her jacket and followed him across the road. The sun was still pounding down and she sweated in her heavy uniform. Dennis wore the tweed blazer she'd seen him in almost every day since she'd joined the team. She wondered how hot he was in it. Sweat beaded his forehead and his hair was plastered down at the back. She grimaced.

He walked ahead of her and rang the front doorbell. Ameena Khan had lived in a pleasant-looking detached house on a wide street, not too far from the centre of Christchurch.

Tina wondered how much houses like this cost. Prices fluctuated around the county. Sandbanks was reputedly one of the most expensive pieces of real estate on the planet, while there were parts of Poole that were run-down and as cheap as anywhere in the north. But here in Christchurch, prices would be high. Wealthy, elderly people from inland retired here, bumping up house prices along with the second homers who gobbled up properties and left them empty most of the year. Locals like Tina didn't stand a chance; she still lived with her mum and dad.

A uniformed constable opened the door. He nodded at DS Frampton. "Sarge."

The DS frowned. "PC Hughes, what are you doing here?"

"I'm the family liaison officer, Sarge."

DS Frampton peered at him. Tina could read his mind. *What's a man doing as an FLO?* But PC Hughes was a good liaison officer, as skilled as any of the women at putting families at their ease and at becoming invisible when they were at their lowest. He was the only man doing this job, and he got his fair share of ribbing from the other male PCs.

"You going to let us in then?" asked the sarge.

PC Hughes stood back. He shared a knowing glance with Tina, who'd worked with him before. She and the sarge filed past him and into a large open plan space at the back of the house. A man sat at a long dining table, his fingers wrapped around a cup of coffee.

PC Hughes followed behind them. "That's Tom Holroyd," he muttered. "The victim's husband."

Tina nodded. "Cheers, mate."

DS Frampton approached the man, holding up his ID. "My name is Detective Sergeant Frampton," he said. "I'm sorry to have to bother you."

The man looked up at him. His eyes were red-rimmed and his face grey. His jowls looked like they might drop down into his chest.

He shrugged. "Who are you?"

37

"Like I say, DS Frampton. This is PC Abbott. We're from the Major Crime Investigations Team, hoping we can find out more about your wife."

The man's mouth dropped even further. "Major crimes? So she was definitely…"

"We can't be sure just yet," said the sarge. "But DCI Clarke, she's the senior investigating officer on this. She wants to get things moving as soon as possible, just in case."

The man lifted his mug to his lips and then placed it back down again. "I think I met her. Tall, blonde?"

The DS nodded. PC Hughes approached Mr Holroyd. "D'you want a top-up, mate?"

Holroyd looked up at him. "Whatever."

PC Hughes took the mug off him and made for the sink. He filled the kettle and turned to look at Tina. "You want one?"

She looked back towards the sarge. He shook his head.

"Not right now, sorry," she said to PC Hughes. "Not for us."

"Fair enough." He filled the kettle.

The sarge sat down at the table, at an angle from Mr Holroyd. Tina rounded the table and sat opposite the sarge, so the two of them flanked the man.

He stared down at his hands, which he was turning over on the table, peering at the fingernails. Occasionally he would lift one to his lips, and nibble at it.

"Where are your children?" DS Frampton asked.

Holroyd looked up. "With their Gran."

The sarge nodded, relieved they wouldn't be interrupted. "You spoke to my boss last night, I understand," he said.

"Yeah, she wanted… I can't remember what she wanted. She told me about Ameena."

Tina curled her toes in her shoes. No matter how many times she'd sat with people like Tom Holroyd, it never got any easier.

"We just need to know if there's anything going on at work or in her personal life, that might mean somebody wanted to hurt your wife," the DS asked.

Holroyd looked at him "Hurt her?"

The sarge nodded.

"Kill her, you mean?" said the man.

The sarge stiffened. "Possibly," he replied, his voice gentle.

The victim's husband shook his head. "I can't believe anybody would be that angry with her. I mean, she's a lawyer. You make enemies, don't you, as a lawyer? I don't know, it's not my bag. I never bothered with it, wish I had now."

"You didn't talk about work? She didn't discuss cases with you?"

Holroyd shook his head. "Good God, no. She was adamant on confidentiality. She was a criminal lawyer, you know. Dealt with… Well, I don't know who she dealt with, but you can imagine, can't you?"

Tina nodded. She could imagine indeed. She wondered if Nevin, Cross and Short dealt with the kind of criminals she was used to. Low-level crimes, burglaries, petty assaults. Or whether they were more accustomed to the criminals that the MCIT tracked down. The DCI was going to the law firm; she'd find out, if anybody could.

She stretched out her hand on the table, leaving it close to the man's but not quite touching. "Could there be anybody who might want to hurt *you*?" she asked.

The sarge flashed her a look.

Holroyd stared at her. "I'm a head teacher. I work at a primary school. No, of course not."

"No parents, no excluded children?" the DS asked.

Mr Holroyd turned to him. "It's not that kind of school. It's just a little place. A community, a happy family, we get along. I mean, of course there are some kids who are naughty. But nothing serious. I haven't had to exclude a child for years."

"And no parents who have taken against you for any reason?" the sarge asked.

Holroyd shrugged. "Why would they? Of course not."

Tina clenched her fists on the table. She could feel grief and despair shining out of this man. Right now, he didn't know how to get from one day to the next, or even one moment to the next.

"How did she seem in herself?" she asked. "In recent days and weeks?"

He looked at her. "She was stressed, I guess. Worried about something. A case, she told me, didn't say what."

"She had a difficult case on right now?" DS Frampton asked.

Holroyd nodded. "I think so. God, you must think I'm a terrible husband. I never talked to her about her work, even when it was stressing her out."

"We don't think anything of the sort," said Tina.

PC Hughes placed a full mug in front of Mr Holroyd. Holroyd grabbed it and drank, long and slow. The three police officers watched him. Finally, he placed it back down on the table and closed his eyes.

"I can't help you," he said. "There's nothing. She was a happy woman, we had a happy marriage, and two beautiful children. She didn't do this to herself and if someone else did it to her, I've got no idea who."

CHAPTER EIGHT

Lesley drove towards Bournemouth, her fingers tapping on the steering wheel. Ironically, the traffic grew thinner as she neared the town centre.

Away from the 'grockles', traffic was more predictable, less seasonal. Here she knew how long it would take to get from one place to another. On the Isle of Purbeck, in contrast, it could take anything from ten minutes to an hour and a half to get from Wareham to Swanage.

Even so, there were signs she was in a tourist area. Adverts for ice-cream stood outside shops, people wore shorts and t-shirts and there was an atmosphere of relaxation and cheer.

Nevin, Cross and Short was in the city centre. Lesley spotted a sign for Boscombe, where Elsa lived, and wondered if Elsa would be at work. Would she admit to knowing the senior investigating officer on this case? Did her colleagues in the law firm even know she was gay?

Lesley wasn't sure how she felt about it herself. Part of her hoped Elsa wouldn't be there, that she'd get to speak to one of the other partners. It had only been yesterday that she'd even discovered that Elsa was a partner at all.

She'd known Elsa worked for a criminal law firm in Bournemouth. She'd known Elsa might confront her one day on a case, but neither of them had talked much about work. It hadn't occurred to her that Elsa would be one of the most senior members of her firm.

Lesley parked in the underground car park in Hinton Road. Bournemouth was part of an urban sprawl, beginning with Poole and stretching into Hampshire. But as she left the car park, she found herself surrounded by low buildings and with a view of the sea. Sprawl or not, it certainly wasn't Birmingham.

She walked to the offices of Nevin, Cross and Short and pressed the buzzer outside. The firm was unprepossessing from the front. Just a darkened glass door in between shops and a sign above announcing the name of the firm.

"Can I help you?" came a voice over the intercom.

She peered in and spotted a camera. She held up her ID. "DCI Clarke, Dorset Police," she said. "I'd like to talk to a senior partner."

"One moment, please."

Lesley stood back. Was this the kind of firm that would instantly admit a police officer, or would they make her wait?

A moment later, her question was answered when the door buzzed. She leaned on it to enter the building. Ahead was a flight of stairs, plaques on the wall telling her that three firms occupied these offices. So Elsa's firm wasn't as big as it seemed.

She hurried up the stairs and found a woman in a crisp black trouser suit waiting at the top.

"My name's Amanda," she said. "I'm Mr Nevin's PA. Can I help you?"

"Is Mr Nevin a partner?" Lesley asked.

The woman nodded.

"In that case, I'd like to speak to him."

"It's not as simple as that. He's got a court case later this morning."

"I'm senior investigating officer in the suspected murder of one of your lawyers. This takes priority."

The woman tugged at her fingers and pointed to a bank of velvet-upholstered chairs. "Please wait here."

Lesley grunted and headed towards the chairs. The woman disappeared through a wooden door. Instead of sitting down, Lesley approached the door and stopped to listen. There was no glass, no view through. She wondered what was beyond. A large open plan office or a warren of pokey corridors? What kind of firm did Elsa work for? Gleaming glass, modern desks, the highest of high-tech, or one of those old-fashioned firms that she'd dealt with in Birmingham city centre? Tiny little rooms up narrow stairs, sitting in the same pokey upstairs offices as they had for decades.

The door opened and Lesley almost fell through. The PA, Amanda, put out a hand but Lesley righted herself before she had to catch her.

"I didn't know you were there." The PA glanced towards the chairs. "I did ask you to…"

Lesley gave her a smile. "He's ready for me?"

The woman looked at her, her eyes full of doubt and distrust. "Follow me."

Beyond the door was a vast open plan office. This space must span three or four shops below, Lesley thought. She wondered how much crime took place in Bournemouth to justify law firms this grand.

She followed the woman through the open space and towards a glass office in the corner. A broad-faced man with greying hair and an orange tan sat inside, bent over

43

paperwork. His ornate oak desk was the only thing here that didn't shine.

The PA knocked on the door and the man raised his hand and beckoned without looking up. The woman opened the door and ushered Lesley through.

Lesley approached the desk. "Mr Nevin?" she asked, raising her ID.

"The one and only." He closed a file and looked up. His hair was slicked back with gel and his suit was tailored, expensive. This clearly wasn't a firm that made its money from Legal Aid.

"What can I do for you?" he asked.

"You've not heard?"

He shifted his face into an appropriate expression of concern. "Of course I have, terrible business. Poor Ms Khan."

Poor Ms Khan indeed, thought Lesley. She'd noticed a hubbub of activity as she'd passed through the office outside. Lively chatter and busy people getting on with their day. Nobody seemed to be mourning the dead lawyer.

She took the seat across from him, despite not having been invited.

"I'm here to find out whether Ms Khan might have had anybody who would wish her harm," she said, getting straight to the point.

Nevin leaned back in his chair and steepled his hands beneath his chin. "You don't mess around, do you? Have I met you before?"

"I've been in the MCIT for six weeks."

"That'll explain it. You've not arrested any of our clients?"

"That'll depend on who your clients are," she said.

"That's our business," he replied.

She'd find out soon enough who their clients were.

"So," she said, crossing her legs. "Tell me about Ameena Khan. What cases was she working on? Who was she working with?"

Nevin glanced out through the glass towards the open plan office beyond. "She headed up one of our teams, had a team of staff working for her. Associates, paralegals, a PA, you know the kind of thing."

Lesley didn't, but didn't say so. "So what was she working on?"

"That's confidential information, I'm afraid."

Lesley sighed. "This is a police investigation, Mr Nevin. If I need to get a warrant to extract that information from you, I will. But it would be much simpler for both of us if you just cooperated."

He lowered his hands to his desk and leaned forward. "My team are going through her files right now, checking what's outstanding. There will be loose ends to tie up, cases to assign responsibility for. I'm sure you understand."

She did. This man was more interested in the smooth running of his firm, than the fate of one of his lawyers. She wondered what it would be like to work here.

She resisted the urge to turn in her seat and see if Elsa was in the office outside. She'd kept her eyes down on the way through, getting a feel for the place but not meeting any eyes.

"So who are the other partners?" she asked him.

"The other partners? Well, there's me, Harry Nevin, I'm the managing partner. Then there's Aurelia Cross, and Elsa Short. Why do you ask?"

"Where did Ameena Khan sit in the pecking order?"

"She was a junior partner," he replied. "Name not on the door yet, but not far off. She was good. Efficient, ruthless, tough. Proper bloody bulldog, she was."

Lesley noticed how easy he found it to slip into the past tense.

She put her card on the desk. "Here's my email address. Where you can forward the details of her current cases."

He sighed. "I suppose I have no choice?"

"Not really."

He picked up the card, holding it between the tips of his finger like he might catch something. "I'm sure one of the paralegals can sort that. Is that everything you need?"

"Not quite," she replied. "Did Ameena have any enemies? Any clients who thought she'd failed them? Cases she lost?"

He laughed. "They all get pissed off when you lose, you should know that. I've seen you lot getting pissed off in court when *we* win."

"I need specifics," she told him. "Any violent criminals that got sent down despite Ameena representing them."

"They'd be in prison though, wouldn't they?" he replied.

"Not necessarily. Not anymore. Or they might have friends on the outside."

"You think a disgruntled ex-client shoved my lawyer off the cliffs?"

"I don't think anything yet," she replied. "I just need to get what background information I can."

"I'll think about it," he said, leaning back in his chair so far she thought he might fall out. He glanced at the card, now on his desk, which was clear except for that and the solitary file. "I'll let you know if I come up with anything."

"And meanwhile, you'll send us over those files."

He nodded. "Of course we will, I know the law."

Yes, she thought. He knew the law all right, and he'd take care to make sure he only gave them what he was legally required to.

Lesley tried not to take against witnesses. But with Harry Nevin, she could tell that wasn't going to be easy. She didn't imagine working with him would be much fun. He didn't seem the type to have given Ameena Khan any support, despite her supposedly being such a good lawyer. Could she have been driven to suicide? *No. He's not that bad.*

"Is that everything?" he said. "I'm a busy man, you know."

Of course you are, thought Lesley. They were all busy men.

She stood up. "If you think of anything, you'll call me?"

He stared back at her. "Of course I will, Chief Inspector. What do you take me for?"

CHAPTER NINE

Johnny walked back to his car, his limbs heavy. The sun was still beating down, and his shirt stuck to his back.

The last two hours had been a waste of time. No witnesses, nothing to learn.

As he opened the car door, he saw Gail walking down from the headland. Her two CSIs, Gav and Brett, were already loading things into the forensics team's van.

Johnny approached them. "You finishing up?"

"Yep," replied Gail. "All done. We've taken the cordon down. We've removed all the evidence we could find, it's all been bagged up and it'll be going back to the lab. My report will be with your boss when we get back to the office."

"Thanks," he said. "Anything useful?"

"Not much," she replied. "There's the bag and the camera equipment. Obviously we'll dust those, check if there's any DNA. You never know, there might be more than just the victim's fingerprints on them, but I doubt it."

Johnny nodded. "You think this is a suicide after all?"

Gail shook her head. "That's not what I'm saying. I just think that if somebody did throw her off the cliff, they knew what they were doing. They took care to cover their tracks. There was only one route through the grass to the spot where her coat was. If there was a killer, he was clever enough to follow the same path she took."

"You photographed it?" he asked.

"I thought I wouldn't bother," Gail replied. "Couldn't see the point."

Johnny gave her a look.

She laughed. "Of course I bloody have, Johnny. What d'you take me for? It'll all be up on your board in Lesley's office by the end of the afternoon."

He smiled at her. Gail was alright, despite the gossip about her and her ex-husband that Dennis liked to allude to.

He heard footsteps approaching from behind: Mike.

Johnny turned. "Any joy?"

Mike looked as downcast as Johnny felt. "Nothing mate. No one saw anything. No strange cars, no individuals they didn't recognise, and nobody seems to have seen Ameena Khan herself. Everybody around here shuts their curtains all night, keeps them closed, doesn't get up until eight o'clock in the morning."

"Lucky bastards," Johnny said, thinking of his own hours, which were about to get worse after his wife gave birth.

"OK." He turned to Gail. "Let's hope you find something useful on that camera."

"Like I say," she told him, "I'm not holding out much hope. See you back at the office, yeah?" She got into the van and drove away.

Johnny looked at Mike. "I'm going up there," he said.

"Up to the cliff top?"

"Where else?"

"But the CSIs have finished up there."

"I want to look at it myself."

"You want to get a feel for how it happened. Stand up there yourself."

Johnny shrugged. He knew that wasn't the real reason he was going up there and so did Mike, but neither of them were about to say it.

"You coming?" he asked.

"Might as well," Mike replied. "Maybe I can get some insight too."

Johnny grunted, knowing that Mike had his own reasons for going up there as well.

They walked along the path in silence. The sea on one side, tangled hedges on the other. Eventually the hedges disappeared and they were on the headland, approaching Old Harry Rocks. In front of them was the promontory leading to the rocks. To the right, the coastal path, across Ballard Down and onwards towards Swanage.

Johnny took the turn towards the spot where Ameena Khan's coat and camera gear had been left. As he reached it, he cast around the area to see if he could spot the path in the grass that Gail had talked about. But it was gone. He couldn't tell where Ameena had been when she'd been pushed off.

"Poor woman," he breathed, looking out to sea. "Horrible way to die."

Mike nodded. He pulled his jacket off and slung it over his shoulder. "Terrifying."

"Do you think she knew?" Johnny asked. "That someone was about to throw her off? How long d'you think she had?"

Mike shrugged. "We'll probably never know. It might have been sudden, might not."

"She came here under her own steam though," Johnny said. "She wasn't brought here."

"That's not what the evidence suggests."

Johnny plunged his hands into his pockets. He turned away from Mike and carried on along the cliff edge, towards Swanage. After a short while, he came to the point where the coastal path met the Purbeck Way, which went inland. He stopped.

He turned towards the sea and stared out, not saying anything. Mike stood next to him doing the same.

After a few moments, Johnny let out a long sigh. "We'd best get back to the office."

"Best had," replied Mike. He looked down, towards the hidden rocks below them. "You're thinking about Mackie."

This was the spot where DCI Mackie had thrown himself off the cliff four months earlier.

Johnny had been up here a few times since. First when it had been a crime scene. Again, after it had been concluded that Mackie killed himself. Finally, and more than once, to attempt to exorcise his own demons.

"Poor bugger," he said. "What must it be like to get that desperate?"

Mike shivered. "No idea, mate."

Johnny turned towards his colleague, facing back the way they'd come. DCI Mackie had the same views on suicide as most police officers. They knew what it meant to clear up the mess. They knew about the coastguard guys, the car or train drivers. The paramedics. Not to mention the family.

He knew that no copper would do that, unless they were truly desperate.

Mackie had retired in January. A retirement that he'd served his time for, one that he'd looked forward to. He'd joked about how he'd fill his time when the rest of them were still working cases, how little he'd miss them. He'd been cheerful about it.

So why had he killed himself?

"Come on," said Mike. "We need to get back. Let them know we found nothing on the door to door."

Johnny nodded. "And I've got the post-mortem."

Mike's face darkened. "That'll be fun."

"Too right," said Johnny, as they walked back towards the car.

CHAPTER TEN

Lesley headed down the echoing stairs of the law firm, pondering what she'd just seen and heard.

Harry Nevin had been cagey. Despite agreeing to hand over the files, there had been an air of defiance about him, a sense that he was hiding something. She hoped the files would shed light on it. And as she'd left the offices, she'd noticed people looking at her nervously. Like they all knew what she was there for, and they weren't happy about it. Of course Ameena Khan's death tainted their reaction to her presence, but she'd felt like there was an extra edge to the atmosphere as she'd walked through the open plan office. Something more than grief, more than shock. Something akin to deception.

As she walked away from the building, she heard a voice behind her. "Excuse me!"

Lesley turned, patting herself down. Had she left something behind? A phone, her notepad? She wasn't carrying a bag.

A young black woman ran out of the office door. She wore a bright pink jacket over grey trousers and looked smart and efficient.

"You're looking for me?"

The woman nodded. She looked towards the windows of the law firm. "You're the detective working on Ameena's case?"

"DCI Clarke. Who are you?"

"My name's Sam, I'm Ameena's PA." Her eyes lowered. "Or I was, I s'pose." She clutched herself, as if suddenly realising that her boss was dead.

"Have you got something you want to tell me?" Lesley asked her.

People pushed past them on either side. The street was busying up now; they weren't far from the main shops.

The woman, Sam, looked back at her, her eyes full of worry. "What did he tell you, Mr Nevin? What did he say?"

"That's confidential, I'm afraid. Why? What do you expect him to have told me?"

The woman's brow furrowed. "No, sorry. It's alright. You don't need me to bother you." She turned away.

Lesley put out her hand and touched the woman's arm, anxious not to grab her in the middle of the street.

She didn't want her to get away. Nobody ran after a police officer if they didn't have something important to tell them.

"Do you have information about Ameena?"

The woman froze, her back to Lesley. She raised her head slowly, looking up at the windows of her employers. She turned to Lesley, her face wary.

"I'm not sure," she said.

Lesley stepped towards her. "Come with me." She ushered the woman towards the building, where they couldn't be seen from above.

As they walked, Sam's gaze kept flicking up to the first floor.

"Are you scared?" Lesley asked her. "Is there something I need to know?"

Sam shook her head. "No. Not scared. Just…"

Lesley cocked her head. "Just what?"

"He won't send you all the files," the woman said.

"Sorry?"

"You've asked him for Ameena's files, haven't you? You've asked him what cases she was working on."

Lesley looked back at the woman. "Yes."

"Look, I watch the TV shows, I know how it works. A lawyer dies, a criminal lawyer. You want to know who her clients are, you want to know if anybody's pissed off with her, if there's someone whose case she's lost, someone who might want to kill her."

"We're not certain that it *is* a murder," Lesley said. "It might just be accidental death."

Sam looked into Lesley's face. Her nostrils flared. There was certainty in her eyes.

"What do you know, Sam? You can tell me in confidence."

She shook her head. "All I can tell you is he won't send you everything."

"What do you mean?"

"He'll send you a bunch of files, they might not even be Ameena's. But it won't be everything, and it won't be what you need."

"In that case, can you tell me what I need?" Lesley's impatience was growing.

Sam jerked away. She looked towards the front door of the building. A man emerged, dressed in a tight-fitting grey suit. Sam pulled Lesley around the side of the building.

"I can't tell you," she said. "I just want you to know that you need to look further."

"If there are important files or an important case that I need to know about, then you need to tell me what it is."

"Sorry, no. Client confidentiality."

"This is a police investigation, Miss…?"

"Chaston. Sam Chaston."

"Miss Chaston, this is a police investigation. I'm sure—"

"I'd lose my job."

"You won't lose your job for helping the police with a legitimate inquiry."

Sam looked back up at the building. She was rubbing her arms, shivering despite the heat of the day.

"I can't tell you, I just want you to know to look further."

Lesley pulled her card out of her pocket and handed it over.

"If you decide you want to tell me more, you call me, day or night. It's important."

The woman nodded. She grabbed the card, folded it up into a tiny square and pushed it inside her blouse. She gave Lesley a final look and hurried away.

Lesley followed her around the side of the building and watched her enter.

The PA shook herself out as she went inside, as if to purge herself of the conversation that she'd just had with the detective.

Lesley looked up at the first-floor windows. There was something going on with this law firm, something that could be relevant to Ameena's death. Nobody inside was telling her.

But what Harry Nevin didn't know was that Lesley had someone on the inside.

CHAPTER ELEVEN

Johnny stood a few steps behind the pathologist, anxious not to get in the way. Classical music blared from a speaker sitting on a sideboard beyond the bench where the body was laid out.

Dr Whittaker looked at him, an eyebrow raised. "Good of you to arrive on time," he said.

Johnny shrugged. It wasn't exactly difficult to arrive on time for one of Dr Whittaker's post-mortems. The man seemed to take hours, if not days, to work himself up to a stage where he would deign to examine a body.

"I'm glad I got here on time, too," he said. "I can observe."

"You're not going up throw up on me, are you?" the pathologist sneered.

Johnny had done plenty of these. As a DC for eight years, he'd attended dozens of post-mortems. He'd seen far worse than this. Bodies bloated from water, scarred by fire. Bodies so decomposed they were barely recognisable as human.

Ameena Khan's body was intact, her injuries relatively mild. Her torso was blotched by black, red and yellow bruising. Her face had been smashed in on one side, and her arms had bruises running all the way down the skin.

Other than that, she looked peaceful. Lying on the table, eyes closed, arms to her sides. She hadn't been opened up yet and looked much as she would have done when the coastguard had dragged her off the rocks below the cliff.

The speaker switched to another track. Johnny glanced at it.

"You don't approve?" said Dr Whittaker. "The music, you think it's too light?"

The music didn't sound light at all to Johnny. He shook his head.

"Fingal's Cave," the pathologist told him. "It felt appropriate. Helps me concentrate."

He looked at the body. "Let's start on external injuries. We don't need to open her up just yet."

Johnny looked down at Ameena. It felt like a violation, what they were about to do to her, the more so given that the injuries sustained in her death had barely broken the skin. The only external bleeding was on her left cheek, which had been smashed open. Johnny hoped the pathologist would be able to tell if it had been smashed by the rocks or by an assailant.

Whittaker took a step towards the body and placed his fingers on her forehead.

"Hmm," he said. "So her face… significant bruising to the left cheek, lacerations along the jawbone and the skin is broken in…" He paused, muttering to himself. "Three places." He nodded to an assistant who stood at the other end of the table making notes.

"Do you think somebody hit her?" Johnny said. "The injuries on her face?"

Whittaker moved her head from side to side, peering at the wounds. "They look consistent with her falling face first onto the rocks," he said. "Jagged scarring."

He squinted. "And there are fragments of rock embedded in the skin."

Johnny nodded. He got his own notebook out of his pocket and made a note. *Fragments of rock. Significant bruising, sustained when she fell.*

Whittaker shifted his attention to the woman's chest. Again, there was significant bruising. Like an abstract painting. Swathes of red, yellow, brown and black peppered her skin.

Whittaker traced his fingers along the edges of the bruises, pushing up the skin. Johnny wasn't sure why. Maybe the skin would change colour with pressure?

"Hmm," Whittaker said, "Bit harder to tell on dark-skinned victims." He looked at Johnny. "But believe it or not, they bruise the same as you and me."

Johnny felt his upper lip curling. He tried to imagine what the DCI would say if she was standing here. He swallowed and said nothing. *Wimp.*

Whittaker bent over the woman's body, examining her chest. "No sign of any stones or rocks here," he said. "But then her clothes would have protected her."

He looked up at Johnny. "I assume your forensic people have the clothes?"

Johnny nodded. He had no idea what the forensics guys had, but he knew that if the clothes were available, they would be examining them. Gail and her team ran a tight ship.

"Here," Whittaker said. "The pattern of this bruising is also consistent with it being sustained when she fell on the rocks. All of the bruising is to her front, nothing on her back. I imagine she fell headfirst and landed face down." He raised an eyebrow. "Do you know how the coastguard found her?"

Johnnie nodded. "Face down." That was all he had been told, but it was enough.

Whittaker lifted one of the woman's arms. "However," he said, "her arms aren't consistent with that hypothesis. She's got bruising here to the upper arm, both sides."

Johnny felt himself perk up. "Inflicted by an attacker?"

Whittaker looked at him. "Top of the class to you, boy. Yes, look at this." He raised Ameena's right arm, lifting it so that her hand pointed towards the ceiling. "See this bruising here."

Johnny moved around the doctor to get a better view. He could hear the pathologist's assistant shuffling out of the way, but his gaze was focused on the victim.

Sure enough, there were distinct bruises on her upper arm. Three small circles, all areas of darkened skin.

"Somebody held on to her very tightly," the pathologist said. "She's got bruising consistent with being restrained. Lifted, maybe. Finger-marks. I can only see three on this arm."

He dropped the arm abruptly. Johnny jumped at the sound of it hitting the table. Whittaker moved around to the other side and examined her other arm.

"Yes, we have four here. Consistent with somebody gripping her arm from behind."

Dr Whittaker dropped Ameena's arm and reached out to Johnny. He grabbed his arm to demonstrate. "See?" He let go.

"So they lifted her and threw her over the cliff?" Johnny rubbed his arm.

Whittaker looked at him. "I'm a pathologist, man, not a clairvoyant."

Johnny held the pathologist's gaze, determined not to be cowed by this man. Whittaker was lazy and slow. He was a decent enough pathologist, but Johnny imagined that the DCI had worked with better.

Johnny, on the other hand, was an experienced detective. He knew how to do a job properly, and he knew when to turn up on time.

He straightened. "So you're saying it wasn't an accident?"

Whittaker nodded. "Nor suicide. Somebody definitely pushed this woman off the cliff."

CHAPTER TWELVE

Ameena Khan's camera was wet, but not so wet that it was ruined.

Gail had taken it apart and removed the SD card. She'd also taken out the battery, which was leaking. Last night, she'd placed the camera and SD card in the kit they used for drying electrical items out: a ziplock bag containing silica and other chemicals designed to dry without causing further damage.

She opened the seal and pulled out the camera and card, hoping the data would be retrievable.

The camera was functional. The buttons worked, the menus were operational. But that wasn't where she was going to start.

She took the card and placed it in the SD slot of her laptop. Swallowing, she brought up the file manager. Would the photos be preserved? Would there even be any?

Only one way to find out.

Gail licked her lips as she flicked through to the external drive. Bingo. Over a hundred photographs, time and date stamped, each with its metadata: where they'd been taken, the camera settings, the GPS location.

Perfect, she thought. Thank God for serious photographers and their digital SLRs.

She navigated through to the photographs taken on Sunday morning. The first was timestamped 4:30am. It showed a man lying in bed, two small children either side of him. All were asleep, the kids draped over their dad like he was just another part of the bed.

Gail felt her heart soften. Ameena had stopped to take a photo of her family before heading out before dawn. This was a tight-knit family.

She shrugged her shoulders to shake away the heavy feeling, and flicked through to the next photograph. It was of the path between Studland and Old Harry Rocks, familiar from her trips back and forth while she'd been examining the crime scene. Ameena hadn't been far from where Gail had parked her van, when she'd taken this photograph. Gail checked the time: 5:12am. She flicked through to the next one.

It was further along the path, with more sky taking up the frame. A smudge of sea was visible above the cliffs. 5:14am.

More photographs followed, a stop-motion video of Ameena's journey up to the headland. Gail felt her skin chill as she worked forward to the moment Ameena would die.

The stop-motion stills were followed by a slew of photographs of the same scene. A vantage point over Old Harry Rocks. They differed in terms of the light and quality, but not the content. The woman had been experimenting with the camera settings. Occasionally there would be another shot out towards the sea, or over towards Bournemouth. She was anticipating the dawn, waiting for the perfect light.

Then there were two shots of a white card: Ameena adjusting her light levels. This woman was serious about her photography.

It was macabre, but Gail could only hope she continued shooting, right up until the final moment. She kept going. More shots of Old Harry Rocks, the light growing now, the settings changing. Occasionally there was a pause for a major setting to be adjusted, and then a few more shots. Slightly different framing, slightly different angle.

Ameena had clearly staked out a location, the spot where she'd laid down her coat. Had she sat on it to keep her clothes from getting wet from the dew? Maybe she'd used it to protect her camera gear.

Gail flicked forward again. The next photograph wasn't of Old Harry Rocks, but of the sky. It was mid blue, facing away from the sunrise. Gail tried to determine the angle. Directly upwards?

Then there was another shot of the sky, this one with a pink tinge to one side: the sunrise. It was followed by more similar shots, all depicting parts of the sky. None of them looked deliberately framed.

There were ten of them, twelve, fourteen, twenty. Gail checked the settings: the camera had been on rapid burst mode. The shots morphed into other images: blurred grass, the sea beyond the cliffs, the rocks, the Isle of Wight in the distance. The framing was random now, chaotic.

Gail tried to imagine where Ameena had been standing when she had taken them, if the word 'taken' was appropriate. It felt like these images had been captured passively, almost by accident. Gail kept going, her chest tightening.

The next image showed a hand. Gail squinted and enlarged it. The hand was shadowy and dark. She pulled in a breath, then turned in her seat and beckoned Gav over.

"Look at this."

He bent over her chair, peering at the screen over her shoulder. "Is this from Ameena Khan's camera?"

She nodded. There was a lump in her throat.

"Whose hand d'you think it is?" she breathed.

Gav bent his head to one side. "Her killer?"

She nodded, her pulse fast. "We need to ID it."

CHAPTER THIRTEEN

Lesley walked into the office to find Mike and Tina staring into their computer screens.

"Boss," Mike said, raising his head. "I've got the email from the law firm."

"The files?" Lesley asked.

He nodded.

"Let's have a look."

Lesley dragged over a chair. He pulled up a set of files.

"Three cases," he said.

"Go on."

"One for aggravated burglary, a Troy Barnes. Sexual assault case, Collin Thrumpton, and then a fraud case, Pauline Silvers."

"I remember seeing that one in the news," said Tina. "She was a GP, defrauded her practice."

Lesley whistled. "Takes all sorts."

"Not," said Mike.

Lesley smiled. "So did Ameena win or lose these cases?"

"The aggravated burglary one, she lost. The guy got a suspended sentence. Sexual assault one is ongoing, looks like she's trying to do a deal with the CPS. The fraud one, that's dragging on. Not got a court date yet."

"OK," said Lesley, "We keep our eye on that one."

"You think this GP might have killed her?" Tina asked.

"I don't think anything," Lesley replied. "I just want to keep my eye on it, in case it leads somewhere. You said it was in the news, see what you can get online."

"Boss." Tina turned back to her computer.

Lesley pointed at Mike's screen, "Check out the metadata. I want to see if there's something missing."

"Metadata?"

"Metadata." She looked at him. "You know what metadata is, don't you?"

He shrugged.

Jesus wept, she thought. She wished she had DI Finch here, and her DC, Connie Williams. They'd be all over this metadata. They'd have stripped it out, turned it upside down and kicked it into next week by now. She'd have the whole lot on the board, and they'd know exactly what was missing.

She took a breath. "The files will have information about the data, details about the files themselves, not just their contents. Things like the dates they were created, when they were last saved, the author, where they were created, whose machine, that kind of thing."

She grabbed his mouse and clicked it a few times. "See, there. Have a look at that." She turned to the PC. "Tina, you got anything on this fraud case?"

Tina looked across at her, her brow furrowed. "Nasty. The other partners in the GP practice are up in arms. They're threatening to sue her."

"While there's a criminal case going on?" Lesley asked.

Tina shrugged.

Lesley shook her head. "They can't start proceedings while the case is ongoing, but… It means the outcome of that case matters to a fair few people."

"But GPs, boss," Mike said. "They're sworn to protect life, they're not going to kill somebody."

Lesley eyed him. "No assumptions, Mike. People can surprise you."

Dennis entered. "Boss," he said. "Sorry, I didn't realise you were back."

"Pleased to see you, Dennis. Anything to report?"

He shook his head. "Not since getting back from the husband's house. Poor guy."

She raised an eyebrow. "Poor guy indeed, but we still need to keep a close eye on him."

Dennis nodded.

"We're looking into the cases Ameena was working on," she told him. "Trying to find the gaps. What have you got, Mike?"

"I'm getting the hang of it," he said, "I've got the last date the files were opened. In two of the cases, it's over ten days ago. The other case, the sexual assault one, was created last week."

"So what was she working on in between?"

"Maybe she was on leave," suggested Dennis.

Lesley shook her head. "Her PA told me there'd be something missing. Whatever it is, it'll be what she was working on in the gap."

Tina raised her hand. Lesley gave her a look. "This isn't school, PC Abbott."

"Sorry, boss. It's just, I've found something else. I thought I'd have a look through the court records. I've got Ameena Khan's name on another case, a Steven Leonard."

Lesley moved round to Tina's desk. "What's he up for?"

"Drugs. Supply, possession with intent."

"How much?" Lesley asked.

"Five hundred ecstasy tablets."

She whistled. "That's one hell of a party. What stage is it at?"

"Sentence handed down end of last week, boss."

"That fits with our timeline. What did he get?"

Tina turned to her. "A fine. Five hundred pounds."

"Five hundred tablets of MDMA and he only got a five hundred quid fine?"

"She's clearly good at her job," Dennis said.

"It went to trial," Tina said. "Magistrates' Court."

"It's unusual for something that big to be dealt with by the magistrates."

"More than unusual," said Dennis.

Lesley tapped her cheek. He was right. Why didn't it go to Crown Court? And she'd have expected him to get a custodial sentence or at least a bigger fine.

"OK," she said. "Do some more digging. Find out what happened that made the magistrate so nice to the bloke. What did Ameena do?"

"Boss." Tina turned back to her screen.

"I'm prepared to bet that's the one that her PA said would be missing, and that could be why. Get everything you can on it, Tina. Look into those court files, find news reports. Find out who the prosecuting officer is, we'll need to talk to them."

"No problem."

The door opened and Johnny and Gail walked in together. Lesley sat back in her chair.

"Good to see the two of you. Have you been conferring?"

Johnny blushed and looked at Gail. "We just happened to get here at the same time."

Lesley laughed. "It's alright, Johnny. You're allowed to walk into the building with a woman, you know. Even an older woman like Gail."

Gail mock-punched Lesley's shoulder. "Oi. You don't know how old I am."

Lesley smiled. "Sorry. So how are you both getting on?"

"Post-mortem was productive, boss," said Johnny. "She's got bruising on her upper arms, fingerprints."

"Fingerprints?" said Lesley. "So now we know this isn't an accidental death."

She surveyed the rest of the team. "That makes what you're all looking into that bit more urgent."

"And there's more," said Johnny. "She had skin under her fingernails."

"Fan-bloody-tastic," said Lesley. She caught Dennis's look. "Fan-*flippin*-tastic. Better?"

Denis grunted.

"So it's been sent off to the lab? Analysed for DNA?"

"Yes, boss," replied Johnny.

"I'll follow up on that," added Gail. "Meanwhile, I've got something else."

"Go on," said Lesley.

Gail sat down in Dennis's chair. Dennis, standing behind Mike's desk, gave her a look of disapproval. Gail shrugged and pulled out an evidence bag.

"So this is Ameena's camera," she said. She pulled out a smaller evidence bag. "And this is the SD card."

"Photos?" Lesley said. "Please tell me you've got photos of her attacker."

Gail flashed her eyes at Lesley. "Sort of."

"Show me."

Gail pulled a file out and opened it to reveal photographs. Images of the sky, the grass, the sea. All blurred.

"I reckon this is the moment she was picked up and thrown over the cliff. And then she must have turned, or at least turned the camera, because then there's this."

She flipped over the last photo. It was a silhouette of a hand against the sky.

"Good work." Lesley bent over to get a better look.

She looked up at Gail. "It's dark. I can't tell if he's wearing gloves."

"Or she."

"That's a man," said Johnny. "Look at the proportions of the fingers."

Gail raised her eyebrows. Lesley caught her expression.

"Nice try, Johnny, but let's not jump to conclusions. Can you get it enhanced?"

"I've already sent a copy to the digital forensics team," replied Gail. "Hopefully they can give us a definitive answer."

"Good," said Lesley. "How long will that take?"

"Should get an answer tomorrow."

"Let me know when you do."

Dennis approached his chair, glaring at Gail as if trying to make her vacate it through sheer force of will. Gail stood up, flashing him a smile.

Lesley looked at her. "Well done. This will give us something to work with until we get the DNA analysis."

CHAPTER FOURTEEN

Lesley's mind wasn't on the TV news, despite her face being no more than a couple of feet away from the screen in her poky living room. The top story in the local news had been Ameena's death: library footage of Old Harry Rocks followed a reporter standing in Studland at the end of the path. They clearly hadn't spoken to anybody involved in the crime, because they didn't have anything to reveal. *Mind you, nor do I*, thought Lesley.

She thought back to the look on the face of Sam Chaston, Ameena's PA, when she'd chased after her in the street. The woman had looked scared. More than Lesley would expect for a breach of employer confidentiality. And then there was Harry Nevin, his reluctance to engage with her questions about the case and about Ameena.

What was going on in that firm?

She switched off the TV and stood up, brushing her jeans down. She had someone she needed to talk to.

Ten minutes later, she sat at the bar of the Duke of Wellington, where Elsa occasionally helped out her brother, the landlord. Elsa was at the other end of the bar, serving two men, chatting to them. Her gaze flicked to Lesley from time to time, but she didn't acknowledge her. Lesley waited, tapping her credit card on the bar.

At last, Elsa finished talking to the men and approached her.

"Hiya." She reached out a hand and brushed Lesley's.

Lesley smiled. "Hi. How's things?"

Elsa shrugged. "Quiet night."

"I don't mean that. What about work? I imagine there's a bit of an atmosphere."

Elsa turned away, towards the till. She jabbed at it, her movements jerky.

"I don't want to pry," Lesley said. "But..."

Elsa turned to her. "D'you want a drink? Gin and tonic? Glass of red wine?"

Lesley frowned. "Red wine, please."

"Coming up." Elsa turned her back and poured out a glass. She placed it in front of Lesley, almost spilling the drink, and grabbed Lesley's credit card. She turned away.

Lesley wondered what had happened to the woman who had brushed her hand affectionately just moments ago.

"Sorry El," she said, "But it would be daft for me not to ask you about this. You're a bloody partner at the firm."

Elsa returned with the credit card machine. Lesley waved her card over it. Elsa grunted and turned away, returning it to the counter at the back of the bar.

"You know I can't talk to you," Elsa said, her back still to Lesley. "You of all people will understand about client confidentiality, and my loyalty to my firm."

"Where were you today?" Lesley asked her.

Elsa rounded on her. "What do you mean, where was I? Who are you, my mum?"

Lesley felt her shoulders dip. "That's not what I meant. I went to your firm. I looked for you. You weren't there."

A couple had entered the pub. Elsa turned her attention to them, chatting and making a meal of taking

73

their order. Lesley watched her, impatience thrumming through her body.

Don't pressure her, she thought. *Let her come to you in her own time.*

But Lesley didn't have time. This was a live murder case. Elsa might even be at risk.

Elsa finished serving the couple and walked to the far end of the bar, tea towel in hand. Lesley knew she didn't need to clean anything. She watched her, waiting. When Elsa passed her, making for the crisps at Lesley's end of the bar, Lesley put out her hand and grabbed Elsa's fingers.

"Don't do that," Elsa said.

"Do your firm know about me?" Lesley whispered. "Do they know you've got a girlfriend?"

"So you're my *girlfriend* now?" Elsa replied. "Last week you weren't even sure if…"

"Nevin was weird with me. I'm not sure if that's because of the case, that he was hiding something about Ameena, or if it's because he knows about my connection to you."

"*Connection?* Is that what it is?"

Lesley clenched her fist on the bar. "Bloody hell El, let's not go round in circles. I know it's awkward for you, but I just want some background. I want to know what Ameena was working on. What her home life was like."

"She was a junior partner. I barely spoke to the woman."

"It's not that big a firm," Lesley said. "Surely you worked with her on cases?"

Elsa shook her head. "Once or twice, maybe. Nothing major. I can't help you, Lesley. You need to ask my colleagues. You need to do this officially."

Lesley swallowed. "So who *should* I talk to? Harry Nevin has been no help."

She considered telling Elsa about Ameena's PA. But Elsa was a partner, and the PA was clearly scared of losing her job.

"Who can tell me what Ameena was working on, what her home life was like, whether she had enemies? And Nevin, is he the kind of man to hide something from the police?"

Elsa met Lesley's gaze. "He's my partner, Lesley. We've known each other for over ten years." She sighed. "What are you expecting me to say? That he's some dodgy dealer who'll lie to the police?" She took a breath. "Of course I'm not. He's a respected criminal lawyer, he's got a good reputation."

"OK," said Lesley. "So why isn't he telling me everything?"

Elsa shook her head. "I don't want to discuss this with you. If you want to talk to me, you come to the office and you do it officially."

Lesley shrank back in her stool. "I'm not trying to put you in a difficult position, El. I just want to find out what I can about Ameena. What if someone else in your firm is in danger? What if *you're* in danger?"

Elsa scoffed. "You don't need to be the knight in shining armour, Lesley. I know you're a copper, but I can handle myself."

"That wasn't what I meant."

Elsa grunted. She turned away, rearranging glasses on the shelves behind her. She looked over her shoulder at Lesley's glass.

"You've finished your drink?" she said.

Lesley pushed the glass towards Elsa, expecting her to refill it.

Elsa shook her head. "I think it's best if you went home. I'm sure you've got a bottle of red in your kitchen somewhere."

CHAPTER FIFTEEN

Lesley stood inside the door to her office, surveying her team. They were gathered around her desk, waiting for her to speak. Dennis had taken one of the chairs opposite her own, and Johnny had insisted on offering Tina the other. Lesley could tell by the look on Tina's face that she found this not chivalrous, as Johnny would have been hoping, but patronising. Tina was ten years younger than Johnny, and no more in need of a seat than he was.

Mike and Johnny hovered either side of the two chairs, both reluctant to take Lesley's chair on the other side of the desk. Lesley, instead of taking her usual place, stayed by the door, keen to get a different perspective. She was closer to the board, and standing up kept her alert.

"OK," she said, "Where are we?"

Tina shifted her chair round to get a better view of the board and of Lesley. "I've looked into Ameena's case files, the ones they sent us and the ones they didn't."

"You managed to get files on the Steven Leonard case?" Lesley asked.

Tina nodded. "Not from his solicitors. But I've got the police file. I spoke to the DS in Bournemouth CID who dealt with the case."

"Nice one. And?" Lesley asked.

"It was a straightforward possession with intent to supply case. He pleaded guilty, went before the magistrate, got a fine."

"Fine?" Lesley asked. "Was it a first offence?"

"Far from it. He's got a history of periodic arrests."

"So Ameena did a deal with the CPS. She was good at her job."

Dennis looked up. "He had five hundred tablets."

Lesley looked from him to Tina. "How did she manage that?"

"I'll follow it up."

"Do that," Lesley said, "We need to find out what happened. Who was the magistrate?"

Tina poked out her tongue and wrote in her notepad. "Maybe he wasn't happy cos she told him to plead guilty?"

"Guy with plenty of previous, I'd doubt it," said Lesley. "And if she did talk him into the deal… Then he should have been thanking her for it, it's a damn good deal for what he was caught with."

Dennis raised an eyebrow.

"Sorry, Dennis," she muttered. "I don't see how a client with multiple offences who got a fine for supply of drugs could be even the slightest bit annoyed."

Johnny shook his head. Mike shrugged.

"Follow it up," Lesley replied, looking at Tina. "It smells a bit off to me."

"Will do."

"OK, so then we've got the forensics." Lesley walked to the board and grabbed the marker pen. She pointed to the two photographs Gail had added. One showed Ameena's fingernails, traces of skin caught under them. The other was the photo of the hand from Ameena's camera.

"Either of these could lead to the killer," Lesley said. "We'll have his DNA from the skin under her nails, and if we can enhance the photo, we might be able to get fingerprints."

"The DNA analysis could take a few days," said Dennis. "The lab has limited capacity."

Lesley sighed. She knew better than to ask for it to be fast tracked.

"Make sure I know as soon as it comes back. Run it against the database."

"If the killer isn't on the system…" Dennis said.

"Let's be optimistic," Lesley replied. "We'll assume that it *will* lead us somewhere, and in the meantime, we've got that hand. Gail's already onto the digital forensics team to see if they can get us a better image. Is he wearing a ring?"

Mike approached the board. He squinted at the photo. "There's a bulge on the ring finger," he said. "Could be a ring, but then if it's a wedding ring, it won't tell us much."

Lesley shook her head. "That's a right hand. The knuckles are visible, and the thumb is on the left. If it is a ring, it won't be a wedding ring. If it's distinctive, it might help us."

Mike nodded. "I can follow it up, if you'd like."

Lesley shook her head, "Gail's already on it. I want you to come with me, speak to the PA."

"Maybe she'll know why Leonard got such a lenient sentence," Tina suggested.

Lesley turned to her, "Good point. I need her address, personal phone number. We'll talk to her outside work."

"On it, boss," Tina replied.

Lesley smiled, glad she'd brought Tina into the team. "Thanks, Tina. You find out where she lives, and Mike and I'll go and speak to her."

"OK."

"In fact, no," Lesley said. "Tina, you've got enough to do with the case files. Mike, you get her address."

He nodded.

"So that leaves Harry Nevin and the other partners. I want to follow up with them, see their reaction when we ask about Steven Leonard. I want to know why they haven't told us the whole truth, and what's still missing."

"Cross and Short," said Dennis. "Aurelia Cross and Elsa Short." He avoided Lesley's eye.

"Why weren't they there yesterday?" Lesley asked. She could hazard a guess as to why Elsa had been absent, but Aurelia Cross?

Dennis shrugged, his gaze on the board. "In court, perhaps?"

"We need to talk to them as well."

Lesley thought of the conversation she'd had with Elsa the previous night. She should declare a personal interest. But her relationship with Elsa hadn't got to that stage yet, had it?

She took a breath. If she hid this, it could backfire. "I know one of them."

Dennis raised an eyebrow. "The partners?"

She met his gaze. He was looking at her in that way people have when they're trying to look natural but are failing. "Elsa Short. She works in my local pub."

"Can't be the same woman," Johnny said. "What lawyer moonlights behind a bar?"

Lesley slid her wedding ring up and down her finger. She was still wearing it, despite everything. "Her brother's the landlord. She helps him out. We've become friends."

"If none of us investigated people we knew from the pub, we'd never get any work done," said Dennis. "It's not a problem."

"I didn't think you were much of a pub-goer," said Lesley.

"Then you'd be wrong."

She raised an eyebrow. Dennis might like the pub, but she knew he wasn't a big drinker. "Still, I'd rather someone else interviewed her. I don't want any allegations of bias."

Dennis shrugged. "I can talk to her, if you want to talk to Aurelia Cross."

"No. You take Johnny with you to Nevin, Cross and Short. Talk to Cross and Short. I want to know their take on what's happened. See if they'll tell us anything Harry Nevin didn't – and ask them what they knew about Steven Leonard."

"Fair enough," said Dennis. He stood up. "Let's get on with it."

Lesley nodded. Finally, the man wasn't dawdling.

CHAPTER SIXTEEN

Dennis and Johnny drove in silence towards Bournemouth. As they approached the outskirts of the town, Johnny cleared his throat.

"Nevin, Cross and Short," he said, "Have you had many dealings with them, Sarge?"

Dennis glanced in his rear-view mirror. A lorry loomed behind, waiting to overtake. He slowed to let it pass, and then focused on the road as he spoke to Johnny.

"I've come across Aurelia Cross a few times, she seems to deal with most of their small time criminal cases. Not sure about the other two. I think the DCI dealt with Nevin."

"I got the feeling yesterday was the first time she'd met him."

Dennis tightened his grip on the steering wheel. "Not *that* DCI, Johnny. DCI Mackie."

"Oh," said Johnny. He placed his hands together between his knees. Neither of them spoke about their old boss much now; his death was difficult to talk about. They drove in silence until they got to the town centre.

Johnny checked for parking spaces as they approached the law firm.

"There's an underground car park around there."

Dennis shook his head. "I'll park on the street."

"It's all pay and display."

Dennis looked at him. "This is Bournemouth, Johnny. My old stamping ground. I won't get a ticket here."

Johnny shrugged. Dennis found a space and got out of the car. Johnny followed him, glancing warily at the pay and display machine. Dennis chuckled.

Johnny reached Nevin, Cross and Short and pressed on the buzzer. A voice came over the intercom. "Hello, can I help you?"

"DS Frampton, DC Chiles," said Dennis. "We're here in connection with—"

A buzzer sounded and they pushed through the door. Ahead was a set of stairs, all metal and linoleum. Not what he'd been expecting from one of Bournemouth's biggest firms.

They hurried up the stairs and found a woman at the top waiting.

"Take a seat there," she said. "We won't keep you long."

"You were expecting us?" Dennis asked.

She shrugged. "I was told to be ready."

Dennis eyed Johnny as the DC took a seat. Dennis remained standing. He couldn't see the point in getting comfortable if they weren't going to be here long.

"They knew we were coming," said Johnny. "Did you call ahead?"

"I never call ahead, Johnny. But I guess if one of your partners has been murdered, it can't be a huge shock that the police are going to show up."

A door behind him opened and a middle-aged man appeared. He had a broad round face with pink cheeks and thinning grey hair. He smiled and held a hand out towards Dennis.

"Sergeant Frampton," he said. "Harry Nevin, pleased to meet you."

83

Dennis ignored the hand. He didn't feel comfortable shaking people's hands, you never knew who you might be arresting one day.

"Come on in," Nevin added. "We're waiting for you."

"We?" Dennis asked.

"I've brought the partners together."

Dennis followed him inside, hurrying to keep up. "I'd rather speak to each of you separately."

Nevin waved in dismissal. "It's a bit late for that. They're all waiting for you."

"You're a criminal lawyer, Sir. You'll understand that people's statements can differ, so long as they're interviewed separately."

"We aren't exactly eyewitnesses to a crime. We're just her colleagues. And besides, we're busy people. You should consider yourself lucky that we're even able to see you at all."

Dennis exchanged a look with Johnny. "With respect, Sir," he said to Nevin. "One of your junior partners has died. I don't imagine you're surprised that the police need to speak with you."

Nevin grunted. He pushed open the door to a glass-walled conference room. Inside sat two women. The closer of the two was in her forties, an attractive woman with thick dark hair and piercing blue eyes. Her colleague was in her sixties, with long grey hair piled on top of her head in a bun. Her clothes and hair made her seem matronly but the intensity of her stare was anything but.

Nevin gestured to two seats and Dennis and Johnny took them. Nevin sat opposite them, between his partners.

"Thank you for seeing us," Dennis said. "Can we take your names?"

The younger woman, the attractive one, leaned over the table. "Elsa Short," she said. "And you are?"

"DS Frampton, DC Chiles," said Dennis, indicating Johnny.

Elsa nodded.

"And I'm Aurelia Cross," the other woman said. "I hope you'll make this brief."

Dennis raised an eyebrow. "It'll take as long as it needs to take, Madam."

Johnny pulled his notepad from his pocket and Dennis shifted in his chair. It was modern and hard.

"We need to know more about Ms Khan's employment history, about the cases she was working on, and in particular about her movements in the last couple of weeks."

"Do you think she was up to something?" Elsa asked.

"We don't think anything," Dennis replied. "But we need to get as much background as possible."

"Surely you got all this from Harry yesterday," said Aurelia.

"We were able to get some information, yes," Dennis said. "My colleague spoke to him."

"DCI Clarke," Nevin added, his lip curling.

"So," Dennis said, "can you tell us about her work patterns over the last few weeks, the cases she was assigned to? Was she in every day, or did she take any time off sick? Any problems with illness or mental health?"

"Mental health?" said Aurelia Cross. "What are you insinuating? You think she killed herself?"

"We're certain now that her death was suspicious," Dennis replied. "So we need to know if her work was connected to her death."

"You think someone here killed her?" said Elsa Short.

"Not necessarily. I imagine it's more likely that—"

"So you want us to hand over confidential client information, so that you can piece together a better picture of Ameena and what she was like?" Elsa asked.

"I understand the need for client confidentiality," Dennis said. "But you'll also understand the importance of forming as thorough a picture as we can in a murder inquiry."

She returned his gaze. "I'm sure we can find a compromise."

He felt Johnny fidgeting beside him. *Don't show them you're uncomfortable, lad.*

"Let's start with last week," he said, turning to Nevin. "Where was she on Friday?"

"Look," said Nevin, "I know you've been sniffing around her cases. You think she was involved in the Steven Leonard case."

Dennis narrowed his eyes. "Was she?"

"You've been speaking to the police who arrested Leonard."

Dennis tensed. How did Nevin know about that?

"I can tell you," Nevin continued, "he was my client, not Ameena's."

"So why is Ameena the lawyer of record in the police files?" Dennis asked.

Nevin shrugged. "She was the first name they got when Leonard was arrested. He gave them her name, but it was me who represented him. The Leonard case has nothing to do with Ameena. You can leave it alone."

Dennis cocked his head. "Steven Leonard was a bit of a minnow, for an experienced lawyer like yourself."

"We don't look at our clients like that, Detective."

"And besides," Dennis continued. "The court records say the same thing. Ameena Khan was the lawyer of record."

"Again," said Nevin, "this all comes from an administrative error made by the police, which got passed on to the Magistrates' Court. You check with Bournemouth CID. They'll tell you they got it wrong. It was me they dealt with."

Beside him, Aurelia Cross leaned back in her chair. Her hands were in her lap, and she was shuffling her shoulders. Elsa Short, in contrast, was calm. She looked between Dennis and Johnny with those steely blue eyes.

Dennis knew already that if there was something to be discovered about the Steven Leonard case, they'd have to discover it without Nevin's help. But he had to defend his old colleagues at Bournemouth.

"DS Biggins at Bournemouth station," he said. "He's a good detective, experienced. I trust him."

"DS Biggins got it wrong," said Nevin. "It's irrelevant, Sergeant. Drop it."

Johnny leaned in. "So we can save your time, could we speak to Ameena's PA to find out her movements in the last few weeks?"

Good idea, thought Dennis.

Aurelia Cross shook her head. "Sam's on sick leave."

"We can contact her at home," Johnny replied.

"I'm not about to give you private information," said Cross.

"This is a murder inquiry," Dennis said. "We're entitled to her mobile number."

Aurelia Cross grunted. "She knows nothing and she's really not well at all. Leave her alone."

Nevin stood up. "I told you we were busy people. That's all for now."

Dennis stayed seated. "We still need to ask you—"

Nevin placed his fist on the table. "DS Frampton, we've got clients who need our attention. We don't have anything more to tell you, you've got the files. Speak to Ameena's husband. I imagine this will turn out to be some sort of domestic incident."

Dennis looked at him. They both knew that there was nothing domestic about Ameena Khan's death. But Dennis would get nothing out of Harry Nevin if he tried to push it.

He stood up, eyeing the lawyer over the table. "If we need anything more, we'll be in touch," he said.

"You do that," Nevin replied.

CHAPTER SEVENTEEN

Lesley took the A352 towards Dorchester. The road was busy in the other direction, holidaymakers heading towards the beach. But her route was clear and she was there in twenty-five minutes.

As she crossed over the A35 on the edge of the town, her phone rang: Dennis.

She hit hands free. "How'd you get on then?"

"Hello to you, too."

She rolled her eyes. "I don't do pleasantries."

"Doesn't hurt to be polite," he said.

She gritted her teeth. Dennis had his foibles. He liked things done the old-fashioned way, the polite way. But he was taking it too far.

"Just tell me how it went," she told him.

"We spoke to all three partners," he said. "Nevin, Cross and Short."

At the mention of Elsa's name, Lesley's foot went to the brake pedal. A car honked its horn behind her. She looked in the mirror and waved in apology.

"Wait a moment, Dennis." She pulled over. When she was parked in a lay-by, she grabbed the phone. "Tell me what they said."

"Not much boss. Nevin insisted that the Steven Leonard case was nothing to do with Ameena, he said it was him."

"But Bournemouth told you…"

"He says Bournemouth were wrong."

"Why would they be wrong?" she asked. "And then there's the court record."

"He's insistent that it was his case, not hers. He says the court record was wrong because Bournemouth got it wrong."

"But you said you spoke to one of your old colleagues."

"DS Biggins. He told me he dealt with Ameena Khan personally."

"So why would Harry Nevin lie about it?" she asked. "He's a senior partner in a major local law firm. Why would he lie to make us think that he was dealing with a minor possession with intent to supply case?"

"I don't know, boss," said Dennis. "But I think we should follow it up."

"I agree. Where are you now?"

"Just outside Bournemouth. On our way back to the office. Johnny's driving, I can't be doing with hands-free."

Lesley smiled. "Get digging when you're back. Call ahead to Mike and Tina and tell them to make a start."

"Yes, boss."

"Good," she said. "I'm on my way to the forensics lab. They should have the enhanced photos for us. Maybe the DNA." She started the car.

"There was something else," Dennis added.

Lesley turned the car off. "Yes?"

"Ameena Khan's PA," Dennis said. "The one who grabbed you in the street yesterday. She's on sick leave."

"She didn't seem very sick to me."

"Aurelia Cross told us she'd gone off sick. Apparently she's *very* ill and we should leave her alone."

"Mmm," said Lesley. "That sounds more than a coincidence to me." She pictured the look on the young woman's face when she'd grabbed her in the street. She'd been scared. Maybe she was right to be.

She drummed her fingers on the steering wheel. Gail could email her those photos. "I'll follow it up. You go back to the office, look into the Steven Leonard case. I'll track down Sam."

"Sam?" Dennis asked.

"The PA," she told him. "She's got a name."

"Of course." Dennis hung up.

She dialled again. "Mike," she said, "Have you got me that address yet?"

CHAPTER EIGHTEEN

Tina stiffened as the sarge and Johnny arrived back in the office.

She preferred it when they were out, feeling more comfortable in Mike's company. Mike didn't look at her like she was an imposter. To be fair, Johnny didn't do it all the time, only when the sarge was with him. Johnny was like a different person when DS Frampton was in the room. But she could tell the DS didn't approve of her. He didn't like having a PC in the team. Either that, or he wasn't good at working with women.

Mike put down his phone. "How'd you get on?"

Dennis's glance flicked from Mike to Tina. "Not too well."

He sat down at his chair and turned on his computer. Mike watched him, waiting for more information. Tina slumped in her chair. She was getting used to this. As soon as she left the room, they would be swapping stories, updating each other on the case. But as far as the DS was concerned, she didn't need to be involved.

Johnny gave her a wink. "Everything OK back here?"

She smiled in response. "All fine."

Mike had wheeled his chair towards Johnny. He spoke to his colleague in a low voice. Tina sighed and went back to her computer.

She wouldn't let this get to her. She would prove that she could do this job, that she was a worthy member of the team. She didn't know if they were being like this because of her uniform or because of her sex. Either way, the only way through it was to knuckle down and get on with the job.

Major Crimes had never had a PC on the team. And if the sarge had his way, she wouldn't last. But she liked working for the DCI. She enjoyed getting stuck into cases like this. She wanted to keep this job, and she didn't want to ruffle any feathers.

She went back to the Steven Leonard file. The man had a string of previous offences: possession, burglary, minor assault, low-level but persistent. He'd had a number of suspended sentences, spent most of his adult life with a collar around his ankle. Before that, there had been two stays in youth detention centres. His first drugs arrest had been at the age of sixteen. His employer was recorded as the responsible adult, it seemed his parents were out of the picture.

The employer was a man called Arthur Kelvin. Tina knew that name.

She checked further into the files. The business Leonard had been working in was Hamworthy Scrap Metal. She'd visited it a couple of times when she was in uniform. CID suspected it was a front for a money laundering operation. But as far as she knew, they'd never made anything stick.

If Steven Leonard had that many prior offences to his name, how had he got such a light sentence for possession with intent to supply? None of it made sense. Unless it had something to do with his employer.

She looked past her screen. "Sarge?"

The sarge looked up. "Yes, Tina?" His voice made her think of a bored schoolteacher humouring the slowest member of the class.

She swallowed. "I think you might want to look at this."

He stood up and strolled around her desk, making it clear he wasn't in a hurry. She pointed at the screen. "Steven Leonard's first offence was when he was sixteen, Sarge. He was working for Hamworthy Scrap Metal at the time. Arthur Kelvin acted as his responsible adult in the police interviews."

Dennis frowned. "Have you spoken to the DCI about this?"

"I've only just spotted it."

"Good," he said. "I'll tell her if she needs to know."

"Of course."

He returned to his desk.

"Do you think here might be a—?" she asked, flinching when he cut her off.

"I doubt that it's relevant, Tina."

"But if there's a link to the—"

"Leave it, Constable," he said. "We need to focus on the law firm. This isn't connected."

CHAPTER NINETEEN

Sam Chaston, Ameena's PA, lived in a narrow terraced house in Springbourne, a suburb east of the centre of Bournemouth.

Lesley parked her car outside and surveyed the street. It was quiet at this time of day, the only movement a woman walking towards a small row of shops at the far end.

She surveyed Sam's house. No sign of life. The curtains in the front window were closed and the front door was firmly shut.

She started up the path, checking the neighbours' houses for movement, and knocked on the door. After a few moments, it opened a crack, the chain still fastened. Lesley held up her ID.

"Sam Chaston? I'm DCI Clarke, we spoke yesterday."

Sam shook her head.

Lesley put her hand on the door. "Can I come in, please?"

Sam looked past Lesley into the street. "What's this about?"

"It's about what you were so eager to talk to me about yesterday."

Sam's eyes roamed Lesley's face. "You can't stay long." She unlatched the chain and opened the door, her movements clumsy. She stood in the doorway, looking at Lesley like she expected her to bite. Her eyes were wide and her skin flushed.

Lesley gave her a smile. She looked the younger woman up and down. Sam was wearing a purple suit and a smart white blouse. She was fully made up and her hair was neat.

"You don't look sick," Lesley said.

"Sorry?"

"Your employers told us you were off sick."

"Oh, no, it's just that with Ameena dead, there's not really anything for me to do."

Lesley frowned. That wasn't what they'd been told.

"Please," she said, "I'm sure you'd rather we have this conversation inside."

Sam peered over Lesley's shoulder, looking across the street. "It's not a good time," she said.

"You seemed anxious to talk to me yesterday, what's changed?" Lesley looked past the woman into the hallway. A collapsed push chair leaned against a wall and toys were scattered at the bottom of the stairs. "You've got a kiddie?"

Sam nodded. "Daughter. She's at nursery."

"Just the one?" Lesley asked.

Sam nodded.

"Are you alone?"

"Yes," said Sam. "Why wouldn't I be?"

"You seem nervous."

"I can't jeopardise my job," Sam said. "I don't want to get into trouble."

"Have you been threatened by someone? Someone from your firm?"

"No, of course not." Sam's gaze flicked over Lesley's shoulder again. Her jaw slackened.

She grabbed the door and pushed it towards Lesley.

"Please, I need you to leave."

Lesley looked round.

A brown Fiesta had parked behind her car and a man was getting out. He had long greasy hair and the kind of face that would make any woman run the other way. His car had long scratches down the side. This wasn't the smartest of locations, but he still didn't fit. She doubted very much that he lived here.

She turned back to Sam. "Is he here for you?"

The door was closed.

Lesley's shoulders dropped. She turned and walked towards the man. As she approached, he frowned at her and turned away. He scrambled into the car and drove off.

Lesley stood on the pavement, watching the car disappear. What the hell was going on?

CHAPTER TWENTY

Gail was working through Google satellite views of the crime scene when her phone rang. She grabbed it, her eyes still on her computer screen.

"Hi Gail, it's Sunil."

Sunil Chaudhary was a member of the digital forensics team. Gail had sent him the photos from Ameena's camera in the hope he could enhance them. In particular, the photo of the hand.

"Have you got anything for me?" she asked.

"Good news," he replied.

She leaned back in her chair, signalling to Brett who was at the desk behind her. "Go on," she said to Sunil.

"I'm confident it's a man's hand. The proportions of the fingers, the thickness of the knuckles, and the ring looks like a man's ring."

She sat up. "What ring?"

"It's indistinct in silhouette, but when you enhance the photo and improve the lighting, he's definitely wearing a ring."

"What kind of ring?" she asked. Brett pushed his chair over to her desk. His eyes explored her face.

"It's a signet ring," Sunil said. "Square. Silver, possibly white gold. I reckon it's silver judging by the scratches on it."

"Any engraving? Any distinctive marks?"

"Can't see any, sorry. Just a ring."

"What finger is it on?" she asked.

"His ring finger."

"Which hand is it?"

She hadn't been able to tell from the original version of the photo. It was either a right hand taken from the back or a left hand taken from the palm.

"It's his right hand," Sunil said, "which means it's probably not a wedding ring."

"In that case, you can make out the square of the signet ring?"

"I certainly can," came the reply. "It should be in your inbox right now."

She opened the email from Sunil. Sure enough, there was an enhanced version of the photograph of the man's hand, the ring clear. It was silver with a squared-off top, and a few scratches on the side. There was an engraving but she couldn't make out the details.

She peered at Brett. "Look familiar to you?"

He shook his head, staring at her screen.

"Thanks Sunil," she said. "I owe you one."

"You can buy me a drink next time we're in the pub," he replied.

"I'll do that."

She turned to Brett. "We need to track this down, find where it came from."

"It could have come from anywhere," he said. "It's just a ring."

She shook her head. "It's chunky, looks expensive. Depending on what it's made of…"

"A ring like that is silver," Brett said, cocking his head. "It costs what, a hundred, couple of hundred quid? Not that expensive."

Gail raised an eyebrow. "D'you buy yourself a lot of expensive jewellery?"

He laughed. "No."

"OK," she said, "We'll give it to the investigating team. See if they can track down the jewellers."

"Do you want me to look at jewellers instead?" Brett asked.

"No, it's their job."

"It might be local," he said. "I've got a mate who…"

"Brett," she told him. "It's not our job to track down jewellers. You carry on with what you're doing. I'll call Lesley."

CHAPTER TWENTY-ONE

Lesley hammered on the door to Sam's house. "Sam, let me in! Who was that man?"

"Go away," came Sam's voice. "I don't want to talk to you."

"Sam, please. Who is he? Why are you scared of him?"

"Your lot must have told them. They know."

Lesley looked back in the direction the man had driven off in. She could have followed him, but she had photos of his car – and number plate.

She flipped open the letterbox and peered through. She could see Sam's feet at the bottom of the stairs. "I know you're scared, Sam, but I'm here to help. If you think of anything, if you want to talk to me, call me. You've got my mobile number."

"Go away."

Lesley sighed. She let the letterbox fall and walked back to her car. She still needed to go to Dorchester, to the forensics lab. She gripped the steering wheel as she drove, her jaw clenched.

She tried calling Dennis but his line was engaged. *Damn. What's he doing?*

She had photos on her phone. The car, the man, the number plates. Assuming the car belonged to him, and those plates weren't false, they'd track him down.

She dialled again; Mike this time.

"Hello, boss."

"Mike, I'm sending you some photos. I want you to identify this man."

"What man?"

"I just went to Sam Chaston's house and this man turned up while I was there. I'm certain she was scared of him. I'm wondering if he was sent to threaten her."

"By the law firm?"

"I don't know. But whoever he is, we need his identity."

"No problem, boss. Send them over."

"I'll email them to you now."

She checked her rear-view mirror and indicated to pull over. She was on a dual carriageway, a parking spot just ahead. She stopped the car and pulled her phone out of its holder. Moments later, she'd fired off an email to Mike with the photos attached.

She was about to drive off when the phone rang. The number was withheld.

She picked up. "Mike, you got them?"

"Who's Mike?"

Shit. She knew that voice.

She started the ignition and pulled away. "Terry, I'm working."

"We need to talk, Lesley," her husband said.

"I just told you, I'm working. I'm on a murder case, and I'm driving too."

"You're on hands-free. It's never stopped you before."

"Have you called just to criticise me, or have you got something to say?"

The last time Lesley had spoken to Terry in person had been when she'd gone home for a surprise visit. She'd had a meeting in Birmingham and had decided to go home the night before. She'd walked into the house and found his mistress standing in the kitchen.

"What is it then?" she snapped, speeding up.

"I was a shit, sorry."

She barked out a laugh. "What d'you want, Terry?"

"I think we should talk calmly. One human being to another. Not through lawyers."

Now she knew why he was calling.

"You've seen the letter," she said. "From my solicitor."

She'd hired a man called Christopher Draper, a friend of Elsa. Elsa said he was a respected family lawyer and would be able to get her what she was due.

"That's not why I'm calling," Terry said.

"Bullshit," Lesley replied. "You think you're going to lose the house. You think you're going to lose custody of Sharon. She told me you've been fighting."

"That's none of your—"

"I'm her mum, Terry. I need to know if you've been getting at her."

"You're two hundred fucking miles away," he said.

"A hundred and forty miles to be precise, and she's been down here every weekend. Clearly she doesn't want to spend time with you and your fancy woman."

"She's not my fancy woman," he said. "Her name's Julieta."

Lesley gripped the steering wheel. She should slow down. She should stop the car.

"I don't want to know," she told him. "I just need a response to my solicitor's letter."

In the letter, she'd said that she was contesting his claim for divorce. He'd tried to claim unreasonable behaviour, saying she worked too hard and had been impossible to live with. But she had bigger guns than that. She had evidence of adultery. For Christ's sake, she'd walked in on the two of them.

She reached the outskirts of Dorchester and indicated to turn right into the town. "I'm working," she said. "You've seen my lawyer's letter, you need to respond formally."

"I think we should go for mediation," he told her. "Talk it through like adults."

She took a left turn, and then a right. She wasn't entirely sure where the forensics lab was, but was driving blindly, making for the town centre.

"I'll think about it," she told Terry.

"Thanks," he replied.

She jabbed at the phone to end the call, her body hot. She was lost, but she didn't care.

CHAPTER TWENTY-TWO

Dennis checked his watch. Five past twelve, an acceptable time to take a break. He looked up from his desk.

"Johnny, you got half an hour?"

Johnny frowned. "Half an hour, Sarge? What's up?"

"Let's go get a pint."

"A pint?"

"It doesn't have to be a pint, Johnny. Let's just get some fresh air, OK?"

Johnny shrugged. He exchanged glances with Mike and stood up. He grabbed his suit jacket and slung it over his shoulders.

"Come on then," said Dennis.

"Just a moment, Sarge." Johnny opened the top drawer of his desk and rifled inside. He pulled out some cash and put it in his pocket. Dennis wondered whether the DC even owned a wallet.

Twenty minutes later, they were in the Ship Inn. It was a homely pub with heavy furniture and a wide fireplace, not lit today. Dennis ordered a pint of bitter shandy and a cheese and tomato sandwich. Johnny had chosen a pint of some new-fangled lager and a fish finger sandwich.

Dennis eyed it. "Fish finger sandwich?" he said. "What's this, nursery?"

Johnny held his hand in front of his mouth, crumbs dropping onto the table. "It's trendy these days, Sarge."

"How can a fish finger sandwich be trendy?"

Johnny shrugged. "Posh fish fingers, I guess. Fancy tartare sauce."

"Looks like the fish finger sandwiches my mum used to give me," said Dennis.

Johnny swallowed and laughed. "Tastes alright." He sat back in his chair. "What's up then, Sarge?"

"You can call me Dennis here." The two of them had worked together for over ten years. They'd moved over from Uniform to CID at the same time, Dennis as a sergeant and Johnny as a constable.

"How's things at home?" Dennis asked. "How's Alice doing?"

Johnny smiled. "She's huge."

"When is she due?"

"September. Little boy."

Dennis smiled. "That's nice. Give her my best."

"Will do, Sarge – sorry, Dennis. How's Pam?"

"She's grand."

"She always is grand," said Johnny. "According to you."

Dennis gave him a look. "That's because my wife is a magnificent woman. Don't you dare criticise her."

Johnny raised his hands in supplication. "I never would." He took another bite of his fish finger sandwich and wiped his mouth with a napkin.

Dennis eyed his cheese and tomato sandwich. Despite the thick hunks of white bread, significantly more expensive than the white sliced Pam bought, it was plain and tasteless.

"So what's this about?" asked Johnny.

"I wanted to run something past you." Dennis leaned over the table. "Just you and me."

Johnny nodded. "Of course. Is it to do with the case?"

"It is. You know the Steven Leonard case, the one the DCI reckons Harry Nevin is hiding from us?"

"I do," said Johnny. "The one Tina found."

Dennis grunted. "He used to work for Arthur Kelvin."

"Who did?" said Johnny.

"Steven Leonard did."

"The same Arthur Kelvin who…?"

"How many Arthur Kelvins do you know?" said Dennis.

Johnny shrugged. He wiped his hands on his trousers, making Dennis wince.

"He was working in Kelvin's scrap metal yard," continued Dennis, "when he had his first arrest. Kelvin stood up for him, gave him a character reference."

Johnny stifled a laugh. "A character reference from Arthur Kelvin?"

"He was masquerading as a respectable business owner. Still is."

Johnny rolled his eyes. They both knew what kind of man Arthur Kelvin was. But they also both knew how he presented himself and how his expensive lawyers had been able to keep him from getting into trouble. So far.

"You think the Kelvins might be connected to all of this?" Johnny asked.

Dennis glanced around the pub, his skin tingling. "Keep your voice down, son."

"Sorry, Sarge."

Dennis scratched his chin. He'd missed a bit shaving. Right in the centre, on the bottom of his chin.

"No," he said. "I don't think he's connected to all this. But I do think we need to watch our backs."

Johnny's face darkened. "After what happened with…?"

Dennis put his hand on the table. "We don't talk about that. Do we?"

"Sorry," muttered Johnny. He pushed his plate away and picked up his glass. He took a long swig, his eyes roaming the pub. Finally, he put his glass down.

"Have you told the DCI about this?"

Dennis shook his head. "She doesn't need to know. It's not relevant."

"So why'd you tell me?"

"I had to talk to somebody about it." Dennis flinched, irritated at having to explain himself. "I just wanted you to know."

Johnny nodded, looking at his watch. "We'd better…"

Dennis put a hand on his arm. "If this does blow up in our faces, we need to be prepared."

CHAPTER TWENTY-THREE

The CSIs worked out of a draughty office on the edge of Dorchester. Lesley sat beside Gail, shivering despite the heat outside, watching the crime scene manager scroll through photos on her computer.

They'd enhanced the photo of the man's hand from Ameena's camera, and a signet ring was clearly visible. Lesley leaned in to peer at it. It was silver with a square top and visible scratches. There was an engraving, blurred in the photo. The hand it sat on was white, with a few knuckle hairs and wrinkles. So this man was powerful enough to push Ameena off the cliff, but not young enough to have smooth hands.

Lesley turned to Gail. "Can we get prints off this?"

Gail shook her head. "It shows the back of the hand. Although skin on the back of the hand can have distinguishing marks, there's nothing useful here."

Lesley twisted her lips. "And this is the only photo we've got of his hand?"

"If we had another one, I'd have shown it to you."

Still, at least they had the ring.

"Have you got any idea where it came from?" Lesley asked, pointing at it.

Gail shrugged. "Brett's got a theory it's from a local jeweller. There aren't too many that sell rings like that round here. Plenty that sell ones with minerals in.

Amethysts, opals, that kind of thing. The whole Jurassic Coast shtick. But most of those are for women. There aren't so many local jewellers selling men's rings."

Lesley eyed it, wishing she could make out that engraving. "He might have bought it online. He might have bought it in a shop outside the area."

"It's worth taking a look," said Gail. "Maybe get one of your guys to check out the local jewellers."

Lesley nodded. "We'll start closest to the crime scene, in Swanage. There are a few jewellers in Corfe Castle. Then we'll look at Bournemouth and Poole."

"That could be quite a few businesses," said Gail.

"I have no idea how many jewellers there are in this county," Lesley replied. "But I'm hoping that there are only a few that sell rings like that."

"And that can remember who bought it," added Gail.

Lesley pointed at the photo. "Is that expensive?"

Gail shook her head. "Brett reckons a hundred, two hundred pounds. Nothing to write home about."

"Enough for them to keep receipts, though," said Lesley. "It's worth a go. I'll get one of the team to follow it up."

Her phone rang. "DCI Clarke."

"Boss. It's Mike."

"Mike, I've got another job for you," she said.

"Oh, OK. I've got a name for you, though."

"The guy at Sam Chaston's house?"

"His name's Danny Rogers, lives in Ringwood."

"How far is that?" asked Lesley. She'd driven past Ringwood in Hampshire when she first moved down from the West Midlands. She had a memory of sitting in traffic for at least Ann hour after that.

"It's nothing," said Mike. "Twenty minutes to Bournemouth down the A338."

Lesley leaned back in her chair. Was this connected to the murder?

"Maybe he's her boyfriend?" Mike suggested.

She shook her head. "She didn't look at him like he was her boyfriend. She looked at him like she was scared."

"Ex-boyfriend, then?"

"Possibly."

One of Gail's colleagues approached Lesley, indicating that he needed to speak to Gail. It was the tall one with the shaggy hair. Lesley shuffled back in her chair and let him pass. He stooped to talk with Gail, their voices low. Lesley tried to listen in while at the same time speaking to Mike.

"Has Rogers got a record?" she asked him.

"Affray, three years ago."

"No domestics?"

"You're thinking maybe he is her ex?"

"Probably not, but we can't discount it. Can you double check his file? Make sure there haven't been any reports from his address, or Sam's. And I want to talk to him."

As Mike read out an address in Ringwood, Lesley had a thought. "Where does he work?"

"One moment."

Gail's colleague straightened up. He gave Lesley a nod as he squeezed past her and moved back to his own desk.

"I've got his workplace," said Mike. "It's a car body shop in Christchurch."

Good, Lesley thought. A bit closer to home. She glanced at Gail's screen.

Mike read out the address. "Can you text it to me?" she asked him. "I'll put it in the satnav."

She was using her satnav a lot lately. She wondered if the roads would ever become truly familiar. Probably just at the point where her assignment ended and she was sent back to Birmingham.

"Before you go, Mike, I've got an image I'd like you to have a look at. Do you know any local jewellers that sell men's rings?"

"Sorry."

Lesley was sure she'd seen Mike wearing a ring on his right hand.

"I'll send it to you anyway. Tell me if you've got any idea where it might have been bought."

She nodded at Gail, who clicked her mouse a few times.

"Have you got it?" Lesley asked Mike.

"Just opening it."

"There's a photo attached," she told him. "Take a look at that ring."

There was a pause while he opened the email and surveyed the photo.

"Any thoughts?" she asked. "Any jewellers who sell that sort of thing?"

"No, boss. But I think I've seen it before."

She felt her skin tingle. "Where?"

"I'm not sure." His voice dropped.

"Mike, you still there?"

"Hang on a minute."

She heard movement at the other end of the phone. "What are you doing?"

"I'm going into your office. You don't mind, do you?"

"Why are you going into my office?"

"I want to look at the board."

Gail's eyes were on Lesley. Lesley shrugged at the CSM. "You've seen it on somebody whose photo is on the board?" she asked Mike.

"I just want to check."

"OK." She could feel her chest tightening. She glanced at Gail, who was watching her face.

After a few moments, Mike came back on the line, out of breath. "I was right, boss."

"Right about what?" Lesley pulled herself upright.

"I *have* seen this ring before."

"On who?" Lesley raked her fingernails across the desk, aware of Gail's gaze on her.

"Nevin," Mike replied. "I've seen it on Harry Nevin."

CHAPTER TWENTY-FOUR

Lesley looked back into Gail's expectant face as she waited for the phone to be answered. Gail stared back at her, her nostrils flaring. Lesley drummed her fingers on the desk.

"Come on," she said. She knew he was there, she'd spoken to his secretary. Why wasn't he answering her call?

At last the phone was picked up. "Detective Superintendent Carpenter."

"Sir, it's DCI Clarke."

"Lesley. You have progress to update me on?"

"Yes, Sir. We have a suspect."

"Already? Good work. Who?"

"Harry Nevin, Sir. He's a senior partner in the law firm where our victim worked."

"And on what basis is he your suspect?"

"We've got a photo from her SD card, a man's hand. The man in the photo is wearing a ring that matches one Mike saw on Nevin's hand when we went to interview him."

"Hmm."

Silence.

Gail mouthed something, Lesley couldn't tell what. She shook her head and looked away. Gail's nerves were adding to her own unease. If Elsa was working with a murderer...

They couldn't afford to wait. They had to go and get Nevin now.

Carpenter came back on the line. "Have you got anything else, apart from this ring?"

"He was acting suspiciously when I went to interview him. He said he would hand over files relating to the victim's current cases, but he missed one. He deliberately withheld information from the investigation."

"That's not murder, Lesley."

"I know, Sir. But this ring…"

"It's not enough, Inspector. You need more."

She sighed. She'd been expecting this. "I'd like to go and interview him."

"That's fair enough," he said. "But try not to rouse his suspicions. Harry Nevin is a respected member of the Bournemouth legal community. He'll know what you're up to as soon as you walk through that door."

She nodded. Harry Nevin might be clever. She was cleverer.

"I'll speak to him, Sir. I'll tell you how I get on."

CHAPTER TWENTY-FIVE

Dennis arrived back in the office, Johnny in tow behind him. Johnny belched quietly as he sat down. Dennis gave him a disapproving look.

"Sorry, Sarge." Johnny stood up. "Coffee, anyone?"

Dennis grunted. "Milk, no sugar."

Mike shook his head. "We've got a development, Sarge."

Dennis peeled off his jacket and hung it over his chair. "Yes?"

"Harry Nevin," Mike said. "He's the man in the photograph."

"What photograph?" Dennis asked.

Mike beckoned him over. Dennis bent over Mike's desk and looked at the photograph on the DC's screen.

"Ameena Khan took this just before she died. Well, I don't think she took it as such, her camera took it automatically. There were a whole bunch of photos, this was the last one."

"It's a man's hand," said Dennis.

Mike nodded. "That ring. I was sure I'd seen it before. I checked the board, I looked at some of the photos we've got of Nevin. He's got a ring exactly like it."

Dennis eyed him. "Good work. But it's not enough to charge the man with murder."

Mike's shoulders slumped. "It's enough to be suspicious of him, surely. The DCI is calling the Super right now."

"She is, is she?" Dennis straightened up. "That's not like her."

Lesley had made her approach to policing clear when she joined the team. Thoroughness, procedure, building a case. She didn't like to alert a suspect until she was confident the CPS would agree to prosecute and a jury would find him guilty.

"Why is she talking to the Super?" he asked. "She's got nothing, it's just a ring."

Mike shrugged. "She spoke to Nevin. Maybe she thinks there's more to it?"

"I spoke to him too," Dennis said. "The man was obstructive. But he's a criminal lawyer, what do you expect?"

Dennis's phone rang: Lesley.

"Boss, what's happening? Mike tells me you've got a link to Harry Nevin."

"It's not enough to arrest him yet, but it's enough to want to speak to him again. Possibly under caution, although I'd rather not. We need to know if he's got an alibi for Sunday morning."

Dennis glanced at Mike. This was more like the DCI. It wasn't like her to go galloping off on a case without solid evidence.

"What do you need me to do, boss?" he asked.

"I'm going to Nevin, Cross and Short," she said. "It's half past six, Nevin should still be there. But he's the boss, he might have left. So I want you to go to his home address. See if you can speak to him."

"You want me to wait for you?" Dennis asked.

"No," she said. "We can't afford to wait. Go straight there, find out where he was when Ameena Khan died. Get backup for his story, speak to his wife if he's got one. Family, anybody who can corroborate."

"Right, boss."

CHAPTER TWENTY-SIX

Lesley parked on the double yellows outside Nevin, Cross and Short. She didn't care now if she got a ticket. This was official police business and she was in a hurry. She ran through the pedestrianised area outside the office and leaned on the buzzer. It rang out, a long tone that she hoped would echo in the offices beyond. She waited. No answer.

She checked her watch: quarter to seven.

She stepped back from the wall and looked up at the first-floor windows. Three of them were illuminated. Lawyers never went home early. There would be somebody up there for hours yet, pulling a late night. Preparing for court tomorrow.

Was Elsa in there, with Nevin?

She returned to the buzzer and pressed it again. At last she heard a voice.

"We're closed. Who is it?"

It was a man, not the woman she'd spoken to before.

"DCI Clarke, Dorset Police. I need to speak to Harry Nevin urgently."

"He's not here."

She thought of the layout of the offices. Nevin in his glass walled office in one corner. Everybody else at their open plan desks.

"Are you sure?" she asked. "Check."

"I can see the whole office from here. He's not here."

Lesley tried to remember where the other end of the intercom was. Was it near the door to the offices or was it closer to Nevin's office? Or could it be accessed from any phone up there?

"I want you to let me in," she said. "What's your name?"

"I'm not letting you in," he replied. "Have you got a warrant?"

Lesley gritted her teeth. *Bloody lawyers*.

"If he's not here," she asked, "Where will he be?"

"At home, I imagine," the reply came. "Try his home."

She swallowed. "I will."

CHAPTER TWENTY-SEVEN

Dennis stood outside Harry Nevin's house, Johnny behind him. He could feel Johnny's nerves coming off him in waves. *Calm down, son.*

Nevin lived in a generous red brick house set back from the road in Canford Cliffs. This was one of the more expensive areas of Poole. Less opulent than Sandbanks, but not far off. More characterful, Dennis thought.

He pushed the buzzer, careful not to press too heavily, and stood back. On a house like this, there would be a camera. He arranged his face into a suitable expression.

A screen next to the door came to life and a woman appeared. She was blonde and looked younger than Harry Nevin.

"Hello?"

"Mrs Nevin?" he asked.

"Yes."

"My name is DS Frampton. I've been dealing with your husband on a case. I'd be grateful if I could come in and speak to him."

"What time is it?" she asked.

"Seven o'clock," Johnny muttered in Dennis's ear.

"Seven o'clock, Mrs Nevin. Sorry to bother you so late, it is rather urgent."

"He's not here," the woman replied.

Dennis eyed Johnny.

"Maybe he's still at the office?" Johnny muttered.

Dennis looked back at the screen. "Is he still at work?"

"Don't ask me," the woman said.

The screen flicked off.

"The DCI's gone to his office," Johnny said.

Dennis nodded. He'd heard nothing from her; he hoped that was because she was with Nevin.

Dennis watched the door. "Let's just give it a couple of minutes."

His phone buzzed. He pulled it out of his inside pocket. It was the DCI. *No sign of Nevin at the office. Is he at home?*

He showed it to Johnny, whose shoulders dropped.

Dennis went to ring the bell again, just as the door opened. The woman stared back at them. She was at least twenty years younger than Nevin, wearing an expensive-looking dress with slippers. Her hair was neatly curled, and her makeup was immaculate.

"Mrs Nevin." He held up his ID. "Sorry to bother you at this time of the evening. Can you tell me where your husband might be?"

She adopted a look of irritation. "Not far away."

Dennis raised an eyebrow. "What does that mean?"

"He'll be in Studland, no doubt," she replied. "He leaves the office at five o'clock, pretends he's coming home to me." She rubbed her nose and looked away. "But he doesn't."

"Why would he be in Studland?" Johnny asked.

Dennis gave him a nudge in the ribs. *Let the woman tell us at her own pace.*

"He's with his mistress," she said. "Fucking bitch."

Dennis felt his cheeks redden. "Do you know exactly where in Studland she lives?"

122

"I don't want to talk about it." She went to push the door closed.

Dennis took a step forward. "Please. We need to speak to him."

She surveyed him. He could tell she was weighing up the consequences of giving them the address, culminating in the police knocking on the door of her husband's mistress. Finally, she smiled.

"OK. I'll get her address for you."

CHAPTER TWENTY-EIGHT

Lesley parked her car on the coast road leading towards the Studland ferry. The address Dennis had sent her was somewhere along here. Nevin's girlfriend lived in one of the apartment blocks looking out over Poole harbour.

Alright for some, she thought.

She'd read that this was one of the most expensive strips of land in the world, and that the houses cost millions of pounds. They didn't look much. But when you turned the other way and took in the view, it was easy to see what the fuss was about.

Ffion Nevin had given them the name of her husband's girlfriend: Priscilla Evans. Lesley wondered what the woman did for a living, how she made enough money to live in sight of that view. She closed her car door and opened up Google Maps on her phone, trying to work out which building she wanted.

A few houses along, she spotted Dennis's car parked at the side of the road. He was inside still, Johnny beside him. She knocked on the window and Dennis lowered it.

"You waiting for me?" she asked him.

"You told me to, boss."

"Thanks," she said, her eyes roaming the flats opposite.

She wanted to be there when they interviewed Nevin. She wanted to see the look in his eyes when he was asked about Ameena Khan's death. She also wanted to check if he was wearing that ring.

"Come on then," she said. "Let's get him."

"I didn't think you had a warrant?" Dennis said.

"You know what I mean." She started walking towards the apartment building she'd identified as the one in which Priscilla Evans lived.

She heard two car doors slam behind her. Without turning to check her colleagues were with her, she strode ahead and found the buzzer for the correct flat. She pushed it long and hard.

They waited for the buzzer to be answered. Lesley turned to Dennis and Johnny.

"As soon as we get in there, we separate them. We need to know if she can give him an alibi without them having the chance to confer."

"Right, boss," Johnny said. Dennis nodded.

The intercom crackled behind her. "Hello?"

Lesley turned to it. "DCI Clarke, Dorset Police. We're here to see Mr Harry Nevin."

"He's not here," the voice replied.

Lesley eyed her colleagues. If not here, then where the hell was he?

"Who are you?" she asked.

"Priscilla Evans, his friend."

"Friend." Johnny smirked.

Stop it, Lesley thought. She pictured Julieta, her own husband's new woman, standing in her kitchen. She couldn't get the woman out of her head. Even if she was in the process of moving on herself.

"Hang on a moment," said the voice. The intercom crackled again and the buzzer sounded.

Lesley pushed on the door and the three of them went inside. Ahead was a broad stairway, carpeted and cleaned to within an inch of its life. They walked up one floor and found the door to the apartment already open, waiting for them. A woman stood in the doorway. She was tall and black, dark wavy hair scooped up on top of her head. Subtle makeup. Not what Lesley had been expecting from Dennis's report of what Ffion Nevin had told him.

"Sorry to bother you, Ms Evans," she said. "We need to speak to Mr Nevin urgently in connection with a murder inquiry."

The woman's eyes widened. "Whose murder?"

So he hadn't told her about Ameena Khan.

"A colleague of Mr Nevin."

"Harry hasn't been here for days," Priscilla said. "Sorry, no idea where he is."

"Would he normally be here in the evening?"

The woman shrugged. "Sometimes, sometimes not. Depends."

"On what?"

Priscilla folded her arms. "It depends what kind of mood I'm in."

Lesley smiled. She liked this woman's attitude. "Can we ask you a few questions?"

"Of course you can. Come in."

They followed the woman inside. The flat was light and airy, with broad windows giving a view over the harbour. The furniture was pale and understated, everything focused on that view.

The woman gestured towards a glass-topped dining table and the three detectives sat down, Priscilla joining them.

"What can I help you with?" she asked.

"We need to know if you were with Harry on Sunday morning," Lesley said.

"Sunday morning… Why?"

"His colleague was killed on Sunday morning. We need to find out where he was."

"You think Harry killed them?" The woman frowned. "No way, Harry wouldn't say boo to a goose."

"Were you with him?" Lesley asked.

"Hang on a moment." Priscilla went to a bookshelf and grabbed a diary. She flicked through its pages.

"Here you are," she said. "Saturday night, we went to see a play in Bournemouth. He came back here afterwards, stayed the night. Left at about ten in the morning, went straight to the office, or that's what he told me." She looked up. "He always says that, but I know he's often going home to his wife. You can check with his secretary."

"Can I take that, please?" Lesley said.

The woman clutched her diary. "How long will you need it for?"

"Not long," Lesley replied. "We'll get it back to you as soon as we're done with it."

The woman didn't let go of the diary. "It's got all my appointments in."

"Like I say, we will return it as soon as we're finished with it."

She wondered if there was anything in this diary the woman wanted to hide. She looked at it, her gaze flicking between the diary and its owner.

Slowly the woman released her grip on the diary. She pushed it across the table.

"Send it back as soon as you're done with it, yes? And there's no way Harry could have killed someone."

CHAPTER TWENTY-NINE

Lesley, Dennis and Johnny sat in Dennis's car. Lesley was in the passenger seat, Johnny in the back. They stared out at the harbour.

"So where on earth is he?" Lesley asked, noticing Dennis's approving look. A few weeks ago, she would have said *where the hell is he*, and earned her sergeant's disapproval. It wasn't always easy, but she was learning to tone down her language.

Dennis shook his head. "Hiding from us, maybe."

"He could just be out somewhere," Johnny suggested. He leaned forwards, putting his head between the two front seats. "Dinner, cinema, a walk?"

Lesley shook her head. "Wherever he is, he's alone. He hasn't taken his wife with him, or his girlfriend. I'm worried he suspects we're onto him."

"I'm not sure *onto him* is the right word," Dennis said. "All we've got is that ring."

"It's enough for me to be suspicious. To want to talk to him."

"So where is he?"

"Maybe he's with a client?" Johnny said.

Lesley turned in her seat. "It's a thought. If one of Ameena's clients has got something to do with all this, he might have gone to see them. Steven Leonard, maybe?"

"It's a possibility," said Dennis. "You think we should go round there?"

Lesley shook her head. "Nevin will be in his office early, if I know lawyers. Dennis, you meet me there at eight am. Wait round the back, I don't want them seeing us."

"No problem."

"What d'you want me to do?" asked Johnny.

"You and Mike follow up this Rogers bloke. I want to know why Ameena's PA was so scared of him."

"Will do," said Johnny.

"And then there's the DNA we might be getting tomorrow," she said. "If it belongs to Nevin, then Carpenter won't stop us arresting him."

Dennis raised his eyebrows, his eyes still on the harbour. The sun was going down and boats were drifting in from the sea. "If that happens," he said, "we've got our man."

She opened the car door. "All the more reason to speak to him as soon as we can. Eight o'clock tomorrow morning, don't be late."

She got out of the car and walked to her own. Sure enough, there was a parking ticket on it. She cursed and ripped the ticket into pieces, then regretted it. She'd need to tell somebody in the admin team to sort it out.

She shoved the pieces into her pocket and got into the car, slapping her hands on the steering wheel. She felt tight, frustrated, hot.

Where the hell was Harry Nevin? Why hadn't he been in any of his usual places? Was he hiding, or was it coincidence?

She turned the ignition. Back to Wareham, she thought. She'd take the ferry over, drive through the countryside. It would take longer than the land route, but would delay the return to that empty house and the reheated take-away that awaited her.

CHAPTER THIRTY

Elsa parked her car at the beach near Sandbanks. She slammed the door and turned to look out at the sea. It was tranquil this morning, hardly a breeze touching the water. Boats were already making their way out to sea, small white dots moving over the blue.

She envied them. Her life was dominated by work, barely a day off. Weekends were spent catching up on emails and reading files in preparation for the week. She longed for the free time to take a boat out. She'd learned to sail when she was a girl, her dad teaching her on the weekends he wasn't working. He was a lawyer too, working long hours, but not as long as hers. Times had changed.

She checked her watch. Five past eight: she was late. He was particular about these things. She hurried to the usual café and ordered a latte. She found a table outside, checking her watch again. Odd that he wasn't already waiting.

She got her phone out of her bag. No messages, no new emails. Nothing from him, nothing from anyone in the firm. She frowned and scrolled through her emails again, more slowly this time. Nothing.

She stood up and looked around her. She was sitting on a small terrace overlooking the beach. The interior, beyond the tall windows, was empty. And he always sat outside when it wasn't raining.

She checked her messages again. She flicked through WhatsApp, Facebook and Twitter. He never used social media to contact her but she was beginning to worry.

She dialled.

"Nevin, Cross and Short, Harry Nevin's office, can I help you?" said his PA.

"Amanda, it's Elsa."

"Hello, Ms Short. How are you this morning?"

"Is he in yet?"

"I'm not expecting him until half past eleven, he's got a court appearance first thing."

Elsa gripped the phone. He hadn't messaged her to say he wasn't coming. The last time she'd spoken to him had been yesterday afternoon. They'd made a firm arrangement, even if it wasn't in either of their diaries. She checked her watch again, eight twenty. He was never late.

"Can you ask him to call me when he gets in?"

"Certainly," replied Amanda. "You might want to try texting him too. Or I can do that for you?"

"I've already tried. He's not answering."

"If the session has started, he'll have turned it off."

If he was due in the magistrates' court, they didn't start until ten. So where was he?

"Can I do anything for you, Ms Short?" asked Amanda. "Where are you?"

Elsa frowned. Their colleagues didn't know that she and Harry had these private meetings on Sandbanks Beach. There were certain cases and certain clients they preferred not to discuss in the office.

She scratched her cheek. "I'll try him again on his mobile. It's not urgent."

She hung up and opened her email app again. She dragged the screen down to refresh it. *Where are you, Harry?*

She called his mobile number. No answer.

She downed the last of her latte and left the café, walking towards the beach. Maybe he was out here on the sand. He liked to watch the boats, too.

But there was no sign of him. A young woman was watching a toddler digging in the sand with a plastic shovel. A middle-aged couple ran after a dog that was playing in the waves. This was one of the few beaches locally that allowed dogs.

She turned back towards the café. She ducked inside and walked around the space one more time. He wasn't here. He hadn't been here in the first place. So where the hell was Harry Nevin?

CHAPTER THIRTY-ONE

It was quarter past eight in the morning when Johnny and Mike arrived at Danny Rogers' house in Ringwood. He lived in a flat above a newsagent, accessed via a door squeezed in next to the shop. The door was scuffed with mud staining on the lower part and a long crack running vertically down the wood. A bag of rubbish sat outside, a tear in its side revealing the remains of a chicken carcass and empty McDonald's cartons.

Johnny banged on the door, wrinkling his nose at the smell of rotting food. No answer.

A man emerged from the newsagent's. He was heavily built, middle-aged and he looked annoyed. "What's going on?"

Johnny held up his ID. "Dorset Police. We need to speak to Danny Rogers. Does he live in the flat above here?"

The man shook his head. "I don't want nothing to do with it, mate."

"It's OK," Johnny replied. "We just want to talk to him in connection with a case."

The man looked up at the first-floor window. "He's nothing but trouble. I keep asking the landlord to get rid of him but…"

"We'll be quick," said Mike.

The man grunted and went back inside his shop.

Johnny banged on the door again. "It's the police, Danny. Let us in."

After a few minutes the door opened. A skinny man in his twenties stared out at them. He wiped his hand across his eyes and yawned. "What d'you want? It's early."

Johnny held up his badge. "DC Chiles, DC Legg. Do you know a woman called Sam Chaston?"

The man screwed up his face. "Sam who?"

"Sam Chaston," replied Mike. "You went to visit her yesterday."

The man looked at Mike with narrowed eyes. "Who says?"

"Our colleague," said Johnny. "DCI Clarke. She was visiting Sam when you turned up in your car, then drove off in a hurry."

"Don't know what you're talking about."

"We checked your plates against the system," Mike said.

"Are you going to let us in?" asked Johnny. "I don't think you want the guy downstairs listening in on all this."

Rogers smirked. "He can listen in on anything he bloody wants to, I don't care about him."

Johnny pursed his lips. "So how d'you know Sam?"

"Who are you talking about?"

"Sam Chaston," said Johnny, patiently. The bloke was winding him up, and he knew it. All he had to do was stay calm and repeat himself. "The woman you went to visit yesterday."

"Sam Chaston?"

Johnny gestured at Mike, who took out his phone. He found a photo of Sam and held it up.

Rogers leaned forwards to peer into it. He smelt musty, like he hadn't washed for a few days, and his breath smelled of beer. "Oh, yeah. Sam. I don't know her surname."

"How d'you know her?" Johnny asked.

Rogers shrugged. "Don't know, just do."

"So why did you go and see her?"

"Just did."

"She looked scared of you."

"How d'you know? You weren't there."

"Our colleague said Sam looked terrified when you turned up."

"That's her problem."

"Is she your girlfriend?" asked Mike.

Rogers laughed. "Of course she's not my bloody girl-friend."

Johnny pushed the phone closer to Rogers. "How d'you know her, Danny? This is part of a murder inquiry."

Rogers raised an eyebrow. "She's dead?"

"No," said Johnny. "But somebody else is. Somebody she worked with."

Rogers cleared his throat, then scratched his nose. "Oh, now I remember. She's a mate of my girlfriend, Jasmine. That's how I know her."

"So why did you go and see her?" Johnny asked.

A shrug. Rogers sniffed. "I returned something, went to give it back."

"But you didn't return anything. You jumped back in your car and drove off."

"What you talking about?"

"You ran away," said Mike.

Rogers looked at him. "I don't bloody run away from anything, mate."

"You saw our colleague, DCI Clarke," Mike replied. "Then you got back in your car and drove off."

"Oh, yeah," Rogers said. "I remembered, I didn't have it."

"OK," said Johnny. "So what was this thing that you were supposed to be returning?"

"I dunno, I didn't have it did I?"

"So did you come back here and get it?" Mike asked.

Rogers eyed him. "No. It was a book. I didn't have it. Jasmine hadn't given it to me after all."

"What book was it?" asked Johnny. He gave Mike a look. Danny Rogers didn't strike him as the book type.

A shrug. "Just a book. Some sort of girly trash that Jasmine wanted to lend her mate."

"OK," said Johnny, "So you weren't returning something to Sam after all? You were lending something to her?"

"Yeah," replied Rogers.

"And if we talk to Jasmine about it, she'll corroborate your story?"

Rogers looked at him. His eyelid twitched. "Of course she will. Ain't no *story*."

"Good," said Johnny, "Where does she live?"

Rogers stared at him for a moment. His gaze went up to the upstairs window. "She lives here with me. What d'you expect?"

"Is she at home now?" asked Johnny.

"She's at work."

"Where does she work?"

Rogers shrugged. "Can't remember, she got a new job last week."

"What time does she get home?" asked Mike.

Rogers scratched his head. "When does anyone get home? Half five, six?"

"OK," said Johnny. "Expect us then, we'll come back and talk to her."

"You don't need to talk to her," said Rogers. "She hasn't got anything to tell you."

"She'll be able to tell us if you were visiting Sam Chaston to return her book. She'll be able to tell us if she knows Sam Chaston."

Rogers shrugged. "Whatever." He backed into the doorway.

Johnny put his hand in his pocket, about to give the man his card.

"I don't want nothing off you, mate," said Rogers. "I'll tell Jasmine to expect you." He shut the door in their faces.

Johnny turned to Mike. "He'll call her. Make sure they get their stories straight."

Mike nodded. "We need her mobile number."

Johnny knocked on the door. "Danny?"

He heard thundering, feet going up the stairs.

"He's not coming back," said Mike.

Johnny sighed. Dennis would give him a grilling for not getting Jasmine's phone number.

He looked at Mike. "He's not."

CHAPTER THIRTY-TWO

Steve Haskins balled his fists in the small of his back and stretched as he looked out to sea. Today was promising to be a warm one. A faint breeze came off the water and the sun had burnt off the clouds from earlier this morning. It was ten am and already he was sweating.

He turned towards his wife Sukhi, who was pulling deckchairs out of the beach hut.

"Hang on, love. I'll help with that."

She put one down and raised a hand to shield her eyes from the sun. "I keep getting tangled up in them but I'll get there. You keep an eye on Max."

"It's OK," he replied. "I'll do the deckchairs, you play with Max."

She sighed. "I play with Max all day every day. It's your turn."

"Fine," he said. He turned to see Max running along the beach. He was chasing a ball, giggling.

"Maxie!" Steve called.

His son ignored him. He swerved to one side and ran towards the other end of the beach huts. Steve took a step forward as his son disappeared past the huts.

Damn.

"Max!"

Steve heard a clatter behind him, Sukhi dropping a chair.

"What's happened?" She'd caught the sharpness in his voice.

"Nothing, sweetie. He's hiding round the back of the huts again."

"I wish he wouldn't do that."

He turned to her. "I'll get him."

The space behind the back of the huts was tight, perfect for a three-year-old. Steve didn't relish going in there after him, he still had the scratches from yesterday.

He strode past the row of beach huts. Sukhi was quiet now, watching him no doubt.

"Max!"

He heard a yelp from behind the huts. His heart lurched.

"Max! Where are you?"

Sukhi was behind him. "Did you hear that?"

Steve turned to her. "He's messing. Don't worry."

Another yelp. Sukhi clutched his shoulder. "He's that way."

He raised a finger to his lips. "Shh."

"Daddy!" came his son's voice. Steve felt his muscles loosen. "He's right over here. He's fine."

"I don't like him going around there. Have you seen the rubbish?"

Steve had. It was filthy behind those beach huts, probably a public health risk. The company that had rented the hut to them claimed the area was cleaned regularly, but it was a natural collecting ground for rubbish. Behind the huts was a steep slope to the cliffs above. People would toss rubbish over from the top, dirty buggers. Steve had gone behind there yesterday, looking for Max's ball. He'd spotted things he'd rather not think about.

"Max!" he called, his voice firm. "Come out now!"

"Daddy!"

Steve gritted his teeth. Max's voice seemed to be coming from behind their own hut. There was a small gap between it and the next one along. Narrow enough for Max to get through, but not for Steve.

Why the hell did they leave gaps like that down the side of beach huts? Why didn't they fence them off?

"I'll go to the end," he told Sukhi. "Work my way around."

He ran past the row of beach huts and skidded around the far end. He inserted himself into the gap between the end beach hut and the grassy slope behind and started wading through the accumulated rubbish.

Not looking down, he pushed ahead. "Max, Daddy's coming," he called. "It's OK!"

"Daddy!"

Steve could see a shape moving up ahead. Max was halfway along the row of huts, past their own. He hurried as best as he could in the confined space. His foot hit something wet and soft and he bit down a wave of nausea.

Max was closer now, his face visible. He turned towards Steve, his face blotchy.

"I'm coming Maxie. It's all right, I've got you."

"Daddy! Daddy, the man!"

What man? Max felt dread grip his chest.

"Keep away from the man," he said.

"Man's asleep, Daddy."

Oh my God. There was a tramp sleeping around the back of the beach hut and Max had found him.

"Come here, Max," Steve said. "Come here, come to Daddy."

Max turned and made for Steve. His small body hit Steve's legs, and Steve gripped him tightly. "It's all right now Maxie, you're safe now. Where's the man?"

He looked past his son, ready to confront the stranger. "Where is he, Maxie?"

Max turned around and pointed. He was crying. "He's there, Daddy, he's asleep. Why is he asleep?"

Steve peered through the gloom. Sure enough, there was a shape lying on top of the litter behind their own beach hut. He took a step forward.

"Maxie, you go back to Mummy."

Max didn't move. Steve considered pushing him through the gap between their beach hut and the next one. But he had no idea if Sukhi was out there waiting for him.

"Max," he said, his voice shaking. "You stand behind me, don't look."

Steve took a step towards the man. He was grey-haired, facing sideways from Steve, the skin pallid on the back of his neck. The edge of one eye was visible: open, staring up towards the sky.

Steve swallowed. Overcome by a reflex, he kicked out and hit the man, pushing him away. The eye was invisible now.

"What's wrong with him, Daddy? Why is he there?"

"It's alright, Maxie, don't worry about it. Come on."

He looked at the man again. He wore a smart suit and a red tie. He wasn't a tramp, nor a holidaymaker.

"Come on, Maxie."

Steve turned and shunted his son along the gap behind the beach huts as fast as he could, breathing heavily. Finally, he emerged at the end like a cork popping out of a bottle. He and Max stumbled out together.

Sukhi was waiting for them. "Maxie! My gorgeous boy." She held her arms out and Steve handed him over.

"There's a man behind there," he whispered to his wife.

"A man?" she looked from him to Max. "Did he hurt Max?"

Steve shook his head. "Have you got your phone?"

She frowned. "Why?"

"Call 999."

CHAPTER THIRTY-THREE

"Turn right," Dennis said. "You can park along here."

Lesley knew they weren't far from Elsa's flat, but still she didn't know these roads. They were on the clifftop in Boscombe, east of the centre of Bournemouth. To her right was the sea, to her left the town.

"Where now?" she said.

Dennis pointed. "Take a right, car park's there."

She parked the car overlooking the cliffs. Ahead of the car was nothing but air. "I can't see anything."

"It's too steep," he replied. "They'll be down there."

She nodded and got out of the car. Once again, this was a pay and display car park. She ignored the signs and turned back to the sergeant. "How do we get down there?"

"Follow me."

She followed Dennis, to a zigzagging path leading down the cliff. They walked along it, gravity pulling them downwards.

"Bloody hell, this is… goodness, this is steep," Lesley said.

Dennis smiled at her. "You're trying, at least."

"I'm very trying, Dennis," she replied.

They reached the bottom. Ahead of them was the entrance to Boscombe pier, ice-cream shops and souvenir stalls. To either side the beach stretched away from them.

Bournemouth beach was one of the longest unbroken stretches of sand along the south coast. Seven miles, Dennis had told her. She hadn't had many opportunities to see it, despite it being only a few streets from Elsa's flat.

Dennis looked past her and indicated with his head. "Cordon's there."

She turned to see a police cordon on the concrete walkway in front of a row of beach huts. The tape fluttered in the breeze. Holidaymakers were gathering on the beach, people staring in the direction of the cordon. *Today's entertainment*, she thought with a frown.

Behind the cordon Lesley spotted Gail and one of her techs. She slipped under the tape and nodded at the crime scene manager.

"What have we got?"

"Middle aged man," said Gail. "Found dead behind these beach huts."

"Have you been round there?" Lesley asked.

"I have. It's not pretty."

"The scene, or the man?"

"Both."

Lesley grimaced. "Take us round."

"It's tight," Gail told her. "You have to go along to the end of the beach huts and then squeeze behind them."

Lesley shrugged. "I've done worse." She was relieved not to be on an exposed clifftop or in a muddy field.

"You're going to need these." Gail handed her a pair of wellies.

Lesley waved them away. "We're not in a field."

Gail looked down at Lesley's feet. "Trust me. You'll be glad of them."

Lesley was wearing her new leather ankleboots. The boots Gail had handed her were black, tall and solid.

Lesley slipped off her shoes and put her feet inside the wellies.

"Where are mine?" Dennis asked.

"I haven't got another pair," Gail said. "These are my spares."

"OK," Dennis sighed. "I guess I'll just have to risk my trousers."

Gail shrugged. "Sorry."

"Come on then," Lesley said. "Let's see him."

"Follow me." Gail led them to the end of the row of beach huts. The huts were set back from the promenade, on a raised concrete platform. They had white roofs and the walls of each were painted a different colour from its neighbours. Around half of them looked like they were in use, but the inhabitants had been asked to leave the area.

They climbed a flight of steps onto the platform and walked around the side of the last beach hut. Gail squeezed into a gap between it and the cliff.

"I told you it was tight," she said.

"You weren't wrong." Lesley elbowed her way along the space, keeping up with Gail. Dennis was behind her. "Do we reckon they brought him in this way?"

"No." Gail's voice echoed in the confined space. "He was pushed off the cliff."

Lesley looked up. The cliff was different from the chalk promontory at Old Harry Rocks. Here, the cliffs were redder, made of clay. They sloped steeply instead of being sheer, and were covered in thin grass. Despite the slope, it was steep enough to throw a heavy object.

Gail stopped and Lesley almost crashed into her. "Here." Gail pointed downwards.

Lesley couldn't see anything. "Where is he?"

"Right here. Sorry."

The space was dark and confined. Lesley couldn't see past the CSM.

"Hang on," Gail said. She leaned into the cliff, trying to move out of Lesley's way. Lesley peered over her shoulder.

Beyond Gail, on the ground between the cliff and the wooden hut, was a man. He had thinning grey hair and a round face. He faced upwards, but the narrow angle between hut and cliff, together with the uneven surface created by the detritus underneath him, meant that the only part of him she could see clearly was the back of his neck.

Lesley cocked her head. "What's that on the side of his head?"

Gail struggled to turn in the confined space. "Looks like an injury. I don't want to move him till the pathologist gets here."

Lesley raised an eyebrow. "Where is Whittaker, anyway?"

"He's here," Gail said. "He texted me a few moments ago."

Texting, thought Lesley. So Whittaker did recognise the twenty-first century. "So where is he?"

"He's waiting on the other side of this beach hut."

"He's what?"

"He says he's not coming round the back here."

Lesley looked up to the sky. *Heaven help me*. "He's a pathologist, he needs to look at this body before we move it."

Gail shrugged. "You don't need to convince me."

"So can we move him before the pathologists have checked him out? Maybe one of his team can do it?"

Gail shook her head. "He doesn't have a team, not one he trusts to come out to crime scenes, anyway."

"So what happens when he's not working?" Lesley said.

"When he's not working, we wait for him to *be* working."

Lesley gritted her teeth. They had to find a better pathologist. Somebody more accommodating, who didn't treat them like his underlings.

Her thoughts were interrupted by the sound of machinery near her right ear.

"What the fuck?"

Behind Lesley, Dennis cleared his throat. She turned. "Sorry, Dennis. I didn't know you were there."

He raised an eyebrow.

Gail pushed her to one side. "That'll be Gav. He's sawing through the back of the beach hut to give us better access."

Lesley ducked down, pulling her body towards the cliff to get away from the wood. "Tell him to stop till we get out!"

"Gav!" Gail called. "Wait five minutes!"

Lesley looked at the back of the hut. "There could be evidence on the wood. We can't just destroy it."

Gail shook her head. "He wasn't brought here." She pointed upwards. "He was pushed."

"You're sure?"

"I'm sure," Gail said. "Look at the tracks running down the cliff."

Lesley looked up. There was damage to the grass above them. A shrub six feet up looked like it had been hit with something heavy.

"He came down that way," Gail said.

"The shrubs?"

Gail nodded. "Plenty of rubbish down here, but nothing solid enough to do that."

"Still, we need to keep all possi—"

"Trust me," Gail told her. "This is my job."

"OK," Lesley replied.

The sawing had increased in intensity now, giving Lesley a headache.

"Let's back up," Gail said. "Then go out through the hut."

Lesley and Gail shuffled backwards, shifting so they were two huts along. Dennis shunted along behind them. Lesley looked at the body on the ground. She hoped they wouldn't damage it.

"They'll make sure the back of that beach hut falls inwards, won't they?" she asked.

Gail looked at her. "You don't have to tell us how to do our job."

"Sorry." She needed to trust Gail. The woman knew what she was doing.

There was a crash and the rear wall fell away from them, towards the front. Someone stopped it before it hit the ground. It was gently lowered and then pulled away.

"Make sure you preserve it!" Gail called. "I want to get any evidence on that wood."

Lesley looked at her. "I thought you said they didn't come down this way."

"That doesn't mean there can't be any forensics on the back of the beach hut. We check everywhere."

Lesley nodded. Thoroughness, that's what she liked.

Gail walked through the beach hut. The back wall had been carried out by her two colleagues and was propped up on the concrete walkway. Next to it, Henry Whittaker stood blinking at them. He cocked his head to look through at them.

"My turn now, I suppose."

Lesley rolled her eyes. "Dr Whittaker. We've been waiting for you."

He grunted. "I'm sure you have."

CHAPTER THIRTY-FOUR

Whittaker bent over the body. "We've got a white man, in his late fifties by the looks of it. Slightly overweight, no injuries visible from this angle. But…"

He moved the man's head, turning it sideways.

Lesley grimaced. The man had a deep gash on the back of his head. Hair stuck to it and blood was congealing around it. It was deep, sticky, blackened.

"Probable cause of death," said Dr Whittaker.

"You're sure?" Lesley asked.

He looked up at her. "I can't be a hundred per cent right now, not until I've taken the chap to the morgue. But a wound like this would kill a man. If not immediately, the internal bleeding would do it." He pointed at the man's head. "See the discolouration around the wound, and on his face? Haemorrhaging. Head wounds can produce a lot of blood."

Lesley looked up the cliff. "Was the blow delivered here, or before he fell?"

"It would take some force to do this. I very much doubt it could have been done in the confined space behind these huts." He followed her gaze. "No. He was hit, then pushed down."

"Not brought behind here from the front?"

"I heard what the CSI people think, and I agree with them. I can't see any evidence of him being dragged behind here. There would be splinters in his skin, grazes where he'd been dragged through. There's bruising on his shoulder – see, here?" He lowered the man's shirt collar and Lesley ducked down to see a bruise beneath. "It's the kind of bruise you get when you hit something, not from being dragged. That'll be where he hit the shrubs on the way down." He looked up. "There's enough of them."

"You're sure he didn't hit his head on the way down? A rock, maybe?"

The pathologist looked up the cliff. "I can't see anything sharp enough to do this. Whatever it was, it was pointed. This was a deliberate blow, a forceful one. The shrubs would have slowed his descent, meaning if he hit something, it wouldn't have been with enough force." He straightened up. "Somebody did this to him."

Lesley nodded. A second murder case in three days.

She turned to Gail. "We need to check for signs of somebody else being here, cordon off the area at the top of the cliff. Check for CCTV cameras. Any houses or flats overlooking it. I want to know if we've got witnesses."

Gail looked at her. "Witnesses aren't my job, Lesley."

"Sorry."

Lesley sighed. She turned to Dennis, who had joined them inside the beach hut. "Dennis, you get all that?"

"Of course," he said. "I'll talk to Johnny and Mike, get them to make a start."

"Good." She looked back at the body. "So do we know who he was? Was he carrying any ID?"

Now he'd been moved, she could see the man's face for the first time, or the little of it that was visible through the thick spatter of blood from the head wound. It obscured his right eye and covered his cheek. Even his nearest and dearest would struggle to recognise him.

Lesley reached out a hand to the wall of the hut. This never got easy.

Gail bent to search his pockets. "Nothing," she said. "Completely empty."

"Could his killer have emptied his pockets?" Lesley asked.

"Not many people have absolutely nothing in their pockets," Gail replied. "So I'd say there's a good chance, yes."

"That's encouraging. They might have left their DNA behind."

"Unless they wore gloves."

Lesley sighed. "Let's hope our killer wasn't that clever. It could just have been a drunken fight at the top of the cliff. Somebody hit him too hard and he went over."

Gail shook her head. "Have you seen the height of the fences up there? You can't push somebody over there by accident. Whoever it was, had to lift him and get him over." She looked at the pathologist. "Is there any evidence of him having been dragged over the fence?"

The pathologist shook his head. "Not from what I can see with him clothed, but obviously we'll know more when we do the post-mortem."

Lesley crouched down to get a better look at the body. A ring on his right finger caught her eye. It was a signet ring.

She looked back at his face. Now she knew what to look for, he was recognisable.

"Oh, sh…"

She glanced at Dennis.

In death, she hadn't recognised the man. There was something about the size of his personality that had made him different in life.

"I know him," she said. "You too, Dennis. We each interviewed him."

Gail twisted to look up at her. "Who is he?"

Lesley swallowed. "His name's Harry Nevin."

CHAPTER THIRTY-FIVE

The pathologist was still inspecting Harry Nevin's body, with Lesley watching on.

Dennis stood back, surveying the scene. He looked up and down the cliff, wondering how much strength it would take to push a large man like Nevin over it. They'd been certain that Nevin had killed Ameena. In which case who'd killed Nevin, and was it related?

He took a step towards Lesley and she turned towards him.

"What are you thinking, boss?" he asked.

"They've got to be connected," she said. "Nevin was looking likely for Ameena's death. Which means somebody could have killed him, because he killed her."

"Or somebody else could have killed them both," Dennis suggested.

She shrugged. "We'll know more when we get the DNA." She looked at Gail. "When are we expecting that?"

"The lab said it will be today or tomorrow. I'll see if they can hurry it up."

"Thanks."

Lesley looked at Dennis. "I'll stay here for a bit, keep an eye on things. But I want you and the DCs to make a start on CCTV and witnesses. I'll come and find you when I'm done here."

Dennis walked away from the crime scene, towards the path that led up the cliff. It would be harder going up than it had been coming down. As he reached the bottom of the path, he spotted Johnny coming the other way.

"Alright, mate," he said.

"I hear we've got a new body," Johnny replied.

Dennis nodded. "Harry Nevin."

"Whoah. The same Harry Nevin who…?"

"The one and only. You've come from the office?"

Johnny gestured behind him. "Mike's with me, we went to see Danny Rogers."

"And?"

"He was obstructive. He insisted that Sam Chaston was a mate of his girlfriend, but I didn't believe him. There's something fishy going on there."

"Right," said Dennis. "Find out if his girlfriend backs up his story."

"Will do," replied Johnny.

"Meanwhile, the DCI wants us to see if any CCTV overlooks the crime scene. And we need to knock on some doors up there." Dennis gestured towards the flats at the top of the cliffs.

Johnny followed his gaze. "No problem, boss."

"Come on, then." Dennis hauled himself up the hill, wishing he was fitter.

Mike was walking down towards them. "Alright, Sarge? What have we got?"

"Harry Nevin, pushed down the cliff. Sometime last night, most likely."

Mike winced. "Really?"

Dennis didn't want to have this conversation again. "I want you to start collating evidence. Forensics, witnesses. You can do that?"

Mike nodded. He looked disappointed. "You want me in the office?"

Dennis scratched his nose. "Uniform are already knocking on doors. I want someone back at base pulling it together." He looked towards the crime scene. The DCI was distracted; he needed to set the investigation in motion. And he'd done this plenty of times before.

"Go on, then."

"Sarge." Mike turned back up the hill, striding purposefully. He was almost thirty years younger than Dennis, who envied him.

"You want me here with you?" Johnny asked, a smile playing on his lips.

"I want you here, yes. Door knocking, those flats. Find out if there's any CCTV. Ask the residents if they saw suspicious activity last night. If Harry Nevin was pushed over, someone must have seen."

"So he wasn't brought in from the road at the bottom, taken around the back of the beach huts?" Johnny asked.

"There's evidence of him going down the cliff. Damage to shrubs."

"That fence is a bit high to be shoving a body over." Johnny looked up, shielding his eyes from the morning sun.

"We might be looking for more than one suspect," said Dennis. "Only one way to find out."

"OK."

Before Johnny had a chance to turn away, Dennis put a hand on his arm. "Wait a moment."

Johnny raised an eyebrow. "Something up, Sarge?"

"That case of Ameena Khan's, the one they didn't tell us about…"

"Steven Leonard?" Johnny said.

"We need to talk to him," Dennis replied. "If the Kelvin family have got something to do with this, we need to know about it."

"Have you spoken to the DCI?"

"Not yet." Dennis looked up the hill. "I'm heading over to his address. You work the door-to-door."

"Of course, Sarge. You sure about this?"

Dennis looked up the cliff, and back at the DC. "I am."

CHAPTER THIRTY-SIX

Lesley answered her phone. She pushed her hair back behind her ear; the wind was picking up from the sea now and buffeting it around her head.

"Dennis," she said, "You've got news for me?"

"Just an update boss," he replied. "Johnny's here, I've sent him up to the flats at the top of the cliff. He'll find out if we have any eyewitnesses or CCTV. I thought I'd go and interview Mrs Nevin, break the news to her. Somebody's got to do it."

Lesley pushed her hair back again, cursing the wind. "No, I'll do that."

"You seem busy at the crime scene."

"It's fine, Dennis."

"Well, I'll go and speak to the partners then. Cross and Short."

She hesitated. It was probably best if she wasn't involved in interviewing Elsa.

"OK," she said, "But call me before you speak to them. I want to inform his wife first."

"Will do, boss." He hung up.

Lesley pocketed her phone and walked back towards Gail. Dennis had been odd on the phone. When she'd spoken to him before, he'd said nothing about disappearing to do interviews. He'd said he would look for

CCTV and witnesses. But Johnny could handle that, and Uniform would be knocking on doors too.

"How are we doing?" she asked Gail.

"Pathologist's finished for now," Gail replied.

Sure enough, Whittaker was packing up his bag.

Lesley approached him. "You still think it was that gash on the back of his head?"

"I can't see anything else," he told her. "Obviously, there's the post-mortem to do and then I'll be able to confirm. I don't like to commit myself before that."

I bet you don't, Lesley thought. "When will you be doing the PM?"

He shrugged. "Tomorrow, I imagine."

"Surely today would be more appropriate?"

"I'm a busy man, Inspector."

She jabbed a fingernail into her thigh. "We've got two related murders, that takes priority."

"I can't just move all of my other work to one side because you're in a hurry." He stood square to her, his gaze level.

"In that case, tell me what you can from your examination here. Any defensive wounds?"

"Nothing," the pathologist said. "His hands are clear."

"OK. See if you can get a shuffle on though, won't you? I'm sure my bosses would be happy if you could do the post-mortem today."

Whittaker raised an eyebrow. "I don't answer to your bosses, DCI Clarke."

She gritted her teeth. Henry Whittaker was a pain in the arse, but if she didn't play nice he might delay even more.

"Just tell me when you're doing it. I'll send one of my guys along."

"Of course." He picked up his bag and walked away.

Lesley stood beside Gail, watching the pathologist striding towards the end of the beach.

"He does my head in," Lesley said.

"I know what you mean," Gail replied. "I've been working with him for years."

"Looks like he was here since the dinosaurs."

"Don't be too harsh on him. He knows what he's doing."

"He's slow," Lesley told her. "He's rude, he's unco-operative and he's arrogant. When I was in West Midlands, we had—"

Gail put a hand on her arm. "You're not in Birmingham now, Lesley. You need to work at our pace."

"But *you* don't work at a snail's pace," Lesley told her. "You're one of the most efficient CSMs I've ever met."

Gail smiled. "Thanks for the compliment. It won't get you any favours."

Lesley laughed. "You don't need compliments to work hard. I'll leave you to it."

"I'll tell you if we find anything else."

"I know you will." Lesley walked away.

She approached a uniformed sergeant who was standing near the cordon. "I need a lift," she told him. "To Canford Cliffs. Can one of your people drive me?"

"Certainly, Ma'am," he said. "Follow me."

CHAPTER THIRTY-SEVEN

Steven Leonard lived in a council flat in the north of Bournemouth. The holidaymakers who came to this town probably never imagined that there were local people living in places like this. They probably thought it was all wealthy retirees, and multimillionaires with their luxury pads in Sandbanks. But like all towns, Bournemouth had its rough patches.

Dennis parked his car and strode to the outside door of the block of flats. It was a low block, six flats in a squat two-storey building. He buzzed flat number three.

The intercom crackled, and a male voice spoke. "Yeah, what d'you want?"

"Mr Leonard?" Dennis said. "My name is DS Frampton. I want to ask you a few questions."

"You got a warrant?"

"You're not under arrest," he said. "I just have some questions."

"You haven't got a warrant then?"

"Like I say," Dennis told him. "It's just background information. I'm sure if you cooperate with us…"

"You ain't got no warrant, you're not coming in," the man said.

The intercom went silent. Dennis looked up and down the row of buttons. At this time in the morning, the trades button would work. He pushed it and the door opened.

He elbowed his way inside and walked up the stairs, his footsteps light.

Leonard's front door was daubed with graffiti. Dennis hammered on it.

"Go away!"

"Mr Leonard, I just want to ask you some questions. I'm not leaving until you talk to me."

"You ain't got no warrant, you can't do nothing."

Dennis placed a fist on the door. He wished he had Uniform here with him, the enforcer that could break through the door. But he had no legitimate reason to force his way into this flat. All he had was the knowledge that Steven Leonard was the defendant in the case that had been missing in Ameena Khan's files. That Ameena Khan's PA had warned the DCI about it. And of course that Steven Leonard had intermittently worked for one of the dodgiest families in the whole of Dorset.

"You still working for the Kelvins?" he said through the door.

Silence.

"You're not answering my question?"

The door opened. An overweight, balding man stood behind it. Dennis knew Leonard was only thirty-four, but he looked twenty years older. He wore a thin t-shirt with holes around the belly and a pair of shorts that looked two sizes too small.

"I don't work for them no more," he said.

"You're sure?" Dennis replied. "I heard you'd been in trouble lately."

Leonard shook his head. "I got off. Remember?"

Dennis looked down to the man's ankle. The fact that he was dressed in shorts made it obvious that he was wearing an ankle bracelet. Dennis and Steven Leonard had very different views on what constituted *got off*.

"How long are you going to be wearing that for?"

Leonard dragged a hand across his face and sniffed. "None of your business."

"You see, it is my business," replied Dennis, "because your name has come up in connection with a murder inquiry."

Leonard scowled at him. "No idea what you're talking about, mate." He pushed the door.

Dennis considered leaning into it, holding it open. But he was alone here and he knew what kind of man Steven Leonard was.

"I'll be back," he told him. "My boss has got questions for you."

Leonard spat on the lino outside the door. "Your boss can fuck off."

CHAPTER THIRTY-EIGHT

Lesley patted the roof of the squad car and watched as it drove off along Harry Nevin's road. She surveyed the man's house. It was broad, made of red brick, and set back from the road. The front garden was filled with healthy looking shrubs and mature trees.

A house like this would put you back a bob or two, she thought. But then Harry Nevin was a senior partner in a prestigious law firm. He wasn't short of that bob or two.

She approached the front door and pressed the buzzer. She pulled her shoulders back, straightening her jacket and tugging at her hair so she didn't look like she'd spent the last hour on a windy beach.

The door opened and Ffion Nevin stood blinking at her. "What is it?"

Lesley held up her ID. "My name's DCI Clarke. Can I come in please?"

"Where is he?"

"I think we should do this inside."

The woman gripped the door. "What's happened? Where's Harry?"

"Please, Mrs Nevin. Let's sit down somewhere."

Mrs Nevin's face paled. She backed away from the door, letting Lesley walk in behind her.

Lesley closed the door and scanned the hallway. Three doors led off: a kitchen, a dining room, and a bright living room. Lesley gestured towards the living room with her head. Mrs Nevin nodded and Lesley walked through.

She took a seat and waited for the woman to do the same. Mrs Nevin lowered herself into the chair, her eyes not leaving Lesley's face. "What's happened to him?" she said. "Was he at his mistresses?"

"I'm afraid he wasn't," Lesley replied. "We went there and she hadn't seen him."

"So where was he? Don't tell me he's got *another* woman."

Lesley leaned forwards. She placed her hands on her knees and licked her lips. She hated this, no matter how many times she'd done it before.

"I'm afraid I have bad news for you, Mrs Nevin."

The woman stared at her. Blotchy red dots formed on her cheeks.

"We found your husband on Boscombe Beach this morning," Lesley continued. "I'm afraid he was dead."

Mrs Nevin grasped the arm of the sofa. "No he's not, you're lying."

"I'm so sorry, Mrs Nevin. I was able to identify your husband myself. But we will need you to come in later on, and do so formally. In the meantime, is there someone who can come here, or who you can go to?"

Mrs Nevin narrowed her eyes. "What happened to him? Did he drown?"

"We found him at the bottom of the cliffs," Lesley said. "He'd fallen down them."

"He killed himself?"

"It doesn't look that way. We think somebody pushed him."

The woman's eyes widened. "Pushed him?"

"That's what we're working on."

"So who? One of his clients? Oh, shit..." The woman looked away.

Lesley cocked her head. "Is anybody else here?" She hadn't heard movement or voices in the house and didn't know if the couple had children.

"No," the woman replied. "It's just me and Harry." She clutched her knee. "Or, it was."

Lesley leaned forward. "Is there anybody who might have wanted to hurt your husband?"

"He's a criminal lawyer. I'm sure there are plenty."

"But anybody specific? Anyone he or his firm had been working for recently?"

"Do you think this is linked to that Ameena Khan woman?"

"We don't know right now," Lesley replied. "We don't want to jump to conclusions. But we will investigate the possibility that the two deaths are related."

She resisted telling the woman that Harry Nevin had been their prime suspect in Ameena Khan's death. Now that he was dead, she was rolling back on that assumption.

"I don't know anything about his clients," Mrs Nevin said. "He doesn't talk to me about work."

"Did any of them come here?" Lesley asked. "Did he have meetings in the house?"

The woman frowned. "Sometimes. Sometimes he had evening meetings here so I wouldn't have to be on my own."

"Who did he meet in the evenings?"

"He'd let them in and take them straight to his study. I didn't see them."

Lesley looked towards the door. "Can you show me where his study is, please?"

The woman stood up, her movements jerky, and led Lesley out of the room and into the kitchen. The kitchen spanned the back of the house, with large windows overlooking a long garden. She took Lesley through a door at the rear of the kitchen, leading back in towards the house. It looked like it might have been a garage conversion.

"It's in here," she said.

Lesley stepped into the room. It was larger than a garage conversion, a spacious room with a handsome oak desk in the centre and a broad bay window to the front. Documents lay in neat piles on the desk and a mobile phone sat beside them.

"Is that your husband's phone?" Lesley asked.

Mrs Nevin shrugged. "I guess it must be if it's on his desk."

"He didn't take his phone out with him yesterday?"

"I don't know. I haven't seen him since he went to work yesterday morning."

Lesley approached the desk. The phone was a basic model, not a smartphone.

Why did Harry Nevin have a burner phone?

She turned to Mrs Nevin. "I'm going to have to take this." She pulled gloves out of her pocket and an evidence bag. She placed the phone inside.

She looked around. "We'll probably need to search this room as well. Take his computer, his files."

The woman nodded. "Do what you need to."

Lesley looked at her. "Do you have anyone you can go to? Any family nearby, friends?"

Mrs Nevin swallowed. "My mum lives in London. I could go there, but I'd rather be here."

"I can understand that," Lesley replied. "Have you got a neighbour you could be with? I don't want to leave you on your own."

The woman shook her head. "It's not that kind of street. The house next door is empty half the time. People who own it use it as a holiday home."

"You must have some friends?"

Mrs Nevin stared at her. "They're not the sort of friends who…" She frowned. "Yeah. I can think of someone."

"Good," Lesley said. "Do you want me to call them for you?"

"I'll do it." The woman's voice was thin.

The woman was genuinely shocked. Whatever her husband had been up to, it seemed unlikely that she knew anything about it or was involved.

"Did you know anything about a man called Steven Leonard?" Lesley asked.

Mrs Nevin shook her head. "Steven who?"

"He was a client of your husband's firm. I'm wondering if he might have come to the house at some point?"

The woman shrugged. "Sorry. Harry sometimes talked about stuff that was stressing him out, but nothing specific. He told me about his arguments with Aurelia Cross, but didn't talk about individual cases. He was a lawyer, he knew better than to do that."

Lesley nodded. "We'll send a family liaison officer here to support you. But in the meantime, you call that friend of yours. You need somebody with you."

Mrs Nevin looked around the room. "I don't know where my phone is."

"It's OK," said Lesley. "I'll help you find it."

CHAPTER THIRTY-NINE

Aurelia Cross had an office in the far corner from Harry Nevin. Dennis sat in a chair, waiting for the woman to appear. A PA had ushered him in, her movements jumpy. She'd offered him a coffee and looked relieved when he'd rejected it.

Dennis gazed through the window beyond the desk. There was a view towards the sea. *Nice place to work*, he thought. He glanced behind him towards the other corner of the offices, where Harry Nevin should have been.

Had the man been in here at all yesterday? Had he conferred with his colleagues about what he was working on? Did they know if he was the man who had killed Ameena Khan?

His phone buzzed: the DCI. She was with Ffion Nevin. Dennis looked up as the door opened and Aurelia Cross walked in. "You again."

He stood up. "I'm sorry to bother you."

She gestured towards the chair. "Sit back down. Let's get this over with."

"This isn't a follow up from our previous interview," he told her.

"No? So what is it, then?" She rounded the desk and sat down. She leaned back in her chair, her hands steepled under her chin.

"I'm afraid I have bad news." Dennis watched for her reaction.

"Bad news? We get a lot of that round here."

"It's your partner, Harry Nevin."

The woman's face darkened. "What's he done now?"

Dennis felt his brow furrowing. "What do you expect him to have done?"

She waved in dismissal. "You know what I mean. I don't really think he's done anything. What's up? What are you here for?"

"I'm afraid he's dead, Mrs Cross."

"Dead?"

"His body was found this morning on Boscombe Beach."

The woman straightened in her chair. She jerked forward and placed her hands flat on the table. "Dead? Harry?" She pulled in a breath. "Harry's bloody immortal."

Dennis winced at the language. "The body hasn't been formally identified yet, but it is Mr Nevin. I've been there myself." He didn't tell her he hadn't seen Nevin's body. The DCI's word was enough.

Aurelia Cross's gaze flicked out towards the outer office. "Who else knows?"

"My DCI has gone to inform his wife. And there were some press at the scene."

"Press? You can keep them away, I don't want any speculating."

"There's not much we can do to control what they print," he told her. "But what I would like is to find out what Mr Nevin has been working on. Who are his current clients? Is there anybody who might want to hurt him?"

171

"You think he was murdered?" The woman's eyes were wide.

"We do. That's a surprise to you?"

A shrug. "You found him at Boscombe, I assumed he threw himself off the cliffs."

"Why would Mr Nevin want to kill himself?"

She raised her hands in a shrug. "Middle aged man. Midlife crisis. Stress at work. Plenty of women on the go. God, the grief his wife gives him. Not to mention his mistress."

"You know about his girlfriend?" Dennis asked, his lip twitching.

"Everybody knows about his girlfriend," she replied.

Dennis shuddered. Men like Harry Nevin treated women despicably. They had no sense of what was proper. "Do you think his wife might have wanted to hurt him because of his being unfaithful?"

Cross shook her head. "No, no. She wasn't that sort of woman. She'll be gutted. She loves him, despite the fact he's a shit to her."

Dennis clenched his jaw. "We need to know the names of the clients he's currently representing, and anybody who might wish him harm."

Aurelia Cross shook her head. "We'll be here for quite a while if you want the answer to that."

Dennis eyed her. "I've got quite a while."

There was a knock on the door. He turned to see Elsa Short outside, looking at Aurelia Cross. Cross beckoned her in and she opened the door.

"Elsa, you need to know what's happened."

Elsa Short nodded at Dennis. "Morning. What is it?"

"I'm afraid Harry Nevin is dead," he told her.

Short raised an eyebrow. "Harry?" She lowered herself into the chair next to him. "Ameena and Harry both in one week?" She looked at Aurelia Cross. "What will our clients think?"

Cross gave her a disapproving look. "I imagine that they'll be concerned for the welfare of Harry's wife, just as we are."

The younger woman scoffed. "His wife, and his girl-friend, and the rest of them probably."

"Let's not speak ill of the dead," said Cross.

Dennis looked at her. She had been speaking ill of him before her colleague had entered. He wondered what kind of relationship the two women had.

Short turned to Dennis. "What happened?"

He recounted the details of Nevin's body being found. She watched him, her expression one of shock. He couldn't tell if it was genuine. Did she know more than she was letting on?

"I need to ask both of you where you were last night," he said.

The two women nodded. "We can do that," said Cross. "Let us check our diaries."

"And I will need the details of Mr Nevin's clients and anyone who might have wanted to hurt him."

Elsa scoffed. "That'll be a long list then."

She was the second person who'd said that. Dennis wondered what Harry Nevin had done to annoy so many people. "Even so," he said, "I'll need the information."

"We'll collate it," said Aurelia Cross. "One of the PAs will send it over to your office."

"Thank you." Dennis pulled two copies of his business card from his pocket and placed them on the desk. "If you think of anything, please call me."

"Of course we will," said Cross. She stood up, indicating that the meeting was over.

Dennis looked up at her. Aurelia Cross had a way of making you feel like an interloper. "Call me," he said. "Anything at all, I want to know."

"Or your DCI," said Short.

"Or my DCI," he replied.

Elsa Short stared into his face for longer than felt comfortable. "We will," she said. She stood up and left the room, leaving Dennis to follow her.

CHAPTER FORTY

Lesley arrived back at the office having managed to get a lift in yet another squad car. Next time, she'd take her own car. Driving with Dennis meant she could be abandoned at a crime scene, or with a witness.

She walked into the outer office to find Tina the only person there.

"Hello, Ma'am," said Tina. "How was your morning?"

Lesley grimaced. "You don't have to ma'am me."

"Sorry."

She sighed. "It wasn't good. Ffion Nevin is a mess."

"Ameena Khan, and now Harry Nevin. How did Nevin die?"

"We don't know for sure yet, but it's looking like he was pushed off the cliffs. Near Boscombe Pier."

Tina frowned. "Boscombe Chine. Lovely there, I took my brother at the weekend."

"Chine?"

"It means a ravine running down to the beach. Local word."

Lesley nodded. More dialect. "You're right. A nice spot for an ice cream and an afternoon on the beach. Not a nice spot to find a body, like that poor family and their toddler."

Tina grimaced. "Poor kid."

Lesley nodded, her face tight.

Tina looked away from Lesley towards the window, both of them lost in thought. Lesley hoped the child was too young to remember what he'd seen. His parents certainly weren't.

Lesley shrugged to pull herself out of her reverie. "We need to get to work. Where's Mike?"

"He went to the evidence store from the Ameena Khan case. Wanted to talk to the Evidence Manager about comparing forensics from the two deaths."

"Good. Anything come in yet?"

Tina shook her head.

"OK. Make contact with Gail, tell me if she finds anything."

"I already left a message with her, boss."

Lesley smiled at Tina. For a uniformed constable, she was showing promise as an investigator.

She leaned back and grabbed a pen from Mike's desk. She tapped her teeth with it. "Ameena Khan and Harry Nevin. I want to know what the connections are between the two of them. Apart from them working for the same firm. Did Ameena work on the same cases as Nevin? Did they share a social life? Did they have any friends? Were they having an affair?"

"An affair, boss?" Tina said. "You think…?"

Lesley stood up. "I imagine Harry Nevin was busy enough already. But a man with one mistress might have a second. I want to find out everything that links them. Start with professional connections, then look at the social aspects."

"Including the Leonard case?"

"Yes," Lesley replied. "Find out how closely Harry Nevin was involved in it. His claim was that he was the solicitor on that and not Ameena, that's why he didn't send us the files. But is that true, or were they both on it?"

"Has the sarge talked to you about the Kelvin link?" Tina asked.

"What Kelvin link?"

"The Kelvin family. Leonard used to work for them."

Lesley shrugged. "Who are the Kelvin family?"

Tina's face darkened. "Only the dodgiest bunch in the whole of Dorset."

Lesley lowered herself into Mike's chair. "Why wasn't I told about this?"

Tina looked back at her, blinking. "I'm sorry, boss. I talked to the sarge. I just assumed…"

"It's not your fault, Tina," Lesley said.

Why wasn't Dennis telling her everything?

"Tell me more," she said to the PC. "Who is this Kelvin family?"

"Organised crime," Tina told her. "Small time compared to what you're used to in Birmingham, I imagine. They run a bunch of businesses, money laundering, a little bit of drug smuggling, that kind of thing. They go in and out of the port at Poole."

Lesley leaned across the desk. "I want to know more about them. What have they been arrested for? Any prosecutions?"

Tina shook her head. "A few prosecutions, but very few convictions. Not of the family, at least. They're clever, they hire good lawyers."

Lesley sank into the chair. She knew a man like that, or she had done in Birmingham. Trevor Hamm, organised crime boss. It had taken years to get anything to stick to him. And in the end, he was convicted of profiting from prostitution, not for the murders he should have gone down for.

"OK," she said. "Tina, I want to know all about the Kelvin family. Who are their solicitors? Was Harry Nevin working for them, and if so, did something happen between him and them? Have they sacked him recently? Or hired him? Has he failed on a case? Anything you can get, I want to know about it, and I want to know yesterday."

Tina nodded. She looked scared. "I'm really sorry, boss."

"Stop apologising, Tina. It's not your fault."

Lesley stood up and turned away from the bank of desks. She strode into her own office and slammed the door.

Bloody Dennis, she thought. Where was he?

CHAPTER FORTY-ONE

The soil behind the beach hut where Harry Nevin's body had been found was dry and sandy. It was far from ideal for preserving footprints, but Gail had found one. She didn't know if it belonged to the father of the toddler who'd found the body, or to Nevin himself.

She doubted it belonged to his killer, seeing as he'd been pushed from the top of the cliff. But she was going to take a cast of it, just in case one of Nevin's attackers had come down to check on him.

It was surprising how many murderers did stupid things like that.

Gav had already photographed it, along with the damage to the vegetation further up the cliff. He was now up at the top in an area they'd cordoned off right above this spot. He was examining the grass there, and the fence, trying to find scraps of clothing that might have caught as Nevin was pushed over the fence.

She stood, stretching her back and wishing she'd been more sensible and crouched instead of bending. Her phone rang. She pulled it from her pocket and looked up the cliff, expecting it to be Gav. It was quicker for them to talk on the phone than to walk up and down the hill.

It was Brett, who was back at the lab going through the samples they'd gathered.

"Hey, Brett," she said. "Tell me you're having a better day than me."

"That bad?" he replied.

She screwed up her face. "I'm trying to pick up a footprint that's just dust."

"Yeah," he replied. "Gav told me it's sandy back there."

She nodded. "You've got news for me?"

"I have," he said. "Good news. Well, news anyway."

"Go on."

"We got the DNA analysis back from the skin cells we found under Ameena Khan's fingernails."

Gail felt her stomach tighten. "And?"

"We've got a match."

She took a step away from the footprint. She didn't want to accidentally stumble into it in her excitement. "Go on then, put me out of my misery."

Brett chuckled. He liked doing this to her. Cheeky sod.

"It was nobody on the crime database," he said. "Nobody who's been arrested. But it was somebody whose DNA we've taken very recently."

"Brett," she said. "Stop it. Just tell me who it is."

"Sorry, Gail. It's Nevin. The DNA under Ameena Khan's fingernails belongs to Harry Nevin."

CHAPTER FORTY-TWO

Lesley sat with her chair angled towards the window, anxious to see when Dennis and Johnny returned. When she spotted Dennis's brown Astra, she left her office.

Tina looked up as she passed, catching her tense expression. "Everything alright, boss?"

"Fine." She pushed through the doors and made for the stairs.

Dennis and Johnny were approaching the building as she left it. She caught Dennis's eye and raised an eyebrow.

The two men stopped as they reached her.

"Boss?" Dennis said.

"Can we have a chat, please?" she asked, ignoring Johnny's expression of confusion.

Dennis turned to the DC. "You go on up, write up the interview notes."

Johnny nodded at Dennis, gave Lesley a wary glance then went inside.

"Everything OK?" Dennis asked. He fingered the stem of his specs.

"Come with me."

Lesley turned to survey the building. She didn't want to do this inside. She led him to the side of the building, a paved area with a bench that looked like it was used by smokers.

Dennis stood behind her, his posture stiff. He had hold of his tie.

"Oh, do stop looking like a kid who's been called to the headteacher's office," she snapped.

He let go of his tie. "Is there a problem? I'm not sure why..." He looked towards the building.

She leaned against the wall and folded her arms. "Tell me about the Kelvin family, Dennis."

A flash of recognition crossed his face. "Er..."

"I'm told they go back decades, maybe centuries. Organised crime."

Dennis nodded. "That's about right."

"And Steven Leonard worked for them."

He met her gaze. "He did."

"Why didn't you tell me this case might be linked to a significant local crime family?"

He pulled his shoulders back. "The link is tenuous, Ma'am. It might have been nothing. There was no need to..."

"You know how I work. We share information, we come together to discuss progress on a regular basis. It helps us to form connections, to push through roadblocks. You've had plenty of opportunity to tell me about this. Why didn't you?"

He looked at her, his eyes roaming her face. She waited while he decided if he was going to lie to her, or at least omit the truth again.

"All I can say is I'm sorry, Ma'am."

"Oh, don't ma'am me. You do that when you're nervous, you know."

"Sorry." His hand went to his specs.

She bit her bottom lip. "So have you uncovered anything more significant than that Leonard used to work for the Kelvins? Were they connected to his arrest?"

"We can't find any evidence of that, Ma'am. Boss. But to be frank, that's their MO. They have a string of low-level employees who do their dirty work. Then they set them adrift after they've been arrested."

"But Arthur Kelvin gave Leonard a reference. He vouched for his character."

"It projects an image, boss. Fine upstanding local businessman protecting his employees no matter what kind of trouble they get into. In a roundabout way, it makes him look less guilty."

She snorted. "From now on, you keep me abreast of any new lines of enquiry, yes?"

He nodded. "Yes. Boss."

"Good. Now come on before the others start to think we've run away together." She eyed him. "Or I've pushed you in front of a bus."

His eyes widened. She smiled. "It's a joke, Dennis. Lighten up."

He nodded. She turned away from him, exasperated.

CHAPTER FORTY-THREE

Lesley walked back upstairs, aware of Dennis dawdling behind her. She didn't like having to reprimand him, but she couldn't have her DS hiding things from her. As she walked into the office, she noticed Johnny and Mike both looking at the DS. Had he talked to them about the Kelvins?

Tina was focusing on her screen, but there was a stiffness to her body language. She glanced up at Dennis as he passed.

"My office, folks," Lesley snapped.

She strode inside and grabbed the board, yanking it out into the centre of the space. The four team members filed in after her, Dennis at the back. Johnny was looking at him, but Dennis didn't meet his eye.

"Where are we, then?" Lesley asked. She poked the board with her fingertip. "The Steven Leonard case links to the Kelvin family. Was Ameena representing them as well?"

"Not as far as we can tell," said Tina. "I've looked into her cases. I can't find any indication that Ameena was dealing with anyone other than Steven Leonard on that case."

"I made some calls too," said Mike. "Bournemouth CID. I've been through all the cases in which they came across her in the last year, and none of them look like they're linked to the Kelvins."

Lesley folded her arms. "So tell me about the Kelvin family, then. Do we need to be interested in them?"

Dennis drew in a breath. "Arthur Kelvin is the grandson of Philip Kelvin, who started the modern incarnation of the family business in the sixties."

"Which is?" Lesley asked.

"Drugs and money laundering, mainly."

"Anything more?" Lesley asked. "Prostitution, violent crime, gun smuggling?"

Dennis shook his head. "Not as far as we're aware. There's speculation that they started out as smugglers. It goes back centuries."

"Family business," Johnny added.

Lesley eyed him. "I don't care if it's a family business. I want to know who they are, and if they're connected to Ameena Khan's death. If she was representing a man who worked for them, and Nevin, Cross and Short are hiding that fact from us, I want to know why."

She thought of Elsa. Would she know what was going on? Did Lesley need to question her girlfriend?

This was getting too close to home.

"Do some more digging," she said. "You must all have contacts associated with the Kelvins. People like that, they'll have fingers in every pie we can think of."

The team all nodded and grunted. Dennis muttered.

"What is it, Dennis?" Lesley asked.

"Nothing, boss."

She gave him a hard look. Dennis was old fashioned and could be a pain. But he was diligent and had shown signs of loyalty. She didn't want to fall out with him.

"OK," she said, "I also want to know about connections between Harry Nevin and the Kelvin family. Who was their usual lawyer for criminal matters? Could they have killed Nevin?"

"Have you got a reason for thinking the Kelvins killed Nevin, boss?" Dennis asked.

"I've not got any reason for thinking anything right now. But I want to rule out any possibilities."

Her phone rang. "DCI Clarke."

"Lesley, it's Gail, I've got an update."

"Wait," Lesley said. "I'm putting you on speaker. I've got the rest of the team here."

Lesley put her phone on the desk and turned on the speakerphone.

"Can you all hear me?" Gail asked.

"Yes, we can," said Tina.

"Go on," said Lesley.

"Right," Gail replied. "We've got the DNA back from underneath Ameena's fingernails, the skin she managed to pull off her attacker."

"Whose is it?" Lesley said.

"It's Harry Nevin," Gail replied.

Johnny whistled. Lesley looked up, surveying the team.

"So," she said. "If Nevin killed Ameena, we need to know why. And if so, who killed Nevin?"

Nobody spoke.

"Where are we with CCTV? Eyewitnesses?"

"Nothing yet," said Johnny. "Uniform is still knocking on doors. It's early though, people are still out at work. We might get a bit more joy when people come home."

"Keep on top of it," she replied. "If we get somebody, one of you goes over there and interviews them. Even better, two of you, so we can cover as many people as possible."

The two DCs nodded.

"What about the forensics?" she asked.

Gail's voice came from the phone. "There's a footprint behind the beach hut. I've taken a photo of it, trying to get a cast, but not having much luck in this soil. And Gav's found fabric on the fence up at the top of the cliff. Could be unrelated. But we'll analyse it anyway, see if we can find out what it's from and where it might have been bought."

"Good," said Lesley. "Anything else?"

"Gav's looking at some tyre tracks in the soil up at the top of the fence. Next to the car park. Not sure how fresh they are but you never know."

"Excellent," Lesley replied. "Glad to see you're making progress."

"I'll keep you posted," Gail told her.

"Good." She looked up from the phone. "What about the post-mortem?"

Dennis took a step forward. His body language was still twitchy. "It's happening later today."

"Blimey," she said. "Whittaker's inhaled rocket fuel."

Dennis shrugged. "Another job got pushed back."

"Pleased to hear it," she told him. "I want you to go along, find out exactly what killed Nevin. If it was that gash on the back of his head, find out what the weapon was."

She looked at her phone. "Gail, I don't suppose there's any sign of a weapon on the clifftop?"

"Oh yeah," Gail said. "Sorry, forgot to mention it. I've got it here in my bag."

"Haha," Lesley replied.

"Sorry, Lesley." Gail laughed.

Lesley hung up.

She looked at the team. "Chop, chop then. You've got things to do."

CHAPTER FORTY-FOUR

Dennis strode out of the building. His whole body sang with irritation and outrage at his new boss. He hated the way she'd dragged him here, taking him to the side of the building as if they were schoolkids. Not stopping for one moment to find out why he might not have consulted her.

But deep down, he knew he had been in the wrong. She was senior investigating officer, and she was his boss. He should tell her all his suspicions about a case, no matter how uneasy it made him.

He yanked open the door to his car and threw himself inside. As he was about to start the ignition, his phone rang. "DS Frampton," he grunted.

"Sergeant, this is the pathology lab. Sorry to call you on such late notice."

Dennis's shoulders slumped. "What is it?"

"Dr Whittaker has been called away. The post-mortem on Harry Nevin will be tomorrow morning."

Dennis looked up at the roof of his car. The DCI was right, Henry Whittaker was slow and inefficient. "What time tomorrow?"

"First thing."

"What does first thing mean for you people?"

"There's no need for that."

Dennis clenched his fists. "Sorry," he said, pushing calm into his voice. "What time do I need to be there?"

"9:30am."

9:30am. Hardly first thing. The DCI would have been in the office for hours by then. The case would have progressed, she'd be expecting the report back. But he knew there was no point in trying to hustle Whittaker.

"Very well," he said. "See you then."

He put his hands on the steering wheel and leaned forward, stopping before his head reached the wheel. He peered up through the windscreen at the office. Nobody was expecting him back in there; it was four o'clock now and the post-mortem should have been his last task of the day.

He wasn't in the mood for going back up there. They'd all stared at him when he'd returned with the DCI. He didn't know which was worse: Tina's smugness, or Johnny's concern.

He started the ignition and drove out of the car park.

Half an hour later, he stopped in front of a set of heavy gates. He opened his window to press a buzzer.

"Who is it?" came a voice over the intercom.

"My name is Detective Sergeant Frampton," he said. "I'm from Dorset Police."

"Wait."

He sat back, surveying the gates. They were tall and wooden, stained a dark brown. He wondered what the house beyond them looked like.

The intercom crackled. "Come in."

He caught his breath and watched as the gates opened, surprised he hadn't been sent away.

The gates revealed a wide driveway with a broad house beyond it. The upper floor was in the eaves, balconies to both sides with views over the harbour behind the house. The front door was open and a woman in a black dress and a white apron was waiting. She pointed to a spot where he should leave his car. He pulled up and got out, hurrying towards her. He had a feeling that if he dawdled, he'd be told to leave.

She nodded at him. "Follow me, please."

He swallowed and followed her inside the house. They were in a wide hallway, broad stairs rising up in front of them. Double doors on both sides, a living room on the left and a study on the right.

Instead of leading him through either of those doors, the woman continued towards the back of the house. She opened a door and they came out into a modest sitting room with vast windows overlooking the sea. Dennis stared at the view. This was why these houses were so valuable. It wasn't the bricks and mortar. It was the view.

"DS Frampton."

He turned to see a man behind a desk beside him. The desk was positioned in the corner along from the door, angled so as to get the best view for whoever was sitting behind it. The person sitting there now was a man in his fifties, slim, athletic. His dark hair showed the first signs of greying around the temples.

Dennis recognised this man. He remembered his father, Sydney. Sydney Kelvin had had a scar running right from his temple all the way down his cheek to his chin. He wouldn't have blended into the millionaire's playground that was Sandbanks. But his son, Arthur, the man sitting in front of Dennis right now, fitted in here like a glove.

"I wondered how long it would be before one of you lot beat a path to my door," Kelvin said. "I wasn't expecting *you*, though."

Dennis straightened. "Who were you expecting?"

"That woman, the brummie. Your new DCI. Did you know she used to work for a man who's disappeared under the witness protection scheme?"

"No," Dennis replied. He had no desire to talk about his boss with Arthur Kelvin.

"You should know," Kelvin told him. He stood up and rounded the desk. He leaned against its front, only a couple of steps away from Dennis. Dennis held his ground, not wanting to be seen backing off.

"His name was David Randall, it'll be something else now," said Kelvin. "He was in cahoots with organised crime up in Birmingham. Rumour is your new boss took him down, and the guys he worked for. He had to disappear, gave evidence against them. Typical bloody copper, can't be relied on for anything."

Dennis raised an eyebrow.

"Maybe she's not as squeaky clean as she makes out, though," said Kelvin. "After all, takes a thief to catch a thief."

Dennis thought of his new boss. Her insistence on procedure, on building a case, gathering evidence, doing everything by the book. Maybe the lady doth protest too much, he thought.

No, she was clean. He could sniff out a bent copper a mile off.

"I only let you in because you're an old hand," Kelvin said, leaning backwards, his hands gripping the front of the desk. "You know how things work. Mackie thought you were good."

"How do you know what DCI Mackie thought of me?" Dennis asked before he could stop himself.

Kelvin laughed. "So naive, Sergeant. Anyway, I know why you're here."

"You do?"

"I do, and I'm not telling you anything."

"Telling me anything about what?" Dennis asked.

Another laugh. "Nice try, Sergeant. What have you got on me? Nothing, I bet."

Dennis met the man's gaze. "I'm not here to tell you about our investigation. I'm here to ask *you* questions."

Kelvin pushed himself away from the desk and approached Dennis. Dennis flinched.

Kelvin stood a pace in front of him, staring into his eyes. He stayed there for a few moments, smiling. Dennis felt his heart race.

Kelvin laughed and turned away. He approached the window and leaned against it, placing his fingertips on the glass.

"Beautiful, isn't it?" he said. "It cost a bloody fortune, but it's gorgeous." He turned to Dennis. "Impresses the women."

Dennis cleared his throat. He wasn't going to comment on that.

"Anyway," said Kelvin. "You can bugger off now."

"We're working a murder case," Dennis told him. "Two. I'm sure you know about them. Ameena Khan and…"

"I know what you're working on, Sergeant. Half of fucking Dorset knows what you're working on. You think I've got something to do with it, but you're barking up the wrong magnolia. You need to look closer to home."

Dennis raised an eyebrow.

Kelvin licked his lips. "Go back to that firm, Sergeant. Nevin, Cross and Short. They're a nasty bunch. Hate each other, all of them. That's why they're such good lawyers. But you'll find your killer there." He stepped away from the window and made a shooing gesture. "Run along then, Sergeant. You're done here."

"I wanted to ask you about the Steven Leonard case," Dennis said.

"Don't know what you're talking about."

"Steven Leonard worked in one of your businesses. Ameena Khan was his lawyer."

Kelvin shook his head. "You expect me to know the name of every little scrote who works in my businesses? I don't have a clue. Now, go away."

Dennis heard the door open behind him. The aproned woman was there again. She looked like something out of a film. Neat, perfectly pressed, not a hair out of place.

"Come with me, please," she said.

Dennis looked back at Kelvin.

He shouldn't be here. He didn't want to generate a complaint.

He followed the woman out of the house and walked to his car. He turned the ignition and started reversing, turning his car in the wide driveway so that he was facing the gates. As he did so, a flash of red caught his eye. He jabbed the brakes and turned to look.

Parked up by the side of the house was a red Corsa. Four years old with a scratch down the side. Not the sort of car Arthur Kelvin would keep.

But Dennis knew that car.

CHAPTER FORTY-FIVE

Lesley got into her car. It was six o'clock. Dennis would be finished at the post-mortem. Why hadn't she heard from him?

She grabbed her phone and dialled his number. No answer. She frowned and called the pathology lab.

"This is DCI Clarke here, is DS Frampton still with you?"

"Sorry, Ma'am, no."

"Has he left?"

"I'm not sure, let me check."

Lesley tapped her fingers on her knees as she waited.

"I don't think he was here, Ma'am."

"Has the post-mortem been finished on Harry Nevin?"

"That was delayed. It's happening tomorrow morning."

"Sorry?" Lesley said.

"Dr Whittaker couldn't do it, he's put it back to tomorrow morning."

Damn. "OK, thanks."

Lesley looked out of the window. Today Dennis had kept information from her. And now he'd disappeared and wasn't answering his phone. What was going on?

She dialled his number again. Still no answer. She sighed and turned the ignition. She'd deal with this tomorrow.

As she drove towards Wareham, her phone rang: Gail.

"Hi, Gail. Any news?"

"This is a bit of a weird one," Gail said.

Lesley felt her flesh chill. "What kind of weird?"

"I know this is odd, but can you meet me at Ameena Khan's crime scene?"

"Ameena Khan, not Harry Nevin?"

"Ameena Khan. I'm heading out there now, it's not far from where I live. Can you meet me up at Old Harry Rocks?"

"Have you got new evidence?" Lesley asked.

"Not quite. Just meet me, I'll explain when we get there."

Lesley hung up and continued driving. She'd already passed the turn-off for her own cottage. Studland was through Wareham, past Corfe and out towards the coast.

She parked her car in the same spot she'd used last time, grabbed her boots and waterproof from the boot of the car, and set off along the path.

When she arrived, Gail was standing near the spot from which Ameena Khan had gone over the cliff, staring out to sea. The sun was setting, illuminating Gail from behind. A soft breeze ruffled her hair. If you didn't know a woman had died here just days earlier, it would look idyllic.

Lesley called out to Gail as she approached, not wanting to startle the other woman.

Gail turned. "Thanks for coming. Follow me." She gestured with her head and started walking towards Swanage, away from Studland.

"What's going on?" Lesley asked as she struggled to keep up.

"Just come with me."

They walked along the coastal path, following the headland until they reached a point where another path came in from the right-hand side. Gail stopped walking. She turned and looked out to sea.

"What's up?" said Lesley.

"This is where Mackie died. Your predecessor."

Lesley followed Gail's gaze over the cliff. "He killed himself."

Gail shrugged. "That's what the coroner said."

"It's not what you think?"

"The angle's all wrong. Look down there." Gail pointed down the cliff.

Thick shrubs were gathered on the edge, blocking the view down to the sea. Lesley could hear the waves but she couldn't see the spot where the sea crashed onto the rocks. She leaned over, trying to get a better view, but it was impossible.

"I presume there was less vegetation when he died," Lesley said.

Gail shook her head. "It's always been like this, for as long as I can remember. I can't understand why somebody would throw themselves off here. There's a chance you could catch in those shrubs, and even if you didn't, you'd have to take a hell of a running jump to get over the edge with the angle it's at here."

Lesley looked out to sea. "So you're saying he didn't kill himself?"

Gail sighed. "He left a note. It was genuine. We got a graphologist in, it was certainly his handwriting. And we analysed the style too, the language he used. It was definitely him."

"So what are you saying?" Lesley asked.

"I don't know," Gail said. "I raised it at the time. I said I wasn't certain about the conditions on the cliff, on whether it would be an ideal place to jump." She pointed back towards where Ameena Khan had died. "If you were going to kill yourself, it would make much more sense to do it up there. The cliffs there are so dangerous that people have gone over by accident. It would be easy."

"Do you think somebody killed him?"

"I don't know," Gail said. "He was found at the bottom of the cliff. The forensics showed that he had gone over the cliff. There was damage from the shrubs and the rocks. The minerals on his clothes were consistent with the cliff face here."

"So he wasn't just dumped down there?" Lesley said. "Somebody didn't bring him in on a boat?"

Gail shook her head. "If they did, they did a damn good job of faking it."

Lesley put a hand on Gail's shoulder. "Do you want me to reopen the case?"

"No." Gail turned to her. "I don't think so."

Lesley tried to imagine how Carpenter would react if she asked him to re-examine the suicide of his previous DCI.

"It's just a feeling," said Gail. "It's not enough, I know. None of my doubts are forensic, it's not my place. This is for your guys."

"But they aren't interested?" Lesley asked.

Gail waved a hand to bat away a swarm of flies. "He was their DCI. The thought of him being murdered…"

"It seems to me the thought of him killing himself is bad enough."

Gail's shoulders sank. "It hit them hard. Especially Dennis. He doesn't like to talk about it."

Gail started walking back the way they'd come. "Ignore me," she said. "I'm talking nonsense. We've got a case to focus on."

"Still," Lesley replied. "If you think there's a genuine reason to doubt that Mackie killed himself, maybe we should do something about it."

They were nearing the clifftop where Ameena had died. Gail stopped, staring towards it. "Let's not stir it up. Forget I ever told you this, forget I brought you here."

She turned away and started walking towards Studland.

CHAPTER FORTY-SIX

Dennis drove out of Kelvin's driveway and parked across the road. He was on double yellow lines, something that made him uncomfortable. But if he parked further away, he wouldn't be able to see when the red car left.

After fifteen minutes the gates opened and the Corsa emerged. It turned away from Dennis and headed back towards Bournemouth.

Dennis followed. Once they were safely out of view of the house, he approached the car and flashed his lights repeatedly. He could see a silhouette inside the car, the driver looking in his mirror, trying to work out what was going on. The car pulled over and Dennis stopped behind it.

A man got out. He slammed his door and strode towards Dennis's car. He stopped when he recognised the car, his jaw falling. He continued towards the car, tugging at the sleeve of his jacket.

Dennis wound down his window.

"Sarge," Johnny said.

"Johnny, what are you doing here?" Dennis asked.

"What are *you* doing here?" Johnny threw back at him.

Dennis shook his head. "No, son. I need to know why you're here."

Johnny's body deflated. "I don't want to talk about it."

"It's too late for that."

"Look, Sarge. We're both on double yellows. Let's drive up to the car park past the roundabout, we can talk there."

"Don't you drive off," Dennis said.

Johnny looked into his eyes. "I won't."

Johnny walked back to his car and slid back inside. He drove towards the car park, his driving slow and careful. He parked in a spot near the beach. Dennis followed and parked a few spaces away from him.

Johnny got out of his car and made for the beach. When he reached the sand, he stopped and sat down. It was quiet here, the sun setting behind them.

"What are you doing?" Dennis said, standing next to him.

"I'm not staying in that car park," Johnny replied. "I don't want anybody overhearing this."

"Overhearing what?" Dennis asked. "What's going on?"

Johnny shook his head.

"What were you doing at Arthur Kelvin's house? I saw your car in the drive."

Johnny turned to look up at him. "I don't get it, Sarge. Why were *you* there?"

"I was following up a lead."

"I don't remember the DCI saying anything about that."

"Don't you dare," said Dennis.

Johnny looked away. "Sorry."

Dennis swallowed. He lowered himself to the ground and sat next to Johnny. His trousers would be covered in sand, Pam would complain. "Tell me," he said, thinking. Johnny had been in the briefing, not long before Dennis had left the office himself. He'd have had to speed over here.

But then, not everyone was as careful as Dennis. "Your car was in the drive," he said. "It was hidden away. Were you hiding while I was there? Did you listen in while I was talking to him?"

"No. I was… You don't need to know where I was."

Dennis balled his fists in his lap. A couple walked past, chasing after a dog. The woman was laughing, the man running to keep up with her.

Dennis's throat was dry. "Tell me, Johnny. What were you doing there?"

"I was following up a lead, like you." Johnny tried to inject confidence into his voice but it didn't wash.

"Don't lie to me," said Dennis. "What's he got on you?"

Johnny's head snapped round. "What d'you mean?"

"Johnny, I've known you since you started on the force. You're a good copper, a good man. You won't have been there unless he's got something over you."

Johnny looked away. "I don't want to talk about it."

Dennis put a hand on Johnny's shoulder. "I don't want to have to report you. You need to talk to me. Confide in me."

Johnny wiped his cheek. "It's my brother." He closed his eyes. "He bought drugs off one of Kelvin's guys. I got a call from them, said they were going to shop him."

Dennis felt his limbs soften. "Why didn't you tell me? You should have talked to me about it."

"And then what?" replied Johnny. He opened his eyes, looking out to sea. "My brother buys drugs, I tell you. What would you do to a person who buys drugs? You'd arrest them."

"Not necessarily."

Johnny's eyes narrowed. "Don't lie, Sarge. You'd have treated him just like anybody else. And the thing is, you should do."

"So why didn't you let them?" Dennis asked him.

Johnny shrugged. "My brother's, well, he's different. He's got learning difficulties. He can't go to prison."

"He wouldn't go to prison," Dennis said. "Not if he's got a mental illness."

"He's never been diagnosed. They wouldn't believe a word of it. I couldn't let that happen to him."

Dennis nodded. He knew what it was like to feel loyalty to your family. He knew how it could conflict with your responsibilities as a police officer.

"Johnny, you need to stop this," he said.

Johnny wiped his eyes. "I can't, Sarge. If I stop then David goes down."

"Is David your brother?"

Johnny nodded.

"You do know that Kelvin's linked to this case, don't you?" said Dennis.

Johnny nodded again. "That's why he wanted to see me."

Dennis raised an eyebrow. "He wanted to know about the investigation?"

Johnny lowered his head. "Sorry, Sarge."

"How much did you tell him?"

"Not much. I don't know much."

Dennis gritted his teeth. He felt loyalty to Johnny, affection. He'd known the man since he was young, he'd seen him develop as a police officer. He'd watched him join CID and blossom into a detective.

If Dennis told the DCI what he'd seen, Johnny's career would be over. He'd have no job, no pension, no future.

But at the same time, if he was helping the Kelvins…

Dennis gulped down a breath. "Come on." He stood up. "You need to get home. So do I, Pam will be waiting for me."

Johnny stood up and brushed down his trousers. "You're going to tell the DCI, aren't you?"

Dennis shook his head. "Not just yet. But I need you to stop."

Johnny looked at him. "I can't stop. My brother…"

"We'll find a way around it," said Dennis, looking into the DC's eyes. "I'll help you."

Johnny's eyes were red. "You will? Really? You'll do that for me?"

Dennis nodded. Johnny was probably the only person he would do this for. It went against all his instincts as a police officer, but it didn't go against his instincts as a friend.

He clamped a hand on Johnny's shoulder and shook it. "Come on. Let's get a drink, and then we can both go home."

CHAPTER FORTY-SEVEN

Lesley dumped her bag on the sofa and walked through to the kitchen. She opened cupboards, impatient. She didn't have the energy to cook, there had to be something quick she could heat up.

Bingo. The remains of a takeaway curry lurked in a plastic tub at the back of the fridge. She got it out, poked at it with a fork and stuck it in the microwave.

Lesley could cook. In fact, she was a good cook. When she'd been living in her spacious four bed terraced home with her husband Terry, she'd even hosted dinner parties, although she hadn't had time for that sort of thing since she'd become a DCI. But here in her cottage, she had a pokey kitchen that smelled of damp and she didn't feel the urge to cook anything from scratch.

She wandered through to the living room while she waited for the microwave to ping. She flicked on the TV, a reality TV show. She grimaced and turned it off. She grabbed her phone and called Zoe, her colleague from the West Midlands.

"DI Finch."

"Hi, Zoe. It's Lesley. How's things?"

"Nice to hear from you, Lesley. Things are good. Mo's taking the inspector's exam and Connie's applying for sergeant."

"I thought the other guy in your team was going for sergeant, the Welsh one?"

Zoe laughed. "Rhodri. We're not talking about it. He took the exam and failed."

Lesley winced. "Ouch."

"He's like a dragon with a sore head right now. But he can take it again. Sorry, Lesley, you didn't call to ask about my team. What can I do for you?"

Lesley lowered herself to the sofa. The microwave pinged in the kitchen. She ignored it.

"You were looking into DCI Mackie for me."

"I hope it was useful," Zoe replied.

"It was," Lesley said. "But there are more questions."

"OK." Zoe sounded interested.

Lesley had asked Zoe to investigate DCI Mackie, because nobody in her new team was prepared to talk about the man. She'd had a feeling right from her first day that this was one of those subjects it was best to avoid.

"One of the CSIs down here," she said. "Her name is Gail. She's…"

"CSI?" said Zoe. "You've moved to America now?"

"Ha ha," replied Lesley. "That's what they call the FSI's down here. They reckon they're in Los Angeles, but really it's more like Midsomer."

Zoe laughed. "So what about her, this Gail, is she good?"

"She is," said Lesley. "She's bloody good. She took me to the spot where Mackie died. It was a clifftop just outside Swanage."

"No idea where that is," said Zoe.

"It's a sleepy seaside town, about ten miles from where I'm living. Near a crime scene I'm investigating."

"Another murder?" Zoe said. "Wow. You've had an influence on the place. Or maybe it is Midsomer."

Lesley scratched her head. "Don't. I'm beginning to wonder... Anyway, Gail doesn't think it was suicide."

"Nor do you, do you?" said Zoe. "I mean, he booked that cruise a couple of weeks before he died."

"People do erratic things," said Lesley. "Even people who are suicidal. Maybe his wife was putting pressure on him. Maybe he wanted to appear normal."

"But you don't think it was suicide?" said Zoe.

Lesley shook her head. "No."

"Are you saying you think it was murder?" Zoe asked.

Lesley sighed. "I don't know what I'm saying, but I certainly can't talk to anyone here about it."

"You can talk to that Gail woman though," Zoe suggested. "Is she not part of your team?"

"No," Lesley replied. "They've only got a couple of CSI teams down here. Gail splits herself between different units, but we get along. She's good, she makes me feel like I'm not in a rural backwater. But she's just a CSI, she's not going to investigate a potential murder, and she could get into trouble too. So..."

"You want me to do some more sniffing around for you?" Zoe said.

"If you don't mind?"

Lesley stood up and walked into the kitchen. She opened the microwave door and pulled out the takeaway carton. It was hot, and she nearly dropped it. "Ow!"

"You alright?" said Zoe.

"Just getting my dinner. It's worthy of your culinary skills, heated up take-away."

"I'm eating a lot of that at the moment. Nicholas has gone backpacking around Europe with Zaf before they go to uni."

Lesley smiled. She knew that Zoe only ate home-cooked food when her son was at home. Otherwise, it was fish and chips from the chippy or baked beans from a tin.

"Which means I'm at a loose end when I'm not in work," continued Zoe. "What do you need me to do?"

"You're sure Frank won't mind?" Lesley said.

"This will be in my spare time," Zoe told her. "DCI Dawson doesn't need to know."

"He's made DCI permanently now?" Lesley asked.

"Nearly. As far as he's concerned, it's in the bag."

"Sounds like Frank."

"Yeah. Anyway, tell me what you need."

"OK. So there's this family down here," said Lesley. "They're called Kelvin. Bit like Trevor Hamm, but older."

"Older?" said Zoe.

"They go back a way. There's rumours they were smugglers centuries ago."

Zoe whistled. "You don't get that kind of thing in Birmingham."

"I want to find out about them. Links to the police, corruption cases."

"Mackie specifically?" Zoe suggested.

Lesley nodded. "Keep it on the down low though, will you? I don't want my Super finding out."

"Of course you don't," said Zoe. "Don't worry, you can trust me. What kind of thing am I looking for?"

"Money laundering, drugs, that kind of thing."

"So small beer compared to Trevor Hamm?"

Lesley scratched her chin. "I don't know yet. Arthur Kelvin, he seems to be the boss. He's got a luxury house in Sandbanks."

"Isn't that that ridiculously expensive place I saw on the TV?" Zoe said.

"It is," Lesley replied. "A house there must be worth a few million, and he didn't get that running scrap yards and launderettes."

"No."

Zoe was thinking of Bryn Jackson, Lesley imagined. Their former Assistant Chief Constable, who'd bought himself a palatial home in Edgbaston on the proceeds of police corruption.

"Anyway," Lesley said. "My curry is getting cold."

"Enjoy it," said Zoe. "I'll let you know if I find anything."

CHAPTER FORTY-EIGHT

DCI Mackie had been cremated at the municipal crematorium in Broadstone on the edge of Poole. It was a nice
enough place, but too impersonal for Dennis. At least the
man's widow had arranged for a plaque to be put in so
there was somewhere to remember her husband.

Dennis stood in front of the plaque, just one in a row of
them inserted into a wall that had been designed to look
older than it really was. The Dorset Police insignia had
been inscribed into it, but there was no epitaph, nothing
to show that this scrap of metal commemorated a man
with forty-five years' public service.

He pursed his lips, trying to remember Mackie's face. It
was fading fast, in danger of being replaced by the image
of his body when they'd found it at the bottom of the
cliffs. He'd been twisted and bruised, his face covered in
scars from the shrubs he'd fallen through. Both legs had
been broken, and blood from a wound on his temple had
mixed with the waves that washed over him.

When Dennis had arrived at the scene, they hadn't
known who the man was. A kayaker had spotted him from
the sea; he was invisible from the clifftop. They'd searched
the clifftop for evidence of where he'd gone over and
found damage to the shrubs but nothing more. There had
been an argument with Gail Hansford over the logistics

of someone throwing themselves off in that location, but he'd closed that down.

The DCI had left a note. Clearly written and confirmed to be in his own hand. He'd taken his own life.

Dennis wished his boss had confided in him, maybe talked about what was troubling him. But neither Dennis nor Mackie were the type of men to discuss their emotions. And Dennis was a lowly DS. He'd revered Mackie, the man's guidance and example was responsible for his own blossoming as a detective. But their relationship had been practical and businesslike.

He blew out a long breath and shivered. He checked his watch. The post-mortem at Poole Hospital was a ten-minute drive away. Parking would be impossible.

He pulled away from the plaque, wishing he'd come earlier. A walk around the crematorium grounds sometimes lifted his spirits, gave him some calm to remember the DCI. It wasn't the same as a churchyard, of course, but it served a purpose.

He turned towards the car park. An attendant was walking towards him, no doubt about to offer some words of platitude. Dennis bent his head and hurried to the car, not in the mood.

CHAPTER FORTY-NINE

Tina liked being the first in the office. When the place was empty, it felt like she owned it. The privilege of sitting alone at the bank of desks that until six weeks ago had only been occupied by detectives felt extra special when she was here in the early morning.

She settled herself in at her desk and flicked on her computer. The DCI had asked her to look into the Kelvin family. Tina could probably do that from memory. Even in Uniform, she'd had plenty of encounters with them.

The Kelvins themselves were careful to stay on the right side of the law. But there was a series of employees, low-level people from their various businesses, who'd got themselves into trouble for drug offences. The Kelvins had plenty of businesses around the county. Scrap yards, launderettes, a nightclub in Poole, even a recycling plant. In recent years it seemed money laundering was going green.

Their junior employees had a habit of selling small quantities of drugs on the streets of Poole and Bournemouth, and getting busted doing it. There'd even been a few arrests of people smuggling drugs into Poole Harbour. Those employees were always sacked and they were never long-serving people, always at the bottom of the food chain. Tina, like her colleagues, knew there were more senior people in the Kelvin businesses who were pulling the strings. But they'd never had the evidence to take anybody down. The Kelvins, it seemed, were good at passing blame downwards.

She trawled through records. The HOLMES database, court reports, arrest records. She made a note of all the cases where the arrestee's employer was listed as one of Kelvin's businesses. At least, one she was aware of. That gave her a thought.

She stopped and went to the Companies House website. She plugged in Kelvin's known address in Sandbanks as well as the known business addresses, and found six more companies. She went back to HOLMES to run those against arrest reports. More, almost half as many again.

She created a spreadsheet: employee names on the left, the business they worked in, their position, how long they'd been in post.

She went back to the records, searching for the names of the solicitors who'd represented these people. She'd found sixty-five names, all people arrested for low-level drugs offences. Surely they didn't have sixty-five different solicitors.

She worked through each one, inputting the name of the solicitor who'd represented them. There were half a dozen names, most only cropping up once or twice. Ameena Khan's name appeared only once, on the Steven Leonard case. Tina continued through the list.

When she'd finished, she sat back and looked at her spreadsheet.

She rearranged the rows by order of the solicitor's name.

One name appeared in fifty-two of the sixty-five cases. She'd represented all of those employees of Arthur Kelvin.

Tina leaned in. The name was familiar.

It was somebody that they'd interviewed, a partner in the firm. Elsa Short.

CHAPTER FIFTY

"You're here," said Dr Whittaker as Dennis entered the post-mortem room.

He shrugged. "Nice to see you, too."

Whittaker grunted.

Music was playing, Vivaldi. Whittaker turned to Dennis, guessing his thoughts. "I thought I'd lighten the mood." He looked at the body on the table. "Necessary, really."

Harry Nevin's body lay face down. "I wanted to start with this gash," Whittaker said, pointing to the back of his head. "It's deep."

The wound had been cleaned up, the hair was no longer matted with blood, and the gash was clearly visible. Dennis could make out splintered bone and brain tissue. He swallowed down bile, forcing himself not to look away.

Whittaker bent over the body and pulled back the skin around the wound. Dennis blinked as he watched. The flesh was torn in places, messed up and mangled.

"Quite a whack," said Whittaker.

Dennis nodded.

"It pierced his skull." Whittaker poked his finger through a hole in Nevin's skull.

Dennis clenched his fist.

"Must have been quite a blow," Whittaker said. "To get through the skull. Poor bastard."

Dennis flinched. "What kind of weapon would do that?"

Whittaker bent further over the body, muttering to himself. He turned as if only just noticing Dennis had spoken. "What was that again, old chap?"

"What kind of weapon do you think did it?" Dennis said.

Whittaker pulled in a breath. "Not a hammer, that's too blunt. A knife, I would expect. It's a heavy blow, and sharp. It would have to be a good quality knife to get through the skull like that."

Dennis nodded. "A kitchen knife?"

"No, no, no. Nothing like that. Look at the skin. Look at the flesh here." He pointed out the lacerations to the back of the man's head. "See, it's jagged. The knife was serrated, definitely not a kitchen knife. And it was strong, made of some kind of reinforced steel."

"How does somebody pierce the back of a skull with a knife?" Dennis asked. "Surely it's not heavy enough?"

Whittaker pulled away from the body. He bent his own head at an angle so that it was facing downwards and brought his hand up to hit the back of his skull. "The blow came from up here," he said. "But the victim must have been lying on the ground. To get enough force, you'd need to have something behind him. So they had him already down."

"Surely he would have been struggling," Dennis said.

Whittaker shook his head. "The wound is too clean and there's no sign of defensive wounds, no practice marks."

"Practice marks?" Dennis asked.

"You know," Whittaker told him. "The little jabs you see when somebody has a first attempt at hitting somebody before they build up to the main event."

Dennis nodded. He'd seen those on other victims. Most killers were nervous of plunging in the knife. Their first attempt wasn't enough, and they needed a few strikes.

Whittaker turned back to the body. "Whoever did this, they knew what they were doing, and they weren't the slightest bit afraid."

With the help of an assistant, he heaved the body over to reveal the face. A dark bruise ran down the side of the nose and there were scratches on the right cheek bone.

"You said there were no defensive wounds?" Dennis said.

"These aren't defensive wounds," Whittaker told him. "This is from him being shoved into the ground. It's road rash. We normally see it in traffic accidents."

Dennis bent over and peered in, glad that he was no longer looking into the man's skull. "So he was lying on tarmac when he was hit?"

"That's what I'd conclude," said Whittaker. "Somebody knocked him down, pushed him along, then stabbed him."

"Could a single person do that?" Dennis asked.

Whittaker wrinkled his nose. "He's heavy. I'd imagine not."

"Maybe he was drugged?"

"We've done a toxicology analysis. Nothing. Approximately five units of alcohol, a trace of cocaine, the kind of quantity you see when somebody has taken it a week ago. Nothing that would have drugged him enough to make him fall to the ground."

"So they surprised him," Dennis said. "Knocked him out, got him on the floor and stabbed him in the back of the head."

"If they knocked him out, the mark would be close to the stab site," said Whittaker. "That's why we can't distinguish it." He plunged his hands in the pockets of his lab coat and surveyed the body. "These chaps knew what they were doing. This was no crime of passion."

"Chaps?" Dennis said.

Whittaker shrugged. "I don't imagine a woman would be strong enough to do this. Do you?"

"You'd be surprised."

"You have two assailants, possibly more," said Whittaker. "One to take him down, one to deliver the blow. He weighs around ninety kilogrammes."

Dennis nodded. "Thanks."

CHAPTER FIFTY-ONE

An email notification appeared at the top of Mike's screen. He opened it, hopeful.

"Brilliant," he hissed. It was CCTV footage from the top of the cliffs at Boscombe Chine.

"Thanks, Johnny," he muttered.

Tina looked at him across the desks. "You got something?"

He nodded. "CCTV."

"Can I watch with you?"

"Sure."

She scooted her chair around the desks and brought it next to his. He clicked on the link.

The first file was from early evening, 7pm to 8pm. He put it on fast forward, only pausing when he spotted movement in the frame. A number of cars came and went, people got out of them, walked away, came back.

So far, so normal. He clicked on the next video, 8pm onwards. He went through the same routine. Again, people pulling up in their cars, a couple looking like they were having sex in the back of theirs, a few dog walkers.

He yawned.

"I'm beginning to wish I'd stayed at my desk," Tina said. "This is dull."

Mike nodded. "Let's check the next one."

The next one began at 9pm. Dusk was beginning to fall, the low sun catching the backs of the cars. Mike watched as people came and went. The amount of activity had slowed, fewer people heading out for walks. He tried to remember what the temperature had been on Tuesday night. Chilly, if he recalled correctly. There'd been rain later on.

He watched as people parked their cars, left them, returned to them, drove away. Still nothing.

"Right," he said, "Next one."

The next one started at ten. Now it was getting darker. Only five cars were in the car park. At 10:15, a dark van pulled up.

Mike sat up in his chair and Tina shifted in closer.

The van parked in a spot on the edge of the car park, its side door hidden from the camera and the other cars. Mike waited, gripping a pen he'd picked up from his desk.

After a few moments, a figure got out of the driver's door and walked to the back of the van, disappearing out of view. Another figure emerged from the passenger side and walked to the back of the van, again disappearing. The two figures reappeared from round the back of the van. Mike couldn't be sure if they were the same two people, or if two more had got out of the back of the van or maybe the side.

He waited. A car parked further along in the car park drove away, leaving a bigger gap between the van and the remaining vehicles.

At 10:20, the two figures disappeared behind the back of the van. At 10:23 they reappeared, this time accompanied. There were three people walking and another being dragged between them.

Mike felt his skin prickle. He glanced at Tina, whose cheeks were flushed.

She licked her lips. "This is it," she whispered.

He nodded, his eyes on the screen.

The three figures moved towards the cliff top, dragging the fourth between them. At this angle, it was difficult to make out individuals. All they could see was the silhouettes of the four people moving towards the cliff top. The one being dragged looked large, consistent with the size of Harry Nevin's body. Of the other three, there were two taller figures and one shorter.

"A woman?" Tina suggested.

Mike shrugged. "Or a short man."

They both leaned in as the group reached the fence. One of the taller figures looked back towards the cars on the other side of the car park. There was no movement there. Mike had already seen people leaving those cars and walking towards the path that led to the beach, meaning the cars were empty. But there were flats behind there, potential witnesses. He would talk to Johnny about that, knock on some more doors. They had a time window now.

He checked the time stamp on the CCTV: 10:31pm.

The three people hauled the fourth up and over the fence that separated the car park from the cliff. The body caught on the spikes on top of the railings.

Mike held his breath. "Fabric. Might have been left behind."

Tina shrugged. "We'll have to check with Gail."

He nodded, his breathing shallow.

Finally, they freed the body from the railings and heaved him over. Before letting go, one of the two taller figures gave him a shove, sending him arcing out into space before he hit the cliff below. The cliff here was a steep slope, not sheer like the cliffs at Old Harry Rocks.

The body disappeared out of the frame. Mike watched the three remaining people, his heart in his mouth.

They turned back towards the van. All of them were formless shapes, wearing nondescript clothing. They either had short hair or wore hats. As they approached the van, the shorter figure stopped. It leaned against the bonnet. One of the taller figures turned to the shorter figure, talking, he thought.

"What d'you think they're doing?" Tina asked, her voice low.

"Don't know," replied Mike. "Just watch."

After a moment, the shorter figure's hand went to its head. Mike had been right, they were wearing a hat. The person pulled the hat off and ran their fingers through their hair.

He looked at Tina. "Long hair," he said.

She nodded.

"It's not clear enough. We'll have to get it enhanced."

"That's a woman," she said. "And she's left-handed, most probably."

He looked at the figure again. Now he was looking for a woman, it was clear. The shape of her body, the way she moved. And her left hand was in her hair. "You're right."

"Jesus," Tina said. "What kind of woman would do a thing like that?"

CHAPTER FIFTY-TWO

Lesley rubbed the skin between her eyes. She'd slept badly, lying awake and mulling over what Gail had told her about DCI Mackie. She was worried someone might find out about Zoe's investigation and trace it back to her.

But no, she thought, she could trust Zoe. If anybody could be relied upon to keep this subtle, it was DI Finch.

She was yawning as Dennis opened the door to her office. She looked up, surprised he hadn't knocked.

"Boss," he said.

She looked past him. Mike and Tina were huddled at Mike's desk, looking at Mike's computer. Johnny sat at his desk alone, his body language tight. He was pulled in on himself, his hands plunged between his knees. Lesley wondered what was going on out there.

Dennis closed the door and put two photographs on the board. They'd divided the board in two now, the left was Ameena, the right Nevin. The photographs that Dennis added were of Nevin's injuries, the front of his head and the back. Lesley rounded her desk and approached the board for a better look.

"You've been to the post-mortem?" she said.

He nodded.

"I thought that was yesterday afternoon?"

He turned to her. "Whittaker put it off, delayed it to this morning."

"So why didn't you come back into the office?"

He swallowed. "I was already there, it was too late to come back. I figured it was best to get up early this morning and go straight there."

She checked the clock over her desk: 10:30am. "This isn't all that early."

"You know what Whittaker's like."

Lesley grunted and turned back to the pictures. She wasn't in the mood for another argument with Dennis. "So what does this show us?" she asked him. "What does Whittaker think?"

"The gash on the back of his head," Dennis said, pointing to it. "That was a single strike, no practice wounds. Whoever did it had killed before. It's clean, but it's a serrated blade. Not a kitchen knife or anything like that."

"And his face?" Lesley said.

"That's from him being shoved on the ground, road rash apparently. Whittaker reckons he was lying face down, knocked out before he was stabbed from behind in the back of the head. Either that or they had very tight hold of him."

Lesley turned her head to one side. "Why would you stab somebody in the back of the head? Why not slit their throat?"

Dennis shrugged. "No idea. But that's what Whittaker thinks happened."

"So he thinks the killer held Nevin down or knocked him out and then stabbed him?"

Dennis shook his head. "He thinks there were two assailants."

Lesley raised an eyebrow. "Two?"

Dennis nodded. "One to get him to the ground, one to stab him. You'd have to use quite some force to pierce his skull with the blade of a knife. It was a sharp knife, a strong one, reinforced steel the pathologist thinks, and whoever did it was confident."

Lesley swallowed.

There was a knock on her door. She turned to see Mike and Tina standing outside, looking expectant. She gestured for them to come in.

Mike opened the door and walked to her desk, Tina following. Johnny was still at his desk outside. Dennis beckoned to him and he followed the other two constables in, not meeting Dennis's eye.

Lesley looked between the two men, wondering what had happened between them. Dennis and Johnny were old friends. She hoped this wouldn't affect their ability to do the job.

"What have you got?" she asked Mike.

"CCTV, boss," he said. "I've emailed it to you."

She bent to her computer and turned the screen around so that they could all see.

"Go forward to 10:25pm, boss, third file," he pointed to her screen. Tina stood behind him, shifting from foot to foot.

She opened the file and fast forwarded to 10:25pm. A van was to the right of the shot, two cars over to the left.

"Is it the van we're watching?" she said.

Mike nodded. "The cars are empty, I saw their occupants leave earlier. On that van, something's about to happen."

She turned to the screen, along with the rest of the team. They all held their breath.

Onscreen, three people emerged around the side of the van, dragging a fourth.

She pointed. "That's Nevin?"

Mike nodded. "It has to be."

Lesley watched as they pulled his slumped body towards the fence separating the carpark from the cliff. It took them a while to lift him and get him over the fence. His body caught for a few moments, clothes snagging on the spikes on top of the fence.

She turned to Dennis. "Have we got any forensics from that fence?"

"I spoke to the CSIs," said Tina. "They've taken scraps of fabric from the spikes."

"Excellent," said Lesley.

She turned back to the screen. Nevin was being launched over the fence. His body flew briefly into the air before it landed with what she imagined was a thud, then disappeared out of shot.

The three people walked back towards the van. Two of them were tall, the other shorter. The shorter one leaned against the bonnet of the van. They put their hand to their head and pulled off what looked like a hat, revealing long hair.

Lesley's breath caught in her throat. The person onscreen ran their hands through their hair.

"That's a woman, boss," said Tina. "At least we reckon it is."

"Could be a short man with long hair," said Dennis.

"Look at the way she moves," said Tina. Tina bent towards the computer. She rewound for a few moments and then played the tape again. They watched as the woman walked back towards the van. Her gait was different from that of the others: softer, more fluid.

"You're right," said Lesley. "It looks like we've got two men and one woman."

"So who?" said Dennis.

Tina stepped forward. "I got the information about the Kelvin family that you asked for, boss."

"Go on."

Tina had a rolled-up piece of paper in her hand. She smoothed it out and pinned it up on the board. It was a printout of a spreadsheet, a list of names and cases.

"These are all the cases I was able to find that are linked to the Kelvin family. People who worked in the Kelvins' businesses. Some of them, Kelvin acted as a referee, others he didn't. But they were all sacked not long after their offences, and they're all drugs related."

Lesley approached the board. Tina pointed at the final column in the spreadsheet. The name of the solicitor working on each case. Lesley's gaze flicked to it and she felt her cheek twitch.

"There's sixty-five of them," said Tina. "Sixty-two of them have solicitors from Nevin, Cross and Short. Fifty-two of those have got the same woman. Elsa Short."

Lesley stared at Elsa's name, repeated down the column. She backed away from the board and leaned on the desk.

"Good work, Tina," she said. She took a breath. "I need to think about this. You all carry on with what you're doing and I'll let you know what we do next."

CHAPTER FIFTY-THREE

Ten minutes later the team were all back at their desks. Everybody seemed to be busy, but Lesley could tell by looking out of her office door that they were distracted.

Johnny's eyes kept flicking towards Dennis, who was avoiding his gaze. Tina and Mike fidgeted in their chairs.

Lesley grabbed her bag and pulled her hands through her hair. She took a deep breath and pushed the door open.

"I've had a call from Gail," she said. "I need to go to the crime scene, be back soon."

She hurried through the office, making it to the door before anybody had a chance to question her. She could only hope that Gail wouldn't call while she was out.

Half an hour later, she was in the underground car park in Bournemouth. The same place she parked when she'd come to interview Harry Nevin.

She slammed the car door shut, trying to keep a lid on her emotions. She hurried to the street where the law firm was based. She took up position in a shop doorway opposite, obscured by the shadows. She took out her phone.

It rang out three times before Elsa picked up.

"Hey, you," Elsa said. "Everything OK?"

"I need to talk to you," Lesley replied. "Come down-stairs."

"Downstairs?"

"I'm outside your office. Come outside, I need to talk to you."

"What's this about, Lesley? I'm busy."

"It's urgent, Elsa. Nobody knows I'm here, I wanted to speak to you before anything got official."

"What are you on about?"

"Please," Lesley said. "Just come down. Don't tell your colleagues where you're going, just say you're nipping out for a coffee."

"I never nip out for a coffee. I've got a PA to do that for me."

"I don't care what you say, just tell them you need a break. Fresh air, whatever, you're going to deliver some files." Lesley gritted her teeth. "Just come downstairs."

There was a sigh at the other end of the line. "Fair enough."

Lesley waited, her eyes on the building. At last the door opened and Elsa emerged.

Lesley waved, beckoning her over. Elsa looked up and down the street and then crossed, giving Lesley a funny look as she did so.

"What's with the cloak and dagger?" she said. "What's going on?"

"Come for a coffee with me," Lesley replied. "I don't want to do this here."

Elsa sighed. "I'm not going for a coffee with you, we'll walk along the beach."

"OK."

Lesley followed as Elsa led her towards the beach. It was quieter today, the sun hidden behind clouds. Lesley

229

felt incongruous walking along the promenade in her suit. People passed them, ignoring them. Busy with their holidays or time out of the office.

Even so, Lesley kept her voice low. "We've been investigating the Kelvin family," she said.

"OK," Elsa replied. "Why?"

"There was a file," Lesley said. "A case. Harry Nevin hid it from us, but Ameena was working on it. I figured that if he was hiding it, then that was for a good reason."

"He might just have been forgetful," Elsa suggested.

Lesley stopped walking and turned to Elsa. "Was Harry Nevin in the habit of being forgetful?"

Elsa shrugged. "Sometimes, recently, he could be distracted. He was acting strange, kept coming into the office late, leaving early."

"He had a mistress, didn't he?" Lesley said.

"He'd always had mistresses. This was new."

Lesley continued walking. "We looked at the Kelvin files, identified all their employees who'd been arrested in recent years."

She sensed Elsa's breath picking up. "And why do you need to talk to me about this?"

Lesley put a hand on Elsa's arm. "We found sixty-five cases where minor employees of the Kelvin businesses had been arrested for drugs related offences. In fifty-two of them you were the solicitor."

Elsa shrugged. "So? I defend a lot of drug cases."

Lesley turned to her. "Where were you on Tuesday night, Elsa?"

Elsa narrowed her eyes. She took a step back, almost hitting a man who was passing. "What are you saying?"

"Where were you on Sunday morning?"

"I think you should go," Elsa said.

"I wanted to talk to you before anybody else did," Lesley replied. "I need to tell them about our relationship. I've already told them we're friends, but if we're investigating you…"

"There's no reason to investigate me." Elsa's face was hard.

"I hope you're right. But you'll understand that we can't—"

Elsa raised her hand as if about to slap Lesley. Lesley's eyes widened.

Elsa stopped, her hand still up.

"I don't know what to think," she said. "I thought you cared about me."

"I do," Lesley told her.

"You care more about your job. You're coming over here to cover your back, to make sure your colleagues don't find out that you're sleeping with me. All you're interested in is your own career."

"That's not true. I came here to warn you. I came here to find out what I could before I have to return with my colleagues and interview you formally."

"You're going to arrest me?"

"No," Lesley replied. "Of course not. But there will be more that we need to know. Be prepared, you'll be getting a call."

Elsa grunted.

"Thanks for the warning," she said, her voice laced with sarcasm. She turned and strode away, leaving Lesley to watch her retreat.

CHAPTER FIFTY-FOUR

Tina stared at her screen, working through all the cases related to the Kelvin family. She'd dug through them every which way she knew, finding out all the information she could. This wasn't her forte; as a PC she was more used to directing traffic and dealing with disturbances. She was still waiting for training to help her fit into the in–between role occupied by a PC working in CID.

The boss had been gone for over an hour now, but nobody had said anything. The atmosphere in the office was tense. The sarge and Johnny hadn't spoken all morning, and Mike was working quietly at his desk, not wanting to get involved.

Tina leaned back, stretched her arms above her head and checked the time. Almost lunchtime.

"Anybody want a cuppa?" she said.

Mike nodded, his eyes on his screen, his shoulders hunched.

"Oh, shit," he hissed.

"What?" she asked.

He shook his head. "Look at this."

Tina stood and went to Mike's desk, glad to stretch her legs. The sarge and Johnny sat at their own desks, still looking into their computer screens, neither of them speaking.

On Mike's screen was the local news, the local reporter Sadie Dawes. She was pretty, always immaculate regardless of where she was reporting from. Even now, standing on the beach at Boscombe Chine, her hair was in place and her jacket didn't have a mark on it.

Mike pointed at the screen. "That's the crime scene."

Tina nodded. "Stands to reason they'd be reporting from a local murder scene."

"Yeah, sorry." He rubbed his eyes. "I don't know why I reacted like that."

She shrugged. "That's OK." They were all tired.

The door to the office opened, and the DCI walked in. She strode towards her own office, not making eye contact.

The sarge looked up. He rose in his chair, about to speak to her. Then he spotted her dark expression and sat back down. Tina watched Johnny, whose eyes were on the sarge, his cheek twitching.

"Mike," she whispered. "What's going on with Johnny and the sarge?"

He shook his head, his gaze still on his screen. "Watch this," he said. "Look."

"What is it?"

"Shh."

They huddled towards the screen, listening to Sadie's report.

"As we reported yesterday, a prominent local solicitor was found dead here yesterday morning. We can now reveal that his body was pushed over the top of the cliff, and not dumped behind the beach huts. We can also reveal that this case is closely linked to another recent case on the Isle of Purbeck."

The camera panned out to take in more of the beach. The police cordon had gone, the CSIs finished.

"The body found here yesterday," Sadie continued, "was that of Harry Nevin, senior partner in local law firm Nevin, Cross and Short. A body found near Old Harry Rocks on Sunday was that of Ameena Khan, a junior partner in the same firm. Police have been investigating connections between the two crimes, and the possibility of a disgruntled client or colleague killing both lawyers. But we can now tell you exclusively that sources close to the investigation have informed us that Nevin was the chief suspect in the murder of Ameena Khan."

Tina turned to Mike.

His mouth hung open. "Where'd they get that from?"

On the other side of the desks, the sarge stood up. "Turn it off. I don't want you watching it."

Mike looked up. "The killer will be watching this as well. We need to know what's going on, what's in the public eye."

The door to the DCI's office opened. She leaned out, her face red. "Everyone, get in here, now."

CHAPTER FIFTY-FIVE

The team hurried into Lesley's office. Each one of them looked uneasy.

She paced between the desk and the board, her laptop turned round on the desk behind her. She'd frozen it at the end of the news report.

She continued pacing as she spoke.

"Close the door," she snapped.

Johnny, standing at the back, did so.

She surveyed the team one by one, her body tense.

"I've just had a call from Detective Superintendent Carpenter." She pointed towards the laptop screen. "Have you seen this?"

The team all nodded, their eyes lowered.

"How did they get hold of this?" She pointed to it again, wagging her finger. "Local news have got Nevin as chief suspect." She stepped towards the team. "Who f… flippin' well told them?"

Dennis shifted from one foot to the other. "We've only known about the DNA since yesterday."

"To a journalist sniffing after a story, that's years." She slammed a fist on the desk. "Jesus Christ, local bloody news. They're normally happy with school pantos and Yorkshire Terriers raising money for charity. They don't have the skill to dig out evidence on a story like this."

Lesley screwed her fist into the desk. Her neck was sore. She raised a hand to it, wincing.

She eyed her team. "Which means somebody told them." She pursed her lips. "*Sources close to the investigation.* Did you hear that?"

Nobody spoke. Lesley waved her hand towards the laptop screen and repeated herself, louder. "Did you hear?"

More muttering.

She looked at each member of the team in turn. Dennis's eyes were on the laptop screen, his hands at his sides, his fingers shifting against his trouser legs. Tina looked straight ahead, blinking, almost at attention. Mike, next to her, was more relaxed, but his expression was grave. Johnny, hovering at the back, had bright red cheeks. He scratched his neck and licked his lips.

"Who?" She shoved the laptop to one side and hauled herself up to sit on the desk. "Who told them?"

She looked between Johnny and Dennis. The two of them hadn't spoken to each other all day. "Johnny? Dennis?" she snapped. "What is it with you two today? There's something going on."

"Nothing, boss," said Dennis.

The two men exchanged glances. Reluctant smiles followed.

Johnny cleared his throat and shifted backwards, towards to the door. If he took another step, he would be outside the room. What was with him?

"Tina," she said. "Mike? Anything you want to tell me?"

Both of them shook their heads. "No, Ma'am," said Tina, her voice reedy.

"No, boss," muttered Mike.

Lesley sucked in a breath. She gritted her teeth and slammed her feet against the front of the desk. Her fingers gripped its edge. She felt like she was full of lead. She wanted to haul them up to Carpenter with her. Let them face the music alongside her.

"Get out," she said. "All of you."

Johnny pulled the door open, relieved to be allowed out. She watched as he slunk back to his desk. Tina and Mike followed, exchanging glances as they sat down at their computers. Dennis stayed behind. He closed the door.

"I've worked with those guys for years," he told her. "They wouldn't do a thing like this."

"You've worked with Johnny and Mike for years, what about Tina?"

He shrugged. "I don't know her so well. But I think I know her well enough… she's not the sort to do that. Look at her, she's mortified."

Lesley jumped down off the desk. Dennis took a step back.

"So why won't Johnny look anyone in the eye?" she asked.

Dennis's hand went to his specs, then dropped. "He's got personal problems. I'm dealing with it, boss. You don't need to worry about it."

"Personal problems? Nothing to do with the case?"

"No," he replied, not returning her gaze. "It's just something he needs to get through. It'll be fine."

She grunted. "Tell him to sort himself out. Now go, I've got to get my arse dragged over the coals by the Super."

"Boss."

He looked down as he opened the door.

She stared at him. "And if you get even a sniff of one of them having done this, you tell me."

"Yes, boss."

CHAPTER FIFTY-SIX

Lesley straightened her suit jacket. She pulled a mirror out of her bag and checked her makeup, poking at her lipstick.

She looked neat, respectable. It wasn't enough, she knew.

She placed the mirror back in her bag and left her office, eyeing the team as she walked past. Dennis was watching Johnny, Mike and Tina were flicking glances between each other. Lesley said nothing as she passed them.

She hurried towards Carpenter's office, forcing herself to slow down as she approached.

Breathe, she told herself. *Calm down*. She had nothing to hide, nothing to be ashamed of.

She arrived at the door to his office and licked her lips. She squared her shoulders and knocked on the door.

"Come in!"

She opened the door and walked inside, her steps measured. She closed the door and stood in front of it. She didn't dare sit down.

Carpenter sat on a sofa in the corner by the window. Another man sat beside him in an easy chair. He was solidly built with grey hair, and wore a chief superintendent's badge on his shoulder.

Damn. Not the best of times for this introduction.

Carpenter looked up. "DCI Clarke," he said.

"Sir."

Lesley straightened her shoulders. She thought of the times she'd been called to a senior officer's office back when she'd been in uniform, and how much more natural that felt. There was something about wearing a uniform that automatically made you stand to attention.

"This is Chief Superintendent Price," Carpenter said.

Lesley nodded at the man. "Pleased to meet you, Sir."

He gave her a lazy smile and put out his hand. She approached, bending over to shake it.

"You're in trouble?" he said, a glint in his eye.

"Sir," she replied. She'd never met this man and didn't know how to respond.

He stood up, gave her a long look, and left the room. As he opened the door, he turned to Carpenter. "See you on Saturday afternoon, yes? Nine holes."

"Surely eighteen," Carpenter said.

"Nineteen would be better," said Price.

The two men laughed. Carpenter's laugh sounded thin.

Price closed the door and Carpenter rose from the sofa.

He looked at Lesley. "So," he said. "Who is this source close to the investigation?"

She swallowed. "I don't know, sir. But it isn't one of my team."

"How can you know that?"

"I've just spoken to them all. I can vouch for their integrity."

"You've only been working with them for a month, Detective Chief Inspector." He paced around her, his eyes on her face.

She stood still, staring ahead. She wasn't going to let him rattle her.

"What about the CSIs?" he suggested.

Lesley blinked. "I haven't had the opportunity to speak to them, sir. I wouldn't know."

"Hmm," he said. "They're not held to the same standards as police officers. There's a chance one of them might have got chatting to a member of the public while they were at the crime scene."

"I really don't think Gail's team would behave like that."

He stopped pacing. "I'll make some calls. We can't have techs blowing their mouths off."

She looked at him. "It's alright, sir. I'll speak to the crime scene manager."

He shook his head. "Leave it with me, DCI Clarke."

She nodded. "Is that all, Sir?"

"There's another possibility," he said. "It could be a witness. Is it in anybody's interest to speak to the press? Somebody from the law firm, perhaps?"

She shook her head. "We haven't informed any of the witnesses that we have a suspect for Ameena Khan's murder." But she didn't know exactly what Dennis had discussed with the partners when he'd interviewed them.

"You check that," Carpenter said. "Make sure they didn't know. Follow it up with the journalist."

"With respect, Sir," she replied. "There's not much I can do about the actions of the public."

His expression hardened. "In that case, you tell your team to take more care in what they tell witnesses in future."

"Sir." Her back straightened.

"You're dismissed," he said.

CHAPTER FIFTY-SEVEN

Johnny picked up his phone as the DCI left the office. You didn't work for fourteen years in CID without making contacts in the press.

Normally, he would discuss the call he was about to make with the sarge. But after last night...

Dennis would protect him, but Johnny was embarrassed. He was mortified. He wanted to scuttle under a rock and avoid it all. But he had to stay here, out in the open, ready to face up to what he'd done.

The phone rang out four times. Johnny was about to hang up when it was answered.

"Matt Crippins."

"Matt," he said. "Johnny Chiles here, Dorset Police."

A laugh. "I wondered how long it would be before I got a call from you."

"How are you, Matt?"

"Let's not waste time on the pleasantries. You're calling me about Sadie's piece at lunchtime, aren't you?"

"I am."

Matt Crippins was the editor of local BBC news. He would know who Sadie's source was.

"I imagine you know what I'm going to ask you," Johnny said.

Another laugh. "You're so predictable."

Johnny smiled. "Who's your source, Matt? Who told you about the suspect?"

A pause. "You know, we journalists like to protect our sources."

"This is a murder inquiry. If somebody has been leaking information, we need to know why. Somebody killed Harry Nevin, possibly the same person who's been talking to you."

Matt scoffed. "I very much doubt it."

Johnny leaned over his desk, cupping his hands around his phone. He had been talking in a low voice and he was confident nobody could hear. But once this call was over, he hoped he'd have something to reveal to the rest of the team.

"Come on, Matt," he said. "Just between you and me."

Matt would be weighing up his options, considering. There was always the possibility that Matt might be interviewed under caution. If so, he might be forced to reveal more information than if he did this informally.

The MCIT didn't like cautioning journalists, they understood the need for a healthy relationship. Matt sometimes had information that helped Johnny identify suspects, and Johnny relied on the local press for witness appeals. So Johnny didn't want to bring in the big guns, but he knew he could.

"Matt," he said, "Are you going to tell me or will I have to speak to my bosses?"

Matt sucked in a breath. "Blimey, mate."

"This is a double murder inquiry," Johnny replied. "My job's on the line."

He waited.

"OK," Matt said, finally. "If it helps you find your killer, I'm prepared to reveal my source for this one. But this is a favour between you and me, yeah? You owe me."

Johnny nodded. He glanced at Dennis, who was peering at him.

He leaned back in his chair. "Go on, then," he said to Matt. "Who was it?"

"It was one of the lawyers," Matt replied. "From Nevin, Cross and Short. One of the partners."

Johnny felt his pulse pick up.

"Aurelia Cross?" he asked. He hadn't liked the woman when they'd interviewed her. She seemed the sort who'd want to derail a police investigation.

"No," Matt replied. "It was Elsa Short."

CHAPTER FIFTY-EIGHT

Lesley walked back slowly, her senses on fire. She hated Carpenter talking to her like that.

As she was about to turn the final corner towards the office, her phone rang.

"DCI Clarke."

"Lesley, it's Elsa."

Lesley stopped walking. "It's not a good time."

"I need to talk to you about something."

Lesley clenched her fists. "I'm in the middle of a murder inquiry."

Lesley thought of the mood Elsa had been in when they'd met earlier. She didn't want to do this over the phone.

"Have you seen the local news?" Elsa asked.

"Of course I've seen the bloody local news. That's what I'm in the middle of." She felt the skin tingle on her back. "Why are you calling me about it?"

"It was me," Elsa said.

Lesley's jaw fell open. "Wait."

She hurried to the stairs and clattered down to the ground floor. She left the building through the front entrance and walked around to the side, the spot in which she'd spoken to Dennis yesterday.

When she was out of sight of the car park she pressed her phone to her ear. "*What* was you?" she asked Elsa.

"The leak, Lesley. I told them."

"Why?"

"I can't talk about this on the phone."

Lesley ran her hands down the brickwork behind her. She dug her nail in, feeling the pressure through her fingertips.

"Tell me, Elsa. Why?"

Elsa said nothing.

Lesley leaned her head back and banged it against the brick. "Elsa, words of one syllable. Please, I deserve an explanation."

"I want to leave the firm."

"So?" Lesley replied. "Hand in your resignation."

"It's not as simple as that."

"Why not?"

Lesley thought about the atmosphere she'd observed at Nevin, Cross and Short. Busy people getting on with their day. There'd been no tension. Harry Nevin had been a bit of a shit. But apart from that...

"What's wrong with the place, Elsa?"

"It's not the firm."

"What, then?"

"It's a client," Elsa said. "They're not the kind of people you walk away from."

"Which client?"

Lesley looked around, checking the car park. Two uniformed constables were walking towards a squad car. She shrunk in further behind the wall.

"Which client, Elsa?"

"Not on the phone."

Lesley sighed. "Are you talking about Arthur Kelvin?"

Silence.

"Elsa?"

246

"Like I say, not on the phone."

"So what the hell does leaking to the local news have to do with it? How does that get you out of the firm?"

Another silence.

"Think, Lesley," Elsa said eventually, "You're the detective, work it out."

Lesley circled on the spot, her muscles tense.

"I get it," she said. "You want the firm to go tits-up so you can't stay."

"I'm not answering that," Elsa replied. "But…"

"You've really ballsed up my investigation. We didn't even tell Mrs Nevin we suspected her husband. Hell, we didn't even tell *him*."

"I know," Elsa replied.

"How d'you know?"

"He and I were partners, Lesley. We talked to each other. He knew you were after him."

Lesley narrowed her eyes. They'd gone looking for Harry Nevin as soon as they had enough evidence to seriously suspect him of murdering Ameena Khan. But he hadn't been anywhere they'd expected. Not at the firm, not at his house, not at his mistress's.

"So what happened to him?" she asked. "Was he at your flat?"

"No," Elsa replied. "He wasn't. I promise you."

"So what happened to him? Where was he?"

"His wife called me. I put two and two together. But I don't know where he went, who killed him. I can hazard a guess though."

"You think it was Kelvin." Lesley thought of the CCTV pictures they'd watched, the two men and the woman dragging Harry Nevin's body out of the van.

"I'm not saying anything," Elsa said.

247

Lesley felt her stomach clench.

"Elsa." Her voice was quiet. "I've got one question for you."

"What question is that?" Elsa's voice too was low.

"Did you have anything to do with Harry Nevin's death?"

Silence.

"Elsa. I know you're there."

"You know I didn't."

"I know you weren't there. At least I'm pretty sure you weren't—"

"Lesley. Don't."

"But Elsa. Did you want him dead?"

"I can't believe you'd think that of me."

The line went dead.

CHAPTER FIFTY-NINE

Tina peered over the top of her computer, watching Johnny muttering with the sarge.

She hated the way they did this. She knew Johnny and the sarge went back years – the way they talked, she imagined they'd known each other since Johnny was a kid. But even so… When Mike was around they'd include him. Her, never.

She needed air.

She stood up and shook herself out. "Just going to the loo."

Johnny grunted.

Tina straightened the sleeves of her shirt and walked towards the door. As she reached it, she stopped. Through the glazed panel, she could see the DCI standing in the corridor. She was on her phone, facing away from Tina.

Tina stood, her hand on the door, watching the boss. After a few moments, the DCI started walking towards the stairway. She was in a hurry. She almost ran down the stairs, then disappeared from view.

Tina pushed the door open just a crack.

Was there a problem? Could she help, or should she leave well alone?

But she didn't want the boss to know she'd been watching her.

She let the door close again. She'd wait to go to the loo, to get that breath of air. She didn't want to stumble into the boss.

She returned to her desk. Johnny raised an eyebrow: *that was quick.* Tina ignored him and flicked on her computer.

What had she been doing? Looking into cases, that was it. The ones associated with Kelvin and his firm, the ones Elsa Short had worked on. Tina was convinced they needed to be looking at Elsa. If she wasn't responsible for killing Nevin or Ameena, then she might know who was. Arthur Kelvin was bad news, his connection to this case made Tina uneasy.

She flicked through the notes she'd made about Elsa. The lawyer had a brother, Tom. He was landlord at the Duke of Wellington pub in Wareham. Should she call him?

He might have background information.

This was the kind of thing she should discuss with the boss, or the sarge. But the DCI had said she liked it when Tina showed initiative. She didn't want the men thinking she couldn't do this.

She dialled the number on the file, her heart in her mouth.

"Duke of Wellington, can I help you?"

"Hello." Tina turned away from her desk so Johnny and the sarge wouldn't hear her. "My name's PC Abbott. I'm calling from Dorset Police. Can I speak to Tom Short?"

"Speaking," replied the man. "Is this about that licensing problem I was dealing with last month?"

"No. It's something else."

"Go on then." He sounded worried.

"Are you the brother of Elsa Short, a partner at Nevin, Cross and Short?"

"Yes." He sounded puzzled.

"Good," she said. "Ms Short is a witness in an investigation we're running. I just wanted to find out some background about her. How long has she worked at Nevin, Cross and Short?"

"Why don't you ask her that?" the man replied.

"Please, Sir. It's a simple question."

She was making a mess of this. Maybe she should talk to Mike. He'd know how to do this. He'd know if *she* should be doing this.

"Hang on a minute," the man said. "Are you working on the Harry Nevin murder?"

"Yes." Tina tensed. "I am."

"Well, in that case you probably work for DCI Clarke, don't you? Lesley Clarke."

Tina frowned. "Er, yes, I do. She's the senior investigating officer."

"You work for Lesley?"

"Yes, Sir."

"Then what the hell are you doing calling me?"

"I'm sorry, Sir. I'm not sure what you mean."

Tina was wishing she'd never made this call.

"Lesley Clarke is Elsa's girlfriend," he said. "If you want to find out how long Elsa's been working for Nevin, Cross and Short, I suggest you ask her."

CHAPTER SIXTY

Lesley hurried back up the stairs and into the office, her heart pumping hard. She'd dealt with that badly.

Of course Elsa hadn't killed Harry Nevin. Lesley's instincts were better than that. She wouldn't have got close to the woman if she was a killer.

She flicked her gaze around the office to see Tina staring at her. Tina's gaze shot back to her computer screen.

Lesley frowned.

Dennis and Johnny were huddled between their desks, conferring on something. Lesley would speak to them shortly, find out what progress they were making. But first she needed time alone.

She walked through to her office and closed the door. She sat down at her desk, resisting the urge to put her head in her hands. They could see her through the glass surrounding the office.

She turned towards the window, her eyes unfocused. She was disturbed by a knock on the door. She turned, to see Tina hovering outside. Lesley beckoned her in.

Tina shuffled inside and closed the door. Her face was red.

"What is it, PC Abbott?" Lesley snapped.

Tina's blush deepened. "I'm sorry, I shouldn't have…"

"What is it?"

Tina's eyes widened.

Lesley sank into her chair. "Sorry, Tina. I'm frustrated. We're not making the progress we should be and I shouldn't take it out on you. Hang on."

She opened the top drawer of her desk and grabbed a bag of crisps. She pulled it open and went to take one out. Before she did so, she remembered her manners and held the packet out. "D'you want one?"

Tina shook her head. "No thanks."

Lesley shrugged. "You're missing out. Keeps me going, junk food." She grabbed a handful of crisps and shoved them into her mouth.

There was another knock: Dennis. Lesley rolled her eyes and beckoned him in, too.

He closed the door just as she was stuffing the second handful of crisps into her mouth.

"Is PC Abbott bothering you, boss?" he asked.

Lesley looked from him to Tina. "I don't know, she hasn't said what she's here for yet."

Tina's face deepened another shade.

"Whatever it is, though," Lesley said, wiping crisp crumbs off her skirt, "it's clearly very embarrassing."

Dennis turned to Tina. "I'm your DS, Constable. You don't come knocking on the DCI's door without speaking to me."

Lesley put up a hand to stop him. "Hang on a minute, Dennis. Tina, is this something delicate? You came in here to talk to me because I'm another woman?"

Tina frowned. "No, boss."

Lesley raised an eyebrow.

Tina shuffled towards Lesley's desk. She stood behind one of the chairs. "Well, yes, boss. Sort of." She glanced at Dennis.

Dennis shook his head. "Is it about the case, Tina?"

"Yes, Sarge."

"Right then," he replied. "Tell us what it is. You've already wasted five minutes of the DCI's time."

Tina looked at Lesley. "I just spoke to Tom Short."

Lesley stared back at her. "Tom Short?"

A nod. "Elsa Short's brother."

"I know who Tom Short is. What the… what the blazes were you doing calling him?"

Tina put her hand on the back of the chair.

"Oh, for God's sake," said Lesley. "Sit down, Tina. You look like you're going to pass out."

"Sorry."

"Come on, Tina," Dennis said. "Let's get out of here. Sorry she's bothering you, boss."

But Lesley knew what this would be about.

"No, Dennis," she said. "Tina, just tell us. It's OK. You don't have to be embarrassed."

"Why would she be embarrassed?" Dennis asked. "Have you overstepped the mark, Constable?"

Tina looked at him. She swallowed. "Tom Short told me that Elsa has a girlfriend."

Lesley leaned her head back, looking up at the ceiling. She'd known this would come out eventually, but had hoped it would be once the case was over.

"Go on," she said.

Tina turned from Dennis to her. "You're sure?"

"Just tell him."

Tina looked at Dennis. "Elsa Short's girlfriend is the DCI."

Dennis spluttered. "Don't be ridiculous, Tina. Lesley is a married… You are a married woman, aren't you, boss?"

Lesley took a breath. Officially, she was still married, but that wouldn't last long.

"She's right, Dennis," she said. "Elsa Short is my girl-friend, she has been for a month."

Tina smiled. "That's nice for you, boss." She blushed again. "Sorry."

"It is, Tina," Lesley said. "It's very nice, but I can see how it would concern you."

Dennis took a step towards the desk. "Wait a minute. Elsa Short is a potential suspect. With her working for Arthur Kelvin and her relationship with Harry Nevin…"

"What *relationship* with Harry Nevin?" Lesley said.

"Professional relationship."

Lesley shrugged. "That's all there is to it. And besides, she isn't a suspect."

Tina cleared her throat. "Er, I found some information about her. She's Kelvin's lawyer."

Lesley shook her head. "It doesn't matter," she said. "She's got an alibi for Harry Nevin's death."

"What alibi?" Dennis asked. "Nobody told us about this."

Lesley fixed her gaze on him. "No," she told him. "That's because she was with me."

CHAPTER SIXTY-ONE

Elsa was pissed off. She was irritated with Lesley for asking her that question. She was annoyed with Harry Nevin for getting himself killed. And she was furious with herself for letting it get to her.

She was the last one in the office, Aurelia Cross having left half an hour ago. She huddled over her desk, hoping to lose herself in her work. Sometimes it was effective, helping her mind to go elsewhere and focus on the minutiae of the day-to-day. But tonight, work and personal life were too closely intertwined.

Her computer pinged and she looked up. She had an email from an address she didn't know, admin@aacar-repairs.com.

She clicked it open. AA Car Repairs was one of Arthur Kelvin's businesses. One of many. Elsa struggled to keep track of them.

The email was short. *I need to meet you ASAP. You know what it's about.* There was no signature, no sign off.

Elsa rubbed her eyes. Ameena's death and now Harry's had got to her. Her colleagues had coped with Ameena dying. Ameena had kept to herself, only made a few friends, not left much of an impression on the firm. But Harry... Harry was the founding partner. Without him, nobody here knew what would happen next. They were all muddling along, pretending there was a plan. There was no plan.

Elsa hoped the firm would disintegrate, and she would be released. But meanwhile, she had this email to deal with.

She typed out a response. *Where?*

A reply came back, with an address in Sandbanks. Elsa frowned. It wasn't like Kelvin to use his home address.

Give me ten minutes.

She stood up and took her jacket off the back of her chair. Her computer pinged again.

Don't tell your colleagues, especially not Aurelia Cross.

Elsa tightened her jacket. Of course she wouldn't tell her colleagues. They knew she was working for him. Harry had given her that role when she'd joined the firm, it was the reason she'd made named partner.

If she'd known, she might never have taken the job.

But despite them all knowing who she represented, she also knew she was expected not to talk about their biggest client, to act like he didn't exist. Despite the amount of money he brought in for the firm.

She turned her computer off and made for the door. She wanted to go home and have a long hot bath. But Elsa knew that when Arthur Kelvin said *jump*, the correct answer, if you knew what was good for you, was *how high?*

CHAPTER SIXTY-TWO

Lesley sat at her desk, poring over paperwork. The team had spent the rest of the afternoon working through everything they had on Harry Nevin. Lesley had checked with Gail, but there were no more forensics yet. They were still trying to identify the weapon from Nevin's wounds.

Dennis and Johnny had gone just before six, the two of them leaving together. Lesley suspected they were going to the pub, to gossip about her.

Let them, she thought.

Tina had left swiftly afterwards, casting an uneasy glance in Lesley's direction. Lesley had given her a wave which Tina hadn't returned.

Mike, by contrast, was still here.

Lesley looked up to see him approach her door. He knocked and she beckoned him in with a nod of her head.

He cleared his throat, his hand on the doorknob. "I'm off now. See you in the morning."

She looked at her watch: seven o'clock. "You got nowhere better to be, Mike? No overtime in CID."

"I'd rather be here than in my stuffy studio flat."

She leaned back in her chair and gave him a knowing look. "I know that feeling. Microwave dinner for one, evening in front of the telly."

He shrugged. "My place is smaller than your office. It's only got a single high window. It gets hot in the summer and cold in the winter."

"But you're on a constable's salary," she said. "You can afford better than that."

"Not around here," he replied. "The grockles push the prices up."

"Grockles," she repeated. The local word for holiday-makers. She was beginning to understand why the locals resented them so much.

"So there's no girlfriend in the picture?" she asked him. "No family?"

He shook his head. "Just me, boss. I had a cat until a couple of years ago, but…" His voice trailed off.

"Sorry to hear that," she said. "See you in the morning."

"Yes, boss." He pulled the door to leave, and then stopped. "I just wanted to say…"

She raised an eyebrow, urging him to continue.

"I just wanted to say, good for you," he said.

"Sorry?" she replied.

"I mean…" He looked down at his feet. "Being gay and all."

She laughed. "I'm not sure I'd label myself as gay, Mike. I'm still married to a bloke called Terry."

He laughed nervously.

"It's OK," she said, trying to feel more comfortable than he clearly did. "I appreciate the sentiment. Not sure about Dennis, though."

Mike looked at her. "He'll come round. The sarge isn't the dinosaur you think he is."

"I'm dating a person of interest in a murder case," she reminded him. "That's a lot to come round to."

"But she's got an alibi."

"An alibi provided by me."

She'd told them that she'd been with Elsa the night before Harry Nevin had died. After they'd left Nevin's girlfriend's house, she'd gone to Elsa's flat in Bournemouth and spent the night there. She'd come straight to the office in the morning and Elsa had gone to her own office.

Based on the time stamp on the CCTV, Elsa couldn't be the killer. That woman on the clifftop wasn't her.

"I know how awkward it is," she said to Mike. "Senior investigating officer providing an alibi for a potential suspect."

He shrugged. "It is what it is."

"That's one way of putting it." She wasn't looking forward to explaining herself to Carpenter if it came to it. She smiled. "See you in the morning, Mike."

"Yes, boss." He closed the door.

Lesley hauled herself up and paced around her desk a couple of times. She was tired and restless. She wanted to move and she wanted to sleep both at the same time. But mostly, she wanted to talk to Elsa. She wanted to tell her what had happened today. She wanted to apologise.

She picked up her phone. It rang out three times.

Lesley drummed her fingers on the desk. "Pick up, please." She hoped Elsa wasn't avoiding her calls.

It clicked over to voicemail.

"Hi Els, it's me. I just wanted to say sorry. Call me back, please?"

She put the phone down on the desk and surveyed the office. That conversation with Mike about going home to a microwave dinner and a night in front of the telly hadn't been far off. Tonight, she wasn't in the mood for her pokey cottage.

She'd been in a meeting room on the second floor a couple of days ago, a sofa against one of the walls. Could she get away with sleeping on it? Spending the night here at the office?

She shook her head. "Don't be ridiculous."

She grabbed her suit jacket and pulled it over her shoulders. Time to go home.

CHAPTER SIXTY-THREE

Elsa approached the building at the address she'd been given. She could see the beach beyond, around the side of the house. A couple walked past her, leaning into each other. It was beginning to get dark and the beach would be quiet, holidaymakers gone for the evening. She could hear the waves beyond the house.

She approached the front door and pressed the buzzer. After a few moments, a voice came over the intercom.

"Can I help you?"

She leaned in, lowering her voice. "It's Elsa Short."

"One moment."

She put her hand on the wall by the door, waiting. After a few moments, it opened and a woman stood in the doorway. She was short, with blonde-grey hair, wearing a suit. She looked businesslike and professional. Elsa didn't recognise her.

"Ms Short?" she asked.

Elsa nodded.

The woman stood back. "Come on in, we won't keep you long."

"Who are you?" Elsa asked.

"Just the help."

Elsa looked the woman up and down. She didn't look like *the help*; that suit was expensive. Still, a person with the money to own a property like this would hire expensive help.

The woman gestured for Elsa to go ahead, up a flight of stairs. At the top was a long hallway with views over the beach beyond. The woman passed her and opened a set of double doors into a vast living room. Elsa followed her inside and, drawn to the view, approached the windows at the back.

As she'd expected, the beach was quiet. An elderly couple walked their dog along the shore front and a solitary man strolled past them. The three people slowed to greet each other and then continued walking. Other than that, the beach was empty.

Elsa turned back to the woman. "How long will…" she began.

The room was empty.

Elsa shrugged and lowered herself into a plush sofa. It was vast, upholstered with cream velvet. She stared out at the view. Her own flat was three streets back from the beach front in Bournemouth. If she hung her head out of the bathroom window and squinted, she could just about catch a glimpse of sea. But here, it was the main event.

She walked back to the window, resisting the urge to place her fingertips on it. The glass was pristine, shiny. The couple walking their dog was still there, the dog playing in the shallows. Elsa watched them, wondering if they could see inside, or if the window had some kind of two-way glass.

After a few moments, she returned to the sofa. She checked her watch: she'd been here twenty minutes. That was longer than it had taken her to get here. She crossed the room to the double doors. They were locked.

Elsa knocked. "Hello?"

No response.

She knocked again, harder this time. "I've been waiting twenty minutes. What's happening?"

She knew better than to lose her temper. Kelvin liked to keep people waiting. This wasn't his home address, but he owned plenty of residential properties. He'd never invited her to one, though. They'd met in neutral spaces: nightclubs, bars, restaurants. Business properties, not personal ones.

She took a step back, surveying the doors. She looked around the room. There was a door at the far end. Beyond it was an empty bedroom, a vast bed dominating the space. She closed the door and returned to the main doors.

She hammered again. "Hello?"

She went back to the sofa and plonked herself down on it.

She shouldn't have responded to that email. She could have pretended she'd left the office already, that she hadn't received it.

Now here she was, shut in for God knew how long.

She pulled her phone out of her pocket.

But who would she call? Certainly not Lesley. Not Harry, not anymore.

Aurelia, maybe? No. The message said not to tell Aurelia where she was going.

She sighed. What did she expect, responding to an invitation like this? She would just have to wait and see what happened.

She leaned back in the sofa, kicking off her shoes and curling her feet underneath her. If she was in for a long wait, she might as well make herself comfortable.

CHAPTER SIXTY-FOUR

Lesley pushed aside the mouldy carrot and sour milk in her fridge. Somewhere at the back of it was the remains of a Chinese takeaway from four nights ago. Sweet and sour pork, rice and prawn crackers.

She pulled it out and placed the cartons on the worktop. The crackers were soggy; she probably shouldn't have put them in the fridge. She opened the door of the microwave and pushed the other cartons inside.

She wandered out of the kitchen while she waited, rolling her head to stretch her neck. She approached the sofa, about to sit down, when her phone pinged. She hoped it was Sharon, they hadn't spoken in a few days and she wanted to check how her daughter's English exam had gone.

It wasn't Sharon, but a voicemail notification from an hour earlier, while she'd been driving.

It was Elsa, her voice clipped.

"I got your message. What you said, it cut deep. I can't believe you'd think me capable of murder, Lesley."

Lesley's shoulders drooped.

She should never have said what she had. Even if she did suspect Elsa of being involved in these crimes, confronting her with it like that was a bad move.

The message continued.

"Don't call me. I need some time on my own."

The message ended.

The microwave pinged and Lesley ignored it.

She slumped onto the sofa. Her limbs felt heavy. She needed sleep but still hadn't got used to the lumpy bed here.

She sighed and stood up.

There was an ugly mahogany chest in the corner of the living room, with a few things inside it that had belonged to the previous tenant. She opened the doors and rooted around inside it.

Perfect. She'd remembered correctly.

She pulled out the more-than-half-empty bottle of whisky from the back. She opened it and shuffled into the kitchen to grab a glass.

She poured herself a generous measure: she needed this.

CHAPTER SIXTY-FIVE

An hour and a half had passed, and no one had arrived.

Elsa sat on the sofa, staring out at the gloom beyond the windows. What the hell was going on?

She went to the doors for what felt like the hundredth time and tugged at them. Again, for the hundredth time, they didn't give.

Back at the patio doors, she tried to slide them open. They too were locked.

Did this flat belong to Kelvin? She'd expected him to have a large house, the man had plenty of money. But in Sandbanks, even a flat cost a small fortune.

The room bore no sign of ownership. Family photos, heirlooms, trinkets: nothing. This place was cold, like it belonged to no one. Maybe it was a holiday home.

She returned to the bedroom she'd investigated earlier and pushed on the window. Locked. In the ensuite bathroom she found a generous shower tiled in marble and a high window above the toilet. That too was locked.

She left the bedroom, her heart rate picking up. There was another door, another bedroom, another vast bed, another ensuite with marble tiles. In both bathrooms, expensive hand wash and body lotion sat on the sink, barely used. The more she thought about it, the more convinced she became that this wasn't anyone's home.

Idiot. Why hadn't she ignored the email? Why hadn't she told someone where she was going?

Elsa hurried back into the living room and took her phone from the pocket of her jacket, which she'd folded neatly on the sofa. Speaking to Aurelia Cross didn't appeal, the woman had been frosty in recent days.

Reluctantly, she dialled Lesley. After three rings, it flicked onto voicemail. She hung up.

After the previous message she'd left, she didn't want to leave a second one. She sank onto the sofa, scratching her forehead. Her eczema was flaring up. She stood again, agitated, unable to sit still now despite having sat in that sofa for over an hour. Through the window, she could only just make out the shadows of waves out to sea, no detail on the beach itself. There could be a crowd of people out there watching her and she would never know.

She went back into the first ensuite bathroom and used the toilet. She returned to the bedroom. Outside was quiet. A few cars parked behind her own, no one walking along the harbour.

In the living room, a tray sat on the glass-topped coffee table in front of the cream sofa.

That hadn't been there before.

Elsa ran towards the doors. She pulled at the handle, but it was still locked. The tray held a pot of tea, a single cup and saucer and a milk jug, and a plate of sandwiches.

Sandwiches? Who locked a person in their flat and provided sandwiches? Whoever it was, they must have known she'd gone to the toilet.

Cameras.

Elsa looked up, scanning the walls. No sign of them. She shuddered and huddled back on the sofa.

The teapot was warm. It, along with the cup and saucer, was made of delicate china. Expensive. She poured a cup of tea, thirst catching up with her. Hunger, too. It had been twenty-four hours since she'd eaten.

She looked back at the doors, half-expecting somebody to appear, to watch her eat. There was no one. She looked back at the sandwiches, stared at them for a moment, then ate it greedily.

CHAPTER SIXTY-SIX

Lesley was woken by her phone vibrating on the coffee table. It buzzed at her, slid across the surface and fell onto the rug with a thud.

She eased herself up from her slumped position on the sofa. Had she fallen asleep here last night? She was too old for this. She put her fingers to her forehead and winced. Her head felt heavy and thick, and her stomach was auditioning for the next season of Strictly Come Dancing.

Lesley pulled herself up, head drumming. At least the phone had stopped shrieking at her.

She squinted at the empty whisky bottle on the table. How much had been in there? More than she'd thought. Or maybe it was the fact she hadn't eaten, or that she was just too old for whisky. She'd guzzled plenty of the stuff as a student, almost thirty years ago. She'd been able to hold ten measures of it and make morning lectures. But now...

What time was it? She squinted at the clock on the mantelpiece. Half past seven. Time for a quick shower. But no, she'd arranged to meet Dennis. Where?

Her phone rang and she glared at it.

"Shut up."

It screeched in her head. She leaned over and pulled it up from the floor. It would be Dennis, wondering where she was.

"DCI Clarke." Her voice was scratchy.

"Lesley, sorry to bother you so early. It's Zoe."

Lesley closed her eyes and prodded her forehead. "Zoe?"

She pulled the phone away from her ear and looked at it. She'd been hoping for a call from Elsa. There was a missed call. Last night, about nine o'clock.

Had she picked up? Had she spoken to Elsa?

No, she wasn't so drunk she'd forget that.

She put the phone back to her ear. "What is it, Zoe?"

"Are you OK?" Zoe asked. "You sound different."

Lesley grunted out a laugh and then instantly regretted it. She sat back on the sofa, trying to get comfortable.

"I'm fine," she said. "All my own fault. What have you got for me?"

It must be urgent if Zoe was ringing her so early.

"I'm sending you an email," Zoe said. "A photo."

"Hang on." Lesley switched the phone to speaker mode. She opened up her email. Right at the top was an email from Zoe with an attachment.

"Shit."

"Am I right in thinking that's the Bournemouth equivalent of Trevor Hamm?" Zoe asked.

Trevor Hamm was a man Lesley and Zoe had targeted in West Midlands Force CID. He was a shitty little man, an organised crime boss who liked to let his minions take the fall for his own crimes.

"Something like that," Lesley replied. "Thanks."

She eyed the photo. Had she been expecting this, or not?

"No problem," Zoe hung up.

Lesley stared at the photo. She didn't need this. Not today, with a hangover and what she'd said to Elsa and – *oh, shit* – outing herself at work. She would have to speak to Carpenter. He needed to know she was in a relationship with a person of interest in a case. If she still was.

Did she need to tell Carpenter about this photo, too?

She'd park that one until the case was over.

She pinched her finger and thumb to zoom in on the photo. Smiling out at her were two men, their hands clasped together.

On the left, Arthur Kelvin. As Zoe had suggested, the Bournemouth version of Trevor Hamm.

And on the right, her predecessor, DCI Mackie.

CHAPTER SIXTY-SEVEN

Elsa woke to find light seeping around the edge of blackout curtains. She yawned and stretched, wondering if she'd overslept, then sat up in bed, blinking.

This wasn't her room. She was lying in a vast bed, in a pale room thinly lit by the sunlight from around those curtains.

She slid out of bed and opened the curtains. In front of her was a view over a street, her own car parked opposite. Seagulls attacked a rubbish bin just along from it, and a man was walking his dog below her. She hammered on the window, but he didn't react.

She turned back to the room. She'd eventually given up on anybody turning up at around midnight, and had decided to get what sleep she could. She'd slept fitfully, worried that someone might be watching her.

She went to the mirror over a dressing table and straightened her hair. Mascara had pooled under her eyes; she rubbed at it. Behind her was one of the ensuite bathrooms. She considered taking a shower, but that felt too vulnerable.

Elsa jumped at a sound from behind her. It was beyond the door to the main living room. Breathing heavily, she gave her hair a final pat down and strode to the door, attempting to put as much confidence into her stride as she could.

Arthur Kelvin would be on the other side. Elsa was ready for him; she'd met him half a dozen times and was learning how to manage the man.

Instead, a woman stood in the double doorway leading to the hallway. It wasn't the woman who'd greeted her last night. This woman was tall and dark-skinned with thick wavy hair that reminded Elsa of her own. In front of her were two squat, light-haired dogs. They strained on short leashes. Elsa eyed them, then looked at the woman.

"Who are you?"

The woman smiled. She wore bright purple lipstick and her eyes were heavily mascaraed. "You don't need to know that." She looked down at the dogs. "Stop it, Bruno."

One of the dogs pulled at the leash, growling under its breath. The woman smiled down at the dogs and then up at Elsa again.

"This is Bruno and Izzy, my babies. They're very protective of me."

Elsa nodded. Her skin prickled.

The dogs' eyes were on her. The growling had stopped but somehow that made them more menacing. The woman gestured towards the sofa by the window.

"Sit down," she said. "We need to talk."

Elsa shook her head. "You've illegally imprisoned me," she said. "You can't possibly expect me to want to chat."

The woman shrugged. "Try and get past me."

Elsa looked over the woman's shoulder into the hallway beyond. The woman and her dogs blocked the way.

The woman loosened one of the leads a little. The dog lurched forwards. Elsa took a step back, hitting a bookcase behind her.

"Like I say," said the woman. "Sit down." She nodded towards the sofa.

Her voice was smooth, with a home counties accent. It didn't sit well with the sight of her holding those dogs. Elsa didn't know much about dogs, but she was pretty sure they were the type that had been illegal at some point, or at least should have been. They were squat and heavy, and looked like they'd go for her neck given half a chance.

She skirted around the edge of the room, keeping away from the woman and the dogs. She lowered herself to the sofa and turned to face the woman, her hands in her lap.

Damn. She'd left her jacket in the bedroom, draped over the bed. Her phone was in the inside pocket.

The woman closed the door and tied the leashes to a hook next to it. One of the dogs licked her hand and whimpered. She gave it a slap. Elsa flinched.

"Good," the woman said. She approached an easy chair at right angle to the sofa and sat down.

"Now," she said, her eyes on Elsa. "I have questions for you."

CHAPTER SIXTY-EIGHT

Lesley nodded at her team as she passed them en route to her office. She needed coffee before she could talk to any of them. She wanted to take stock as well.

She pushed open the door to her office and slung her bag into a chair, then rounded the desk and sat down heavily. She bent her head over the desk, rubbing her eyes. Never again. She was too old for whisky.

There was a knock at the door: Dennis. She beckoned him in.

"We've had developments, boss. New evidence came in overnight."

She leaned back in her chair, trying to conjure up energy. "What kind of evidence?"

"They found Nevin's car, a couple of streets away from the top of the cliffs."

"What state was it in?"

"Undamaged. No sign of a break-in."

"You think somebody might have forced him to the side of the road and then taken him to the cliff top?"

"He was in that van," said Dennis. "None of it makes any sense."

"Maybe they got him into the van from his car," she replied. "Left his car behind."

He nodded.

The rest of the team filed in behind him.

"Go on," Lesley sighed. "What else have we got?"

Johnny walked to the board and pinned up a photograph. It showed a woman's scarf, pink with yellow swirls.

"We found this in the car," Dennis said. He looked at her, his expression pointed. "I recognise it."

So did Lesley. "It belongs to Elsa Short."

He nodded. "Puts her in his car before Nevin died."

Lesley shook her head. "It puts her in his car at some point before he died. Not necessarily on the same evening."

Was she defending Elsa too strongly? Was she treating her differently from any other suspect? She'd been with Elsa when Harry had died.

Could Elsa be involved?

Dennis cleared his throat. "She was wearing that scarf the day before he died. I saw it on her when I went to speak to her and Aurelia Cross. If it was in his car, that means she left it there between that interview and his death."

"Unless somebody else put it there," said Lesley.

"Why would someone do that?"

Lesley leaned back. "I don't know."

Her stomach growled. She took a breath, wishing she could go home and sleep. "What else have we got?" Her gaze flicked over the rest of the team.

"Mike has—" began Dennis.

Mike stepped forward. "We're working through CCTV from a shop opposite Nevin, Cross and Short."

Lesley leaned forward. "Any particular reason?"

"With both of them dead," said Dennis, "we wanted to see who came to that office on Tuesday night."

"OK. Have you watched it yet?"

"Not yet, boss," said Mike. "That's my next job."

"Good," said Lesley. "Tell me if you see anything."

"Will do."

"I've been going through Nevin's computer," said Tina. "We found a laptop in his car."

"Excellent. Anything useful?" Lesley asked.

"There's an email exchange between him and Elsa Short. She was threatening to leave the firm, sell her partnership."

Lesley tensed. She knew how Elsa felt about her position at Nevin, Cross and Short.

"And?" she said.

"He told her she couldn't," Tina replied. "It was impossible for him to release her from her contract."

"It might give her a motive," said Dennis.

"I've already provided her with an alibi."

Tina and Mike exchanged glances. Dennis looked down. Lesley stared at them.

"Don't tell me you…" She stopped herself and looked at Tina. "Tell me if you get anything else on that contract. Mike, keep me informed on the CCTV. Dennis, was there anything else in Nevin's car? Signs of a struggle? Bloodstains?"

"Nothing," he replied. "The car has been impounded. Johnny and I were planning to head over there."

"Good," she replied. "Get on with it, then."

The team filed out of the office. Lesley leaned her head back, staring up at the ceiling. She felt sluggish and heavy. She thought of the message Elsa had left, the missed call.

She picked up her phone from her desk, about to call her back.

But if the emails incriminated Elsa, then Lesley needed to take a step back. She couldn't warn a potential suspect.

She stood up and stretched her arms, then yawned. *Get a grip*. She needed coffee, and she also needed to talk to Carpenter.

She'd stop by the kitchen and then go and see her boss. She should tell him about her relationship with Elsa. Better that it came from her now.

As she approached the door, she saw Mike lurking behind it. She yanked the door open.

"Mike, what is it?"

His eyes widened. "It's the CCTV boss. You're going to want to see this."

CHAPTER SIXTY-NINE

Elsa looked back at the woman. "I don't want to chat," she said. "Let me go, I need to be at work."

She glanced at the dogs by the door. "And call off those idiotic dogs." She wasn't going to let the woman frighten her.

The woman snapped her fingers and one of the dogs barked, making Elsa jump.

Elsa gritted her teeth. She clenched her hands together in her lap. "I refuse to let you frighten me," she said. "Where's Arthur?"

The woman shrank back. "Arthur?"

"Arthur Kelvin. This is his house, I assume."

"No, this is my flat."

"You work for him then?"

A shadow passed over the woman's face. "No, that's not why you're here."

"No, you don't work for him, or no, he didn't summon me here?" Elsa asked.

The woman gave her a long look. "Both," she said eventually.

Elsa stood up and pulled in a breath. If this had nothing to do with Kelvin, there was no reason for her to be afraid, and the dogs were simply a bluff. She approached the door, considering putting out a hand and fussing one of them. They were probably docile idiots just there for show.

One of the dogs snarled and she withdrew her hand.

"You can't leave," the woman said. She was standing by the window overlooking the harbour.

Elsa glared at her. "Why not? What's going on?"

The woman put her hands on her hips. "You need to tell me the truth."

Elsa sighed. "The truth about what?"

"About Harry."

"Harry?" Elsa said. "Harry Nevin?"

The woman nodded. She looked across at the dogs, then at Elsa. She stared at her for a long moment. Elsa met her gaze.

Finally, the woman took a step forward. "You fucking bitch."

Elsa was about to take a step back before she remembered the dogs. "Just let me go," she said.

This woman was a client of Harry's, perhaps, pissed off that he'd died, that he couldn't represent her anymore. She needed to get some perspective.

The woman shook her head. "You and Harry," she said. "You were sleeping with him, weren't you?"

CHAPTER SEVENTY

Lesley walked to Mike's desk. Tina, at the next desk, looked over. Lesley grabbed a chair from by the wall and pulled it over to Mike's desk.

"Go on then," she said.

Tina was leaning over, looking across at Mike's screen. Lesley gave her a frown and she returned to her own computer.

The image from the CCTV was black and white, and grainy. But Lesley could see that it was the street where Nevin, Cross and Short were based. Below the offices was a newsagent, next to that the doorway leading up to the offices. On either side, coffee shops. The street was empty.

Mike shuffled his chair towards the screen.

"What have you seen?" Lesley asked him.

"I rewound it eight minutes, boss, so you can see it all."

"Go on then." She leaned forwards and clasped her hands on the desk.

Mike started the video.

"What time is this?" Lesley asked.

He pointed to the top right of the screen. "7:16pm, Tuesday last week. Five days before Ameena Khan died. It was the first recording we got, lucky."

Lesley nodded.

Onscreen, a woman emerged from the office. She closed the door slowly, looking up and down the street.

Lesley squinted. "Is that her?"

Mike nodded. "That's Ameena Khan."

"Can you zoom in?"

He clicked his mouse and enlarged the centre of the screen. Sure enough, it was Ameena Khan. She wore a dark suit and carried a briefcase.

"What's she doing?" Lesley said.

Ameena moved to one side and stopped in front of the newsagent. She kept checking her watch and looking towards the office door.

"She's waiting for someone," said Lesley.

Dennis stood behind them. "What have we got?"

"CCTV from opposite Nevin, Cross and Short," said Mike. "Last Tuesday evening."

"And?" Dennis asked.

"Wait," said Mike.

Onscreen, the door to the offices opened and Harry Nevin emerged.

He ignored Ameena, instead looking up and down the street. After he'd checked both directions, he turned to her. They faced each other. They seemed to be talking.

"I'll fast forward it," says Mike. "They talk for four minutes."

"Four minutes?" said Lesley. That was a long chat outside the office between the managing partner and a junior colleague.

"Can you run it faster instead?" she asked. "I don't want to skip it."

Mike leaned in and adjusted the settings to run at double speed. Lesley leaned back and folded her arms across her chest.

"What are they talking about?" she wondered aloud.

"Steven Leonard case, maybe?" said Dennis. "They were working on it together."

"Possibly," replied Lesley. "But why wouldn't they have that conversation in the office? Why the cloak and dagger?"

"We're about to find out," said Mike.

He clicked his mouse again and slowed the video to normal speed. The timestamp showed 7:22pm.

Onscreen, Harry Nevin put his hand on Ameena's cheek. Lesley sucked in a breath. She sensed Dennis tensing behind her.

Nevin leaned in and kissed Ameena on the lips. She grabbed his hand, holding it to her cheek. After a moment she pulled away and looked behind her. Another moment passed and then she kissed him again.

Lesley, Dennis and Mike watched in silence. Tina had given up on what she was doing and was watching from her desk.

After two more minutes of Nevin and Ameena kissing, Ameena pulled away. She turned her back to Nevin and walked off, her pace measured. She turned just before going out of shot. He waved. She turned and left the shot.

When Ameena was out of view, Nevin walked away in the opposite direction. The street was empty again.

Tina whistled.

Lesley looked at her. "So," she said. "Harry Nevin had a wife and *two* girlfriends."

CHAPTER SEVENTY-ONE

Elsa couldn't help herself. She laughed.

"Of course I'm not sleeping with Harry. I'm sleeping with a fucking pol…"

She stopped herself. If this woman was associated with Arthur Kelvin, Elsa didn't want her knowing that she was seeing a DCI.

"Who are you, anyway?" she asked.

The woman shook her head. "You don't need to know that."

"Look," said Elsa. "I know what Harry was like. If you were one of his women, then you can take it from me. I was *not* one of your rivals. Just let me go, yeah?"

She hurried to the door, gritting her teeth and steering a path round the dogs. One of them gave a low growl from the bottom of its throat and came at her. It shoved its face into her crotch. She held her breath. When all it did was bury its nose in further, she laughed and looked down at it. "Is that all you've got?"

She turned to the woman. "These dogs are soft as blancmange."

"You're lying. I know you were meeting him."

Elsa put a hand on the doorknob. "No, lady. I'm really not."

She yanked open the door. On the other side, two men faced her. Elsa's shoulders dropped. Both men were tall and solidly built. One had a shaved head and a bright blond beard, the other had a scar above his right eye. They stepped towards her.

"Who the fuck are you?" She wasn't going to show fear.

"Stop her!" the woman shouted.

The man with the yellow beard grabbed her. The other, Scarface, hit her across the face. She spat at him. He grabbed her by the shoulder. Both men had their hands on her. She struggled to pull free.

"This is ridiculous!" she said, letting her outrage block her growing fear. "Just let me go. I'm no threat to you!" she shouted back to the woman.

Harry was dead. What did this woman care who he might or might not have been sleeping with?

Elsa turned to the men just as a hand obscured her vision. She felt a slap across her eyes and stumbled, falling against Yellowbeard. She staggered and fell to the floor.

CHAPTER SEVENTY-TWO

"OK," said Lesley. "So now we have a motive for Harry Nevin killing Ameena Khan."

"You reckon she dumped him?" asked Mike.

Lesley shrugged. "It doesn't matter what happened. We've got his ring on that photo and we've got the two of them having an affair."

"It might not have been an affair," said Tina.

Lesley gestured towards Mike's screen. "What we just saw isn't a one-off."

She looked at the image onscreen of the empty street. "You don't do that after a first kiss. If something like that happened spontaneously outside the office, they'd either have left together, or there'd have been some kind of fight. At the very least there'd be awkwardness. No, that's an established relationship."

"So something went wrong between them and he killed her?" suggested Tina.

"Looks like it," said Lesley.

"I've got more," added Mike, flicking through screens on his computer.

Lesley clasped him on the shoulder. He flinched.

"Sorry," she said, removing her hand. "What do you mean, more?"

"More CCTV, the next morning. Hang on a minute."

Lesley leaned over him. "More of Nevin and Ameena?"

He shook his head. After a few moments, another similar image appeared. The outside of the offices, black and white, grainy. The light was different this time, the sun shining from the opposite direction. After twenty seconds, Nevin walked into shot. He was arm in arm with a woman.

"That's not Ameena," said Tina.

Dennis cleared his throat. Lesley frowned at him.

"You're right," she said. "That's definitely not her."

Ameena had long, straight hair that ran halfway down her back. This woman had thick, wavy hair, that stopped at her shoulders. She had her back to the camera and was leaning into Nevin.

"Is that Elsa Short?" asked Dennis.

Lesley squinted at the picture. Elsa and Harry might have been arriving together, but they wouldn't have been arm in arm like that.

"Colleagues don't walk like that," she said.

"Still," said Dennis. "Maybe he was having an affair with her too."

Lesley felt her skin prickle. Surely not…

She looked back at the screen. The woman had long, dark wavy hair, and a confident stride. Her hair was like Elsa's. But it couldn't be her.

The couple arrived at the door to the offices. Nevin turned to the woman, who was still facing away from the camera. He gave her a light kiss on the lips and opened the office door. She pulled away and turned towards the camera.

Lesley felt her body relax. "That's not Elsa."

Mike gripped his mouse. "It's the other one."

"The mistress," said Dennis. "Priscilla Evans."

"How many women did Harry Nevin have?" said Tina.

They watched as Nevin disappeared into the office. A moment later, the door opened again and he re-emerged. The woman was still outside, with her phone to her ear. She looked up as he appeared. They faced each other and looked like they were talking, their movements jerky. Nevin shook a fist at her.

"They're having a row," said Tina.

The woman shoved Nevin into the doors. She turned and walked away. She didn't look back.

"Maybe she found out about Ameena Khan?" suggested Mike.

"Either way," said Lesley, "I want to talk to her. Rewind it a minute, will you?"

Mike went back to the point where Nevin re-emerged from the office.

"Bit further," said Lesley.

He took it back another minute.

"There," she said.

He paused it.

"Run it again, half speed."

Mike did so.

The woman was pulling her left hand through her hair, scraping it back. Lesley had seen that gesture before.

"Tina," she said. "Get up the CCTV from the clifftop from when Nevin was thrown over."

Tina slid her chair to her own desk and flicked through files on her computer. She brought up the CCTV from the night in question, and paused it at the point where the woman had removed her hat and run her hand through her hair.

Lesley stood back and looked between the two screens. "It's the same woman."

In both shots, the woman had her back to them. It was the same long dark, wavy hair, similar to Elsa's. But that gesture. Elsa was right-handed.

"It's her," she said. "She was the one on the cliff."

"You're sure?" asked Dennis.

Lesley turned to him. "We're going to see Priscilla Evans, now."

CHAPTER SEVENTY-THREE

Lesley hurried into her office and grabbed her jacket. As she emerged, the whole team was staring at her. Waiting.

"Right," she said. "Tina, you go back to Harry Nevin's emails, see if there's anything between him and Priscilla that might give us an idea of what their relationship was like. We need to find where Priscilla works, we've already got her home address. Dennis, you and I are going to head over there now. Mike, Johnny, find out where she works. Go there. Wherever she is, I want to talk to her."

"We're going to arrest her, boss?" asked Johnny.

"Not yet," Lesley replied. "I'll talk to Gail in the car. Find out if there are any more forensics. But Priscilla Evans is a person of interest."

Dennis nodded. Lesley looked at him, wondering what he was thinking. Would he assume she was trying to move the blame away from Elsa?

It didn't matter. They needed to see Priscilla Evans. They'd asked her to provide an alibi for Nevin on Sunday morning and she'd said she was with him. That alibi looked somewhat different now she was a suspect.

"Come on, then," she snapped. Dennis followed as she hurried out of the office and towards the stairs. She ran down, almost tripping in her haste, and sped out into the car park.

"We'll take your car, Dennis," she called to him. "You know the roads."

"Yes, boss." He ran towards his Vauxhall Astra.

"How long will it take?" she asked as she strapped herself in.

"Forty, forty-five minutes? Not sure at this time of day."

Lesley checked her watch. It was quarter past nine, the rush hour would be ending. They would have to drive through Poole. At least rush hour traffic in the town was more predictable than holiday traffic on the Isle of Purbeck.

"OK," she said, "Put your foot down."

"I'm not breaking the speed limit," he told her. "It's not an emergency, I can't put the blue lights on."

She gritted her teeth. "Let's just get there."

He left the car park and they drove towards Wareham.

As they passed the town, she turned to him. "I want to get this out in the open. About me and Elsa Short."

His face was still, his eyes on the road. "None of my business."

"You know I gave her an alibi," she said. "You believe that alibi, right?"

He glanced at her and then back at the road. His fingers gripped the steering wheel, his knuckles white. "Of course I do. Why would you lie?"

She stared ahead. The traffic ahead had slowed. They were approaching the outskirts of Poole.

"I didn't lie," she said. "But I also didn't tell you I was in a relationship with her. I didn't tell anybody."

"Like I say boss, none of my business."

She put her hand on the dashboard. "She was a witness in a case, Dennis. I should have come clean."

The car slowed and they came to a halt at traffic lights. Dennis turned to her.

"I know you think I'm a dinosaur, but you're wrong. I can understand why you didn't want to talk about it. It's awkward. You hardly know us, we hardly know you. Nobody's judging you."

"Good." She didn't know if he was talking about the fact she was dating a woman, or the fact she was dating a suspect.

The traffic started again and Dennis turned away from her.

"When we get there," she said, "we need to ask her where she was at the time of both murders."

"Do you think she was involved in Ameena Khan's murder?" Dennis asked. "I thought we have Harry Nevin for that?"

"She said she was with him. They could have been working together."

"What, and then she turned on him?"

"He would have been a witness to her being a murderer. Maybe she wanted to get him out of the picture?"

"But that would work both ways."

Lesley shrugged. "I don't know. We can look into motive. But we've got her on that clifftop, I'm sure of it."

She grabbed her phone and called Gail. Engaged. *Damn*. Hopefully the CSM was talking to one of her team.

"Maybe she was annoyed with him?" said Dennis. "That video, the CCTV outside the office."

Lesley nodded. *Hurry*, she thought, wishing they could put the blue lights on. She hadn't spoken to Carpenter.

She knew she didn't have enough for an arrest warrant. But her senses were tingling.

"I'm calling Tina," she said.

Dennis nodded, taking a left turn.

"Where are you going?" she asked him.

"Shortcut," he said. "I know these roads."

"Fair enough."

She dialled. "Tina, is there anything else in those emails?"

"Sorry, boss. Nothing yet. Plenty between Nevin and Priscilla, lovey-dovey stuff, that kind of thing. But nothing about Ameena, nothing about an argument."

"When was the last email that she sent him?" Lesley asked.

"One moment... Last Tuesday."

"And did he reply?"

"I can't see anything. Oh, wait... No, no, there's an autoreply. But no, last email between them was last Tuesday night."

Lesley looked out of the windscreen at the residential streets Dennis was taking. She was glad she'd told him to drive. She had no idea where she was.

"So the last time that Harry Nevin and Priscilla Evans made email contact was the night we saw him kissing Ameena Khan?" she said.

"The night before they had that row," Dennis added.

"You're right," Lesley said. "Tina, have Johnny and Mike got her work address yet?"

"They just left, boss. She works in Poole."

"Where in Poole?" she asked.

"I didn't catch it. Johnny said something and ran out the door."

"OK. Keep trying Gail for me, will you? I need to know if there are any more forensics from his car."

"Will do, boss."

They were passing through the centre of Poole, turning towards the coast. Lesley drummed her fingers on her knees, impatient, wishing they could get there quicker. But the traffic had cleared and this was about covering the miles now, not about getting through the jams.

At last they arrived in Sandbanks. There were no parking spaces near Priscilla's flat. Dennis parked on double yellows and Lesley jumped out.

She eyed the building that Priscilla Evans lived in. The woman's flat was on the first floor, windows overlooking the road and the beach behind.

She glanced both ways and started to run across the road. As she did so, the door to the apartment building opened. Three people emerged.

Lesley's eyes widened. "What the hell?"

CHAPTER SEVENTY-FOUR

Elsa felt the wind knocked out of her as she fell against the man. She slid to the floor, her hip hitting it hard.

The woman stood above her.

"Tie her wrists," she said.

"No you bloody don't!" Elsa screeched. She kicked out, hitting the woman in the ankle.

The woman yelled and grabbed her ankle, losing her balance. Yellowbeard threw out a hand to stop her falling, and she righted herself.

Now was Elsa's chance. She jabbed out with her foot, kicking him in the calves. He stumbled.

She pushed herself up and shoved her elbow into Scarface's groin on the way up. He opened his mouth wide and doubled over. His face was red.

Elsa pulled in a breath and straightened, trying to ignore the pain in her hip where she'd hit the floor.

She turned and ran for the stairs, almost smelling freedom.

As she reached the stairs, she felt a hand on her ankle. She turned to see Yellowbeard behind her. He lay flat on the floor, his arm stretched towards her, hand clasping her ankle.

Elsa kicked out, but it was too late. She threw her hands out, panic making her skin tight. The stairs were made of concrete, under that plush carpet. She remembered walking up them last night, thinking how solid they were.

She lunged forwards, her outstretched arms giving her unwanted momentum. She screamed as she went down. Her head hit a step, the blow jolting though her. She tumbled over, twisting again and again as she shuddered to the bottom of the stairs. Her hip screamed at her as she went, making her cry out.

She came to a stop at the bottom. Her ankle was twisted to one side, possibly sprained. She gritted her teeth, checking herself.

Touching the side of her forehead, she found a lump. Warmth, wetness. She swallowed. She turned and tried to untwist herself. Her ankle screamed at her.

She reached her arms out towards the front door of the building. Where was the other woman? The one who had opened the door to her last night, the one who let her in?

"Help!" Elsa cried. She dragged herself towards the front door, unable to stand. If she did, that ankle would take her down.

She was a foot away from the door. She stopped, feeling a weight on her back. It was sharp, a stiletto heel. The woman. Elsa grimaced as the woman ground her heel into her back.

"Help!" she screamed.

The front door was solid, but she had to hope someone would hear. She clawed her way a few more centimetres towards the door.

"Put her in the van," the woman snapped.

"Where d'you want us to take her?" asked a male voice. Elsa couldn't tell which of the men it was.

A pause. "Boscombe Cliffs," the woman said.

"Again?" he replied. "It's broad daylight, there's no way we'll—"

"Just do it."

Elsa squinted as the front door opened. Sunlight fell across her face. *Please let there be someone out there. Please let them see me.*

Hands dug under her arms and dragged her upwards. She kicked out, then screamed at the pain in her ankle.

They pulled her up and out of the door, her injured foot dragging on the ground. Her breaths came out as whimpers. It was broad daylight, someone had to see. But this was Sandbanks. The houses were spaced apart, the frontages set back from the road. People kept themselves to themselves.

The hands loosened and she crashed to the ground. Elsa closed her eyes. *This is it*, she thought. *They'll kill me before they put me in the van.*

But then she heard it.

Footsteps, running towards her from the road.

A voice. A familiar voice.

"Police! Don't move a goddamn muscle!"

CHAPTER SEVENTY-FIVE

Lesley stared at the house. The door of the building that Priscilla Evans lived in was open, and two men were walking out. They were staggering, dragging a woman between them.

Lesley hesitated, her mouth opening. Was that Priscilla between them? Who were the men?

She ran towards them.

"What's going on?" Dennis called.

"Run!" Lesley shouted.

She pointed ahead of her towards the men. She sprinted across the road, oblivious to a blaring horn, and reached the pavement on the other side. She was focused on the three people, her stride not faltering.

As the men left the building, a fourth person emerged behind them. A tall black woman with dark wavy hair. Priscilla Evans.

Lesley looked down at the other woman, the one they were dragging between them. Her head was bowed. Her hair, like Priscilla's, was shoulder-length and wavy.

"Oh my god," Lesley breathed. "Stop right there!" she called.

She almost tripped in her panic, but then caught herself and carried on running. She picked up pace, speeding towards the men. One of them had a shaved head and blonde beard, the other had a scar on his right cheek. Behind them, Priscilla Evans was limping.

One of the men, the one with the beard, looked up and saw Lesley. He dropped the second woman.

Lesley gasped.

"Police! Don't move a goddamn muscle!"

She ran to the woman on the ground.

"Are you OK?"

Elsa looked up at her, recognition filling her eyes. "Yes. Stop them!"

Lesley sprang up. She grabbed the first of the men, the one with the scar. Dennis had already grabbed Priscilla. Lesley slapped handcuffs on the man and Dennis did the same with the woman.

"Where is he?" she yelled, looking around her.

The second man, the bearded one, had disappeared.

"He won't get very far," said Dennis.

"He could hurt somebody!"

She stood, turning from side to side, her senses ablaze. Where was he?

She grabbed her phone. "This is DCI Clarke." She barked out the address. "Ambulance urgently required. Murder suspect on the move. Backup needed, right now."

She turned to see that Dennis had secured Priscilla and the man to the railing of the fence outside the building. She nodded at him. "Good thinking."

An ambulance pulled up and two male paramedics got out.

"That woman, over there!" Lesley called, pointing towards Elsa. "Her name is Elsa Short, she's been attacked."

"What about this pair?" said the first of the paramedics. Priscilla Evans was leaning against the railing, complaining of pain in her leg.

"Worry about Elsa first."

Her phone rang: Tina. "Boss, Uniform will be with you in two minutes. Do you need anything from me?"

"No," said Lesley. "I just need Uniform to get here."

"Where is he?" Tina asked.

"How do you know?" Lesley said.

"PC Mullins called me. He's been called to the scene."

PC Mullins was her colleague, the one Tina had been with when Lesley had first met her at Corfe Castle.

"He's probably on the beach," Lesley said.

She heard drumming above her head and looked up. A helicopter approached from the west. It flew over her head and made for the beach. Lesley panted, watching it disappear over the rooftops.

"I have to go find him," she said. She hung up.

"No boss," said Dennis. "Uniform will get him, you stay here."

She glared at him. "Don't give me orders."

A squad car pulled up behind the ambulance and two officers jumped out.

"PS Wright," he said, "Who's in charge?"

Lesley turned to him, pushing down her irritation at Dennis. "DCI Clarke. We arrested two suspects, but there's a third, a man. He's got a shaved head and a blonde beard. He's about six foot tall, heavily built, wearing jeans and a yellow t-shirt."

Sergeant Wright nodded. "Which way did he go?"

"That way," Lesley pointed towards the beach.

Wright's radio crackled. "The helicopter has spotted him, Ma'am. We'll get him, don't worry."

Another squad car pulled up and two more officers got out, along with a third from the car that PS Wright had been in. Wright turned to them, called out orders, and the five of them ran off in pursuit of the man.

"Quickly!" Lesley called after them. "There are people on that beach." *Grockles*.

She turned to see a paramedic approaching, making for the ambulance. The man pulled out a wheelchair and hurried back to the building. Lesley followed him. The second paramedic eased Elsa up off the ground and helped her into the chair.

Lesley bent over and grabbed Elsa's hand. "Are you OK?"

Elsa stared back at her, blinking. She nodded and then closed her eyes.

"She's lost consciousness," one of the paramedics said.

"Quick. Get her in the ambulance," the other replied.

Lesley pulled back, watching as they hurried Elsa towards the van. They closed the back doors and pulled away, sirens blaring as they drove towards Poole.

CHAPTER SEVENTY-SIX

Dennis kept his eyes on his two detainees as the ambulance sped away.

"Boss, I need some help here!" he called.

Lesley approached. "Have you arrested them?"

"I have. We need to get them in my car."

"No," she said. "We'll put them in the squad cars."

Three of the uniformed officers had run off for the beach. The others had gone in different directions, searching the roads.

"Boss," he said, "You're not thinking straight. I can't have them attached to the fence like this."

She turned to look at him. She looked at his car, then along the street, then at the suspects, and finally back at Dennis.

"What?" she said.

He narrowed his eyes at her. She was distracted. She'd watched the ambulance drive away with her girlfriend in it and she hadn't snapped back to reality.

"Boss," he said. "You take her, I'll take him. We'll get them in the back of my car."

Priscilla Evans laughed. "What is this? Keystone Cops?"

Dennis turned to her. As he moved he winced. Pain in his leg. How had that happened?

"You're injured," said Lesley.

"I'm fine." He shook his head. "He kicked me, that's all, nothing I can't handle."

Lesley frowned. She looked off in the direction the ambulance had disappeared. Her eyes faded and then brightened again.

"Dennis," she said. "You take him, I'll take her."

"That's what I... Never mind."

Lesley looked at the man. "What's your name?"

"No comment," he replied.

Lesley balled her fist. She raised it and stepped towards him.

"Boss," Dennis hissed.

Lesley stared at the man, her chest rising and falling. Slowly she let her fist fall to her side and took a pace back. Dennis stepped in between her and the suspect. He unfastened the man's cuffs from the railing and to his own wrist.

"I'm taking you to the car," he said.

As Dennis approached the car, PS Wright returned. Two of his men were behind him, the third suspect between them.

Thank the Lord, thought Dennis. He raised a hand to touch his shirt, the crucifix beneath it.

"Is anybody hurt?" he asked. "Did he get anybody on the beach?"

PS Wright shook his head. "Too busy running away from us."

"Good," said Dennis. "Can you take these two? Put them in your cars, take them to the nearest station."

"No problem," replied Wright.

He took the man from Dennis. One of the PCs went to take Priscilla Evans out of Lesley's hands. Lesley was staring at Priscilla, saying nothing. Her hand kept going to the back of her neck. Dennis watched her, wondering when she was going to come back.

The uniformed officers bundled the arrestees into two of their cars and drove away. Dennis breathed a sigh of relief and bent over, prodding at his shin.

"That damn well hurt," he muttered.

Lesley's head went up. "Dennis," she said. "You swore!"

He gritted his teeth. "I'm in pain, boss."

She smiled at him. He started to smile back then grimaced.

"Do you need an ambulance yourself?" she asked.

"Of course not. It's just a kick."

She blinked at him. "Will she be OK, do you think?"

Dennis nodded. "She'll be fine."

"Yes," the boss replied. "She's made of stern stuff, Elsa."

He raised an eyebrow. He wondered what had happened inside that building. How Elsa had managed to avoid meeting the same fate as Ameena Khan and Harry Nevin.

"Reckon she is," he said.

Lesley sighed. She looked at him, as if noticing him for the first time.

"Come on, Dennis," she said. "We've got interviews to do."

CHAPTER SEVENTY-SEVEN

Elsa woke to an unfamiliar smell, disinfectant mixed with a perfume she didn't recognise. She put her hand out, only to grab at air.

Where had they taken her? Was she in that flat still, or somewhere worse?

Did she dare open her eyes? Were they sitting nearby, watching, waiting for her to wake up?

There was breathing nearby.

Oh, God.

It was the woman. Or maybe the two men.

Elsa still didn't know who that woman was. Was she an employee of Arthur Kelvin? Kelvin was a hardened criminal, but he'd never threatened Elsa. She was his lawyer, for God's sake. What had the woman said about him? Elsa had asked her, but she couldn't remember the answer.

She couldn't lie here all day, giving them the upper hand.

She blinked her eyes open. Her head hurt and her ankle felt like it was pinned down.

She was lying on a soft bed. Not on the floor, at least. She closed her eyes again.

Slowly, she turned her head towards the source of the breathing and readied herself.

She opened her eyes.

The woman sitting next to the bed was plump with grey hair piled on top of her head and thin lips painted a bright pink.

Elsa frowned. "Aurelia?"

Aurelia Cross put a hand over Elsa's. "Elsa, thank God, you're awake. What happened?"

"I don't know," said Elsa. "I don't remember."

"It was Priscilla Evans," Aurelia said. "Harry's girl-friend. She attacked you. You were at her flat."

"Harry's girlfriend?" Elsa's throat was sore. Her face hurt.

"Priscilla Evans," Aurelia repeated. "What were you doing there?"

Elsa turned and looked up at the ceiling. It had tiles and fluorescent lights. It was dull and institutional. Where was she?

She tried to remember, but her brain felt thick, the memories indistinct.

Aurelia patted her hand. "It's OK. You don't need to remember anything right now. There's plenty of time. The police will be wanting to talk to you, though."

Elsa nodded, then regretted it. Her head pounded. Her hip was sore, she remembered hitting it falling down stairs.

"I need to report an assault," she croaked.

Aurelia leaned over her. "Not just an assault, Elsa. She killed Harry. Ameena too, I expect."

"What?" Elsa turned towards the other woman. She couldn't remember any of it, it was all too hazy.

Aurelia squeezed her hand. "I'll let you get some rest."

Elsa closed her eyes. She lay in silence for a few moments. The light was red behind her closed eyelids. She wished she could close the curtains, but she didn't have the strength to even sit up in bed.

"I heard you put up a hell of a fight," said a woman's voice.

Elsa opened her eyes. She smiled: Lesley.

Lesley bent over her. She was smiling, looking into Elsa's eyes. "How are you?"

"My ankle feels like shit and I'm… Have they put me on painkillers?"

Lesley nodded. "Morphine."

"That explains it. I feel like someone's put my brain through a car wash." Her voice was breathy.

"You broke her leg, you know," said Lesley.

"What? Whose?"

"Priscilla Evans, when you kicked her."

"What? How…?"

"We've interviewed her, Elsa. Twice. You've been in and out of consciousness for the last two days."

Elsa squeezed her eyes closed. "Who was she? Is it true she…?" Her voice tailed off.

Lesley sat down in the chair that Aurelia Cross had vacated.

"She was Harry Nevin's girlfriend. So was Ameena Khan. Priscilla was the jealous type, it seems."

Elsa, puzzled. "That's why she…?"

"She thought you were sleeping with him, too," said Lesley.

Elsa could remember someone else asking her about that. She closed her eyes, she needed sleep.

"You weren't, were you?" Lesley asked.

Elsa shuddered. She opened her eyes. "No. Of course not."

Lesley nodded. "We found images of you and him meeting at a café on Sandbanks beach." She looked worried. She cocked her head, looking into Elsa's face as if trying to read her mind.

Elsa shook her head. *Ouch.*

"Business," she muttered.

"But you worked in the same office."

"Confidential business. Can't talk…"

Lesley squeezed her hand. Elsa turned to her and wiped her eyes. Lesley could see through her, she knew it. She was a detective.

She should never have got involved with a detective.

Lesley let go of her hand. "I'll let you sleep."

She kissed her fingers and placed them on Elsa's forehead. Elsa felt warmth radiate through her skin.

"Thanks," she whispered.

"What for?" said Lesley.

Elsa remembered hearing Lesley's voice when the men were dragging her out of the apartment block. Seeing her appear over her, when she was slumped on the ground.

"For doing your job," she whispered.

CHAPTER SEVENTY-EIGHT

Lesley walked into the living room of her house in Wareham. At some point, she would stop thinking of this as a temporary base and start thinking of it as home. Elsa and Sharon were on the sofa, playing a game of cards. Elsa had her leg in plaster, resting on the coffee table. Her ankle had been broken in two places, and it would be weeks before she could walk again.

Sharon looked up. "We're playing rummy, Mum. D'you want to join in?"

"Let me make a coffee," Lesley replied. "Then I'll be in."

She walked into the kitchen. Sharon came in behind her. "Can I have one?"

"Since when do you drink coffee?"

"Since you've started drinking that decent stuff your friend Zoe bought you."

Lesley poured coffee grinds into the machine. "She's not my friend, she's my colleague."

"You don't work with her any more."

Lesley turned. "I will, though." She glanced past Sharon, towards the living room. "It's been a month. I'll be back in Birmingham in five."

Sharon nodded. "You'll have to buy a house."

"Who says?"

Lesley already had a perfectly good house. She'd paid half the mortgage. She'd decorated it.

Sharon shrugged. "Did you know Julieta has a kid? She's moved him in."

Lesley felt her stomach dip. She put her hand on her daughter's shoulder. "I'm sorry, love. What's he like?"

Another shrug.

The coffee bubbled behind Lesley and Sharon indicated it with a nod of her head. "It's ready."

Lesley noticed that Sharon hadn't answered her question. "How old is the kid?" she asked.

She turned to pour coffee into a mug.

"He's three," Sharon said.

Lesley turned back to her.

"Three!"

"Yeah. Wakes up in the night crying, gets up at half past five. Dad hates it."

"How old is Julieta, then?"

"Late thirties, maybe? Not sure."

Lesley poured a cup of coffee for herself. She poured half a cup into a mug for Sharon and topped it up with water from the sink.

"What are you doing that for?" Sharon asked.

"Doing what?"

"Watering down my coffee."

"I don't want you getting addicted to it."

"I'm fine, Mum. I'm sixteen."

Sharon grabbed the mug. She poured half of it into the sink and topped it up from the coffee machine.

"Are you OK with me and Elsa?" Lesley asked her.

Sharon grinned. "I think she's OK. It's cool, my gay Mum and her glamorous girlfriend."

311

"It's not the fact she's a woman I'm worried about," replied Lesley. "Me and your dad have both brought new people into your life. It can't be easy."

"I'll get used to it," Sharon said.

Lesley gave her shoulder a squeeze. "Talk to me, yes? If you're finding it hard. You're my priority, you'll always come first."

Sharon shook her off. "That's not true and you know it."

Lesley froze. "Sharon. You have to understand, you're more important to me than Elsa is."

Sharon averted her eyes. "I'm not talking about Elsa, Mum. Or Dad, when you two were together. I mean properly together." She sipped her coffee. "This is good stuff. You've always loved your job the most, though." She walked out.

Lesley stared after her. Was Sharon right? Did Lesley put her job first? She'd taken this secondment to Dorset for her mental health. Sharon was sixteen, busy with her friends and her exams, and Lesley hadn't had much choice in the move.

She walked into the living room, her nerves tingling. Sharon looked up and smiled. Lesley gave her a sad smile in return.

Elsa raised her eyebrows: *You OK?*

Lesley nodded. She sat between the two of them. "So," she said. "Tell me the rules."

"Mum!" Sharon said. "You know how to play rummy."

"Nope, never played it. Never had the time."

"I bet," Sharon said.

Too busy with work, she thought. She should do something about that.

"Then we'll teach you," Elsa said. She started dealing cards onto the coffee table.

CHAPTER SEVENTY-NINE

Lesley looked up from her desk to see Dennis walking into the outer office. Johnny got up to help him to his chair, but Dennis waved the younger man away. Lesley walked out and leaned against the door post.

"Dennis," she said. "Good to have you back."

"It's a big fuss over nothing," he said. Then he smiled. "Still, it's nice to have Pam looking after me at home."

Lesley nodded. "You pulled a cruciate ligament," she said. "Not nothing at all."

Dennis straightened up and winced. He leaned against his desk. "I did no such thing. The suspect did it to me."

He smiled. He was right, she thought. Assaulting a police officer didn't make much difference to a murder conspiracy charge. But it didn't hurt.

Mike appeared with a mug of tea and put it on the desk in front of the DS. Johnny fussed around his boss: arranging his chair, moving files around his desk, turning his computer on. Tina watched in silence, her body language stiff. She needed to stop telling herself she was an outsider.

Lesley walked past the desks. "I have to go and see Superintendent Carpenter. I won't be long."

"Nothing to worry about, I hope?" Dennis asked.

Lesley eyed him. How much did he know about what she was about to discuss?

"Just routine," she said. "Wrapping up the case."

Mike looked up. "Boss, I finished checking out that bloke for you, the one Ameena's PA was so scared of."

"Danny Rogers. And?"

"She knew him. They worked together six years ago."

"What did he do to her?"

"Nothing, she says. But the place they worked…" He rubbed the side of his nose.

"It's one of Kelvin's places?" suggested Tina.

Johnny looked at Dennis. "I thought this was all about Harry Nevin and his sex life."

Dennis returned the look. "It is." He turned to Lesley. "All done and dusted now, boss?"

"Pretty much." But Lesley shelved the names in her memory, just in case. Sam Chaston, Danny Rogers. Not to mention Steven Leonard and Arthur Kelvin. "Thanks, Mike."

Mike gave her a shrug. Dennis was watching Johnny. Lesley could only hope those two had resolved their differences.

Five minutes later, she was standing in Carpenter's office. He stood by the window looking out over the car park.

"So," he said. "Your second double murder case. I think we should send you home, you know. You're not good for the death rate."

She gave him a tight smile. "Sorry, Sir."

"Anyway," he said, "You've got enough of a case against Priscilla Evans? CPS happy?"

She nodded. "Her and the two men. They were her cousins. They were all on that video, and we found Harry Nevin's DNA in their van."

"And Ameena Khan's too?" Carpenter asked.

"It was Harry who killed her. His skin was under her fingernails."

"Motive?"

"An old-fashioned crime of passion, Sir. She'd told his other mistress about their relationship. He'd never gone for a colleague before. And we think Priscilla encouraged him. Blackmailed him, possibly. Although we're still working on that angle."

"Conspiracy?"

"Possibly. We have her on his murder, anyway. As well as false imprisonment and assault of Elsa Short."

Carpenter sucked in a breath. "Nasty business. Not sure the firm will survive."

Lesley pursed her lips. She knew that Elsa was hoping it wouldn't.

"I've read your letter," he said. "About your personal involvement."

She pushed her shoulders back. "I wanted to be upfront, Sir. At one point we thought Elsa Short might be a suspect. But she almost became the third victim."

"And you're going out with her?" Carpenter said.

Lesley nodded. "Four weeks now."

Carpenter raised an eyebrow. "I thought you had a husband, a daughter?"

"We separated, Sir."

Lesley bit down the urge to tell him about Julieta, to pass the blame away from herself.

Carpenter walked to his desk and sat down. He leaned back in his chair. "You're not the first copper to be sleeping with the enemy. I wouldn't worry about it."

Lesley felt her face heat up. "The enemy, Sir?"

"Criminal lawyer," he replied. He leaned forward. "I trust you to act professionally though, whoever's on the other side of the table."

"Of course."

He gestured towards the seat opposite him and she took it.

"You've got something else you want to talk to me about?" he asked.

She swallowed. "Yes, Sir. Another matter."

She glanced towards the window and then looked back at him.

"A delicate one?" he asked, giving her a meaningful look.

"You could say that."

"You're leaving us?" he said. "Going back to West Mids?"

"No, Sir. It's about my predecessor, DCI Mackie."

Carpenter rubbed the bridge of his nose. He fixed her with his stare. "I was expecting this."

"You were?"

He nodded. "There's a DI from the West Midlands who's been poking her nose into his records. Anything to do with you?"

Lesley stiffened. "Entirely my fault, Sir. Not her idea. I had my suspicions and I asked if she could—"

"Why not ask your team?"

"With respect, I thought they would react—"

He raised a hand to stop her. "If you have suspicions about officers in this force, DCI Clarke, current or former, you speak to me, understand?"

"Yes, Sir."

"Can she be trusted, this DI Finch?"

"Absolutely. Zoe was one of my best."

"She won't go gossiping to your old mates in Birmingham?"

Lesley shook her head. "Never."

"That's something, then." He rocked his chair forwards
and backwards. "So what have you got?"

"I don't think…"

"What has she dug up? It must be something, or you
would have dropped it."

Lesley looked at him. She pulled out her phone and
flipped to the photo of Mackie and Kelvin. He leaned
forwards to peer into the screen.

"That's all?"

"And there's the crime scene," she said. "There's reason
to think he couldn't have jumped off from that spot."

"So Gail Hansford's been talking to you."

"I don't want to…"

Carpenter stood up. He walked around the desk and
perched on its edge, right next to her. She could feel heat
emanating from his body, hear him breathing. He glanced
at the door, then bent down to look into her eyes.

"You keep this between you and me, understand?"

"Of course," she replied. "Am I onto something, Sir?"

"I'm not answering that question. And I'm going to
pretend we never had this conversation. But if you do find
anything else, you bring it straight to me."

He stood up and walked away from the desk. He
opened the door to the office, and gestured for her to
leave.

Lesley stood up and smoothed down her skirt. She
looked at him, trying to read his expression. Was he
making sure she didn't take this further, or saying he
would help her? There was only one way to find out.

"Yes, Sir," she said. "Thank you."

She walked past him and out of the room, the door closed behind her.

She headed for the corridor, pulling her phone out of her jacket pocket, and dialled Zoe.

I hope you enjoyed *The Clifftop Murders*. Do you want to know more about DCI Mackie's death? The prequel novella, *The Ballard Down Murder*, is free from my book club at rachelmclean.com/ballard.

Thanks,

Rachel McLean